DIRTY suede

DIRTY suede

. . .

Ken Law

Library of Congress Control Number
Registration Number: Txu 1-916-006

Universal ISBNs:
ISBN-13: 9780692971635
ISBN-10: 0692971637

Printed in the United States

Table of Contents

To all the individuals who never lost sight of the light within me even during my darkest moments.

BUSINESS ASSOCIATES & CONTACT LIST

MOMDADJASONJARRETTTERRAJUNCLEALUNCLEMACCHRISTONYCHRISTYRACHEL
BETHCNIELARASHAWNSKYLARBHMORGANERICKEVINSCOTEMILYAMYSTACYLPCGTAYEPAM
KELLYCORYROSSQJMRPOWELLSEANNMRJACKSONMRENGLISHMSBYRDMSDRAKEMILTONRICE
CHRISTINAREBECCAMSKINGGGTROSTMELVINSPRIGGSFELTONCIARANKAPLANEDKEDB
PETECOURTNEYTIFFANYSWANNSYLVIABETHMRSJACKSONKESSLERDREANDREAAMANDA
MAMAPNUPURPAYALDRSATISHCABATTSASHAAUNTLOUUNCLEJOKENNYBECKYBJBRANDI
BOBBYMARVINCSAGCANDICEMRMRSMALEHORNMATTYCOVALESKIERUEBENDAMON
MSREGINADAVIDDEMONDDMCCAROLINAMARIAELISABETHHERBERTFAITHWESTSIDE
NORTHWOODLISAMRMRSTHORNTONREGGIECOURTNEYGRANDMAGRANDPAKIRSTIEYAN
GWENNHANESJOEYMRMRSRUCKERJAMIEJAREDJENJASONELFERTJESSICAJUSTINTRACY
KELLYEVEKYLEMARKMcGRAWMICHAELFINKLEVINMRCOLLINSMRROSSMSMINORANIAH
LOGRANDEMRMRSMCKNIELANDNICKNIKKIPATPEARLMANROBINROYBROOKEDINGLECOCO
FRYEHUDSONSHELLEYMRSNELSONSIBOHNGRACERICHARDSONMARTINSTORKSUECASEYXIXI
TINABILLYRUBYJOSIEEVEWENDYDOLLYAMYBECKYSMURFBABSBRETTALMAGSLORENJENPHILLIP
LINCOLNMSSTOKESGREGDAVIDTANYADAMIANCHRISRONNIELISAGOULSETKRISTINSUBRENALL
MELANIEKENTTYMBERLEESTEPHENBRIANDANIELBRONCOTYLERGARYTIMJULIEERNESTO
KENNETHPINSONBRENTJEFFENRIQUENOTORIOUSBIGJZTUPACFUGEESMORCHEEBASTPMARIPOSA
PORTISHEADESTHEROLAMBSNEAKERPIMPSPUSHATTRIBEOUTKASTSADEGNRKRAVITZNIRVANA
DANGELOSEVENPUBLICENEMYDIGABLEPLANETSDASFXSNOOPPEANUTSMXDMXBOBMARLEY
TCORPORATIONCRYSTALAMSTERDAMBELGIUMPUERTORICODREPUBLICAVEGASNYCCHARLOTTE
VIRGINISLANDSDCLONDONFRANCESWITZERLANDHAVANAHCUBA

Prologue

● ● ●

-These events may or may not depict actual people or real-life circumstances or conditions. Reader discretion is advised.

July 24, 1988

FAITH IS THE ANTITHESIS OF proof. Seeing is believing, and drama is portrayals of symbols that parallel reality.

I was a child of six. Nature was my generation's digital playground. To the interested eye, Darwinism was on display daily. This fine summer's day, my father took me on a field trip to peer into the grassy underworld of our backyard. Between each blade of grass, there was a dark place where the prey that were preyed upon prayed for the death of their predators. My father had filled my ears with tales of epic battles between beetles and fire ants and artistically spun spider webs that entranced and then entangled all types of unsuspecting victims. But there I sat, eyes glued for four straight afternoons, and the only thing that I watched was the grass grow.

"Be patient, Clint. It will happen; you just have to give it enough time." My dad had an uncanny way of being able to sell any dream to anyone that was willing to listen to his dream.

We waited until patience had become grueling. I was ready to go play some video games.

"Clint, look!" his left index finger pointed my eyes in the direction of the tiny sounds of mayhem.

A black cricket had haphazardly hopped onto the back of a yellow jacket. The sudden jolt startled the yellow jacket, and his body's defensive reaction triggered a chemical reaction. Testosterone mixed with cortisol instantly coursed throughout the yellow jacket, covering every cell from its antennae all the way through the suede-like black-and-yellow fuzz at the base of its wax-paper wings. Ill equipped, the cricket's demise was sealed. Retreating, hands up, he signaled that he wanted no part of this fight. Yet without warning, several precise stabs of the yellow jacket's stinger paralyzed the cricket. With each passing breath, his chirps grew weaker as his four legs took turns twitching. The yellow jacket wasted no time; although it was still breathing, the cricket became food. I can still hear the crunching of the yellow jacket feasting. Captivated, I watched in fascination from the beginning until the stuffed yellow jacket hopped up and struggled to fly away. Meanwhile, my father collected the cricket's corpse with a pair of tweezers and slid it into a short, orange plastic vial.

"Let the cricket be a lesson. Be aware of your friends. Stay hip; don't lose focus of your surroundings, and never, ever assume anything." My head bobbed in agreement, my eyes only focused on the vial; his words crawled into my left ear and ran out my right ear.

CRACK!

"Daddy! Daddy! Wait—don't go!" I screamed as I started to regain my consciousness.

CRACK!

Twenty-plus years later, here I was wishing that I had followed my father's words. The blows from the gun left my ears ringing as my vision went dark. I was teetering in and out of consciousness. I wasn't sure of my surroundings. What seemed real proved to be false. The only certainty of the moment was the feeling of continuous blows to the back of my head.

CRACK!

"Your daddy isn't here. Shut the fuck up and start walking," his gun aggressively poked my back, and I obliged.

We hadn't even entered Crook's apartment, and I could smell the pungent aroma of nitroglycerin, sawdust, graphite—all the components of gunpowder and death. We walked through the half-opened front door and into the first floor of a split-level apartment. Blood was everywhere. The scene resembled a *Cocaine Cowboys* dustup. Two people lay dead in the kitchen, one portly Hispanic man was slumped over the dining-room table, and three more bodies were on the stairwell landing. A couple of nameless dead faces were riddled with holes just outside the upstairs bathroom. My knees buckled; my mind raced into every possible corner as I plotted my escape.

CHAPTER 1

Clint's Interview

• • •

THE KNOCK AT THE DOOR was barely perceptible as my girlfriend rose to answer its call. Upon opening the door her eyes were greeted by a familiar face. My doctor was a tall, well-built gentleman, with receding greyish, blonde hair, a softly lined face, and black rimmed eyes. Contrary to last week's visit, this time he was wearing blue-jeans, a wrinkled white shirt, and a light brown jacket. This was our second meeting; his first visit did not fare too well. Sadly, my mind had not worked properly over the past several months.

"How is he feeling today?" he asked as my girlfriend took his jacket.

"The headaches come and go. His doctor said that a full recovery may take another 3-4 months," she replied.

"Do you think we'll be able to at least start the interview this time?" he inquired while slowly turning in my direction.

"I would imagine, he's slightly medicated. This may be your best chance, we have an early flight tomorrow," she smiled and rubbed my right hand before she sat on the sofa beside me.

"Good, I really think his story needs to be heard," he responded.

"Okay, do either of you need anything before you get started?" she questioned while her left hand rubbed my right thigh.

"No, I am fine. Would you like something to drink, Dr. Wiesenthal?" I asked.

"That is kind, maybe later. If it's okay, I would like to start the interview," his voice brightened as he spoke.

"No problem, I understand. Honey, could you leave us alone for the rest of the day?" I questioned.

Surprised, she replied, "Sure, of course. I'll be in the next room."

"Babe, I think it might be better if you are not here. I need to protect you, some of the things that Dr. Wiesenthal and I discuss could be detrimental to your health." A quick, sharp pain caused my head to ache as I spoke those words.

"Clint, that's not fair, you always shut me out!" Shouting, she stood up in protest.

"My head!" I moaned as I pressed both hands against my left and right temples.

"Oh, Clint. I am so sorry, is it the same pain you felt last night?" she quickly massaged the back of my neck.

"Yes, it is," I responded as I buried my face into both palms of my hands.

The room filled with bated breath as everyone focused their attention upon me.

I paused, then inhaled until my lungs were full. Seconds later, I slowly released the trapped air.

"That's it, Clint. Breathe in slowly and exhale slowly. Envision each gulp of air as a purifying agent to free your mind from all of its pain," Dr. Wiesenthal calmly advised.

"Clint, baby!" In an effort to console me, she rubbed her right hand up and down my back.

"Babe, I think I'll be okay. I left some money inside my top desk drawer. Take it and get yourself something nice," I said, still trying to shake the pain.

"Baby, I don't want something nice, I just want you!" she replied.

"You are sweet. I promise, I'll be okay," as I spoke, my voice was barely louder than a whisper.

Confused and concerned, she sat in silence as her eyes began to fill-up with tears.

"It will be okay," I said as I smiled into her damp, sorrow-laden eyes.

Begrudgingly, she agreed. Before she left, as a precaution, she gave Dr. Wiesenthal her cellphone number. Then, Lourdes kissed me several times on my neck and forehead.

I waved goodbye as I stood in front of the large, wooden framed living room window. On the outside, I was the picture of stoicism but on the inside my mind trembled with fear regarding the story I was about to tell.

"Clint, are you ready to start?" asked Dr. Wiesenthal.

"Yes, on one condition," I replied.

"And what is that condition?" he inquired.

"May I call you, Dr. W.?" I calmly asked.

"Sure, I don't have a problem with that," he responded.

"Okay, now I am ready to begin," I said.

"Before we start, I need you to sign this consent form," Dr. W. stated as he pulled out a small, black audio-recording device.

Clumsily, I scribbled my name just above the form's signature line.

"Let us get started," he said as he collected the consent form.

I nodded my head in agreement and he pressed the button labeled *"Record."*

"Do you, Clint Stoener, to the best of your ability, solemnly swear that the statements you provide today are an accurate account?" he asked.

"Yes," I replied.

"Can you describe your childhood?" he questioned as he shifted his body weight from the left side to the right side of the tan padded, leather arm chair.

"My childhood? I can't remember that far back," I retorted.

"Is it because of the explosion?" Dr. W. asked.

"Yes, yes, it is," I softly stated.

"I understand. Can you tell me what you remember about your life after your father left?" he interrogated.

My head dropped as memories of my father's face seemingly sent small, needle-like daggers into my brain.

Sensing my discomfort, Dr. W. said, "Clint, use your breathing tool."

Eyes closed, I grabbed and released several deep breaths.

Dr. Wiesenthal quickly grabbed the recorder and pressed the button labeled "*Stop*."

"Clint, I know you are on prescription drugs, but my experiments with medical marijuana have revealed serious benefits for victims of severe head trauma. Would you like to try some? he inquired.

"Marijuana? I haven't used that drug in a long time," I sheepishly responded.

"This strain is a proven remedy for what ails you," he confidently stated.

"My pulmonologist said that I should refrain from smoking," I replied.

"I agree with your pulmonologist's caveat. But, this tablet is condensed THC. It is all natural and is healthier and more beneficial for your overall health," Dr. W. countered.

"Okay, doc. At this point, I am open to anything," I said as I extended my right palm towards his right hand.

Dr. Wiesenthal gently placed the tiny capsule into the center of my palm.

"Thank you, how long does it take for me to feel its effects?" I asked.

"About 45 minutes," he replied.

I looked Dr. Wiesenthal into his face, paused briefly, then muttered "salud" as I chased the small green capsule down my throat with a gulp of water from a clear, plastic bottle Lourdes left on the coffee table.

"What time will Lourdes return?" he asked after examining his watch.

"In a few hours," I responded.

"Okay, shall we resume our interview?" he asked.

"Yes, we can try. Where did we leave off?" I quizzed.

"I asked you how you dealt with your father leaving you and your mother," he retorted.

"Here goes," I said.

About nine years ago, today, I was seventeen and freshly finished with my first semester at the University of Southern California when my father abandoned me and my mother. Despondent and engorged with rage, I started lifting weights in an attempt to channel my anger. Eventually, through patience and dedication, I morphed my once frail physique into that of a sculpted man. Still furious, I wanted to fight my father, but he was nowhere to be found. And whenever I questioned my mother about our family history, she was always vague in detail, and only revealed that my maternal grandmother was allegedly responsible for my full, black, wavy hair that habitually fell over my perpetually sheepish eyes.

"I'm sorry Dr. W., but that is all that I can remember about my family," I remorsefully announced.

"That's fine Clint. Can you please describe for me what happened on May 1, 2008, the day you came back to the East Coast?" Dr. Wiesenthal politely asked.

"I think so." Once again, I paused, took several breaths and continued.

"You landed in New York, correct?" he questioned.

"Yes," I responded.

"Good. Now close your eyes and imagine that you just exited the airplane and you are walking inside of the airport. Can you see this image?" he asked.

Initially, I paused, then I stated, "I remember now," I replied with my eyes still closed.

"Okay, now talk me through it. Describe what you felt," Dr. W. probed.

The afternoon I returned to the East Coast, the combination of extreme ninety-degree heat and elevated humidity outside formed a cocktail that threatened to create thunderstorms. Inside JFK Airport, despite the air conditioning, the cramped, crowded conditions were stifling. I needed an ATM, a stiff drink, and a place to breathe and contemplate. In concert, both of my pupils danced from left to right as my eyes scanned the airport's littered array of franchises. The options were too numerous to absorb. Several minutes later, I finally discovered an ATM sandwiched between a hamburger shop and a hot-dog vendor.

Unfortunately, other people were in need of this automated teller machine. I stood third in line behind a hump-backed elderly woman and a medium-build boy who looked too young to have an ATM card of his own. After he approached the machine, the boy immediately had a difficult time executing his transaction. His face was smothered in confusion as he turned away from the demanding machine.

"*Hablas Español?*" he shyly muttered in my direction.

"*Si...Hablo un poco de Español...Tu necesitas ayuda?*" was the best I could offer. Quickly assessing the situation, I pressed a few buttons and instructed the boy to input his PIN.

Moments later, my Spanish-speaking friend was well on his way, *dinero* in hand and a smile on his face.

"*Gracias, mi amigo, muy bien!*" he exclaimed as he walked off into the crowd.

"*De nada, chico,*" I retorted, but he couldn't hear my words as they were swallowed alive by the ever-moving, never-stopping airport crowd.

Speaking of money, helping that boy somehow jump-started my mind and fueled a personal review of the jobs that I'd possessed to this point of my life. Long in number but short of longevity, none of them had lasted longer than twelve months. Perhaps I was mired in the depths of fearing the threefold nexus of neurotic bosses, seventy-hour workweeks, and gross dollars earned that were only worth cents. Perhaps I was just too hip for my own good. Either way, my lifelong dream didn't include being pushed around until I was jaded, disillusioned, and dissatisfied about exhausting half of my life chained to a mindless job. Frankly, I'd never been able to grasp any of my ten fingers around the ideology of working for someone else.

So, one day, just like that, I woke up and filled out an application to become a drug dealer. Over time, I dealt with the procurement and distribution for profit of prescription drugs, marijuana, ecstasy, and cocaine. If every drug dealer was assigned a mantra, mine would be "Buy, sell, or go to hell."

Fully lucid, I understood that this is a dirty business. I sell dirty products to collect large sums of dirty cash. As I glanced deeper into the rearview mirror of my life, a recollection of my initial "business transaction" became all too familiar, similar to the touch of an old lover's inner thigh or the taste of Grandma's tuna casserole.

The first deal of my life took place during college. Strangled by single motherhood, my mom crumbled. I was beleaguered and distraught over my father leaving us with a refrigerator filled with poverty and barren wooden cabinets that contained neither the bread nor the meat to make sandwiches. During that time in my life, there were several things that I did not understand. My mother had been beautiful, smart, and witty, and to this day I still can't fathom how the loss of a man not even worth the cost of a used stick of gum could send her into severe depression and then into drugs. No matter how much she fought the urges, the urges always won. Her drug of choice shifted from alcohol to more alcohol and then more alcohol and prescription pills. Perhaps not surprisingly, my first drug deal involved prescription pills stolen from my mother's medicine cabinet.

I officially became a drug dealer on a rather idyllic mid-June afternoon, one of those days when the sun burned brightly enough that the moon could take the night off. With the last name Stoener, the few friends I had called me Stoney or Stone. Other, less familiar people only knew me as *Ralph Nader*. The deal had been arranged; I was scheduled to meet one of the local frat boys in the parking lot of a taco establishment.

Supplied by the federal government and provided by my mother, Valium, OxyContin, and Percocet were quite popular. "Oxys," or "oxes," as the coeds called them, went for fifty-five dollars a pill for eighty milligrams, but the hundred-milligram pills were fetching eighty-five dollars. I had a mild case of anxiety, but the deal went off like I was a professional.

Months later, I was making money hand over pill. But life would not be life without adversity. After years of overindulgence, my mother's abuse had become so volatile that her doctor ordered that she be admitted into a 180-day rehab program. Somewhere, in one of my old file cabinets or tucked in a box in my closet, is a folded, faded prescription notice. I can still feel the feverish warmth of embarrassment as I walked past everyone in line after the pharmacist informed me that Dr. Handlesmen had denied my mother's prescriptions.

PRESCRIPTION HAS AN ANTI-COPY COLORED BACKGROUND ON THE FRONT, AND A WATERMARK ON THE BACK

ALLISON HANDLESMEN, MD
Internal Medicine
56789 Random Building
SUITE 420
123-555-0068*Fax: 123-555-0069

-[**DENIED**]-

NAME: <u>EDIT NAME</u>   DOB: <u>EDIT DATE</u>
ADDRESS: <u>EDIT ADDRESS</u>   DATE: <u>EDIT DATE</u>
Rx
OXYCODENE 80MG
_ Dispense as written
_ Generic Substitution Allowed
Refill 20 Times

ALLISON HANDLESMEN M.D.
DEA: ANP4206821

Now that prescriptions were no longer an option, I took the money from my pill sales and invested it into low-grade marijuana, or, as the coeds called it, "swag." Saying the word "swag" made me giggle. But this silly-sounding nickname proved to be quite profitable; the imported watch on my left wrist was evidence of that. I loved that watch. I bought it right after my first two-pound transaction. I paid the salesperson in cash for this sterling, large-faced British green Tag Heuer. The first time I opened the suede-trimmed gift box, I was overwhelmed with pride and satisfaction. Comically, I can even recollect the quizzical glances the salesperson offered as he counted varied bundles of bills: ones, fives, tens, twenties, fifties, and hundreds. Meeting his condescending gaze, I almost dumped a shoe box of quarters, dimes, nickels, and pennies onto the glass counter when it came time to pay the tax. We both knew where the money came from, and he was hungry for the sale, and I wanted the watch. This innocent transaction was just another beautifully dirty example of capitalism.

Lost amid my frayed thoughts, I'd almost forgotten the reason I was in JFK on this day and at this time. There, waiting for me at gate 5B, was my girlfriend. Rebecca was a stylish, well-built woman in her mid-twenties, pretentious by design. Her mother was a former model, and her father an all-American quarterback at Cornell. They married and consummated the relationship, and the result of their passion was Rebecca—a pretty woman with pretty hair, pretty toys, and a pretty life. But her parents had spoiled Rebecca rotten and she knew it yet did nothing to change her perceptions about life.

Thoughts of what I had to do forced intermittent ripples of anxiety throughout my soul. Rebecca and I had been together for more than three years. In the same way my anxiety came and went, our relationship featured periods of being together and being separated. Now was the time to make the periods of togetherness permanently separated. I didn't want to scar anyone. I shook my head, but I knew all the head shaking wouldn't deny me the culpability of the scarring that I was about to commit. These guilt-laden thoughts strengthened my thirst for a strong beverage.

SIPS N' SUDS, or *SNS*, as seen on employee shirts, brimmed with a schizophrenic vibe. One side featured revelry, as a group of frat boys doused their livers with shots of bourbon. The right side of *SIPS N' SUDS* offered a somber atmosphere. I settled a few stools from three owl-faced Toronto-bound businessmen who slowly sipped cool, dark liquor poured into short, wide glasses with ice.

Perched atop my stool, I surveyed the scene, and a vivacious collection of Air Jamaica stewardesses captivated my curiosity. They wore thin heels and spoke patois as they effortlessly dragged their miniature roll-on suitcases.

"What can I getcha'?" he wore a name tag that read Cleo, and highlighted brown hair covered the top of his head. A huge man with a soft, high-pitched voice. His size didn't match the pitch of his voice.

"I'll take a vodka tonic—no, make that a Johnny Walker Black," I replied as I examined the menu.

"Did you want that on the rocks?" he asked.

"Yes, and may I have an order of French fries, please, with a bottle of ketchup. Could you point me to the men's room?" I questioned.

Cleo extended his long, right arm in the direction of a door labeled *JANITOR'S CLOSET.* I walked past a booth where a man and woman were drinking coffee and talking about their favorite Tarantino movie. Stepping under the grass-green *EXIT* sign, I pushed the restroom door open, but the lights were out, and my nose was stunned by the overwhelming smell of beer-scented urine. After several failures groping and grasping in the dark, I finally found the light switch. It took some time, but my eyes adjusted to the cheap, fluorescent lightbulbs and were greeted by a calico-stained toilet stall and a lonely sink crouched under a severely cracked mirror. Turning back to the door, I pulled it shut and locked the door. My right shoulder gave the door an investigative push to ensure its security. Bending over the sink, I cupped my hands as I splashed my face with water. Slightly refreshed, I reached inside my track jacket and patted a peep pocket that contained a well-wrapped plastic bag. What I needed to ease my mounting anxiety was just a few fingertips away. But a clear head is sometimes better than a high head. Suddenly there was a knock on the door, and the cheap lock rattled as Cleo said, "Your order's ready."

"Cool," I said as I continued to splash my face. Empty and cracked, the paper-towel dispenser offered no help, so I used my jeans, snapped the lights out, and exited the bathroom.

A few unaccounted-for drops of water rolled off my face as I slid back onto my stool. No longer hungry, I ignored the fries and went straight for the liquor. Two guzzles later, I ordered another JWB. Following the second one, I rose from my stool, left one ten-dollar bill and one twenty-dollar bill on the bar, and walked out of *SNS*.

"Hello, excuse me! May I talk to you for a second?"

I heard Cleo's voice yelling in my direction, so I turned around.

"What's wrong?" I asked, uncertain of his intentions.

"Umm, I'm sorry, but I normally don't do this sort of thing, but I was wondering if you'd like to come back to the bar and have a drink with me?" he sounded nervous, almost jittery.

"I am not thirsty. Thanks for the service," I replied as I started to turn and continue upon my journey.

"Wait!" he yelled.

"Yes," I responded.

"Well, if you're not thirsty, maybe I can have your number so that we can have dinner together?" this time his voice was calmer.

Aware of what was happening, I paused and responded, "Hey, look at that clock over there—the one against the far wall. Can you see it?" I retorted.

"Yes, yes, I can see it!" he exclaimed.

"Cool, because I am like six o'clock or nine fifteen," I answered.

"Huh, what does that mean?" he replied.

"That means I am straight." And just like that I completed my turn and walked away, leaving Cleo to figure out the correlation between the hands on the clock and my refusal to share my number.

Several strides later, I was headed to rejoin Rebecca. My objective was to make this situation as surgically neat as possible. I could ill afford to have the situation mushroom out of control. With a potential bloodthirsty drama queen and the "package" that I had in my possession, the last thing I needed was police scrutiny. Rebecca turned as I walked around and down a row of blue, padded low-back seats. I made another left and walked down the aisle where she was seated. My anxiety spiked when our eyes locked. Just before I reached her, I angled my body in a parallel manner as I sucked in my stomach and slid by a corpulent man wearing a tight white T-shirt that read, *Jesus Saves*.

After several twists and turns, here we were, sitting right beside each other. She smiled as she rubbed the nape of my neck with her right hand. There was little doubt in my mind that she loved me. But she'd messed up several months ago, and as a result I was certain that our relationship had run its course. She spoke as she placed her left hand on my knee.

"How do you want to do this, honey?" she asked.

Somewhat off guard, I bought a few extra seconds with a lame chuckle; then I quickly regained my composure.

"Do what?" I despondently inquired.

The surrounding crowd of strangers began to swell. A big crowd could serve as a buffer, I thought.

"Split the cost for the trip, silly," still smiling, her teeth were brighter than the streetlights I'd seen in Belgium.

"How much did you pay for my ticket?" I asked. The total was inconsequential; like an indentured servant, I was prepared to pay any amount to acquire my freedom.

She had been reading a magazine article about Kate Moss and Johnny Depp. Before she spoke, I grabbed her right hand and filled it with an ample number of twenty-dollar bills.

"I don't think I can take this trip with you. In fact, I don't think I'll be seeing you anymore," the albatross around my throat vanished once the words exited my mouth. Now it was time to brace for her reaction. In less than three seconds, I watched her face shift shapes from confusion to hysteria.

"Are you breaking up with me?" she said, lashing out. People started to stare, and everything became silent. Rebecca stopped yelling and started to chew on her left thumb as her right knee started bouncing erratically.

"You aren't going to say anything? So...am I supposed to fill in all the blanks for myself?" between statements she gnawed on her thumb like a starved dog on a grizzled bone. As her voice became even stronger, almost frantically mad, I remained silent.

"You're a work of chickenshit art!" the more she spoke, the more she chewed her thumb until a thin stream of blood rolled down the outside of her left palm.

I tried to explain my position, but everything that came out of my mouth was like throwing water on a grease fire.

"So, I get it! Fuck me all weekend; then throw me away!" Rebecca was furiously screaming at the top of her lungs, and her eyes filled with blood.

"I didn't go into this with such intentions. It just happened this way," I barely believed my own words.

Now Rebecca's anger had gone full tilt. "Get the hell away from me! I am through with you!" she shouted. She was crying; her eye shadow mixed with her tears.

When I turned and walked away, she started screaming every syllable that came into her mind. Her tirade quickly attracted the type of attention that made my skin crawl.

"Clint, come back! I'm not through with you! Clint! Clint, you've got what's coming to you! You son of a bitch!" she was beyond angry, furious, irate, incensed, and apoplectic.

My feet weaved me in and out of the crowded, faceless thoroughfare as my cell phone rang.

"Hello," I muttered.

"Man, where are you!" asked the voice on the other end.

"I am on my way," I said.

"What's the deal? Are you going to be on time!" asked the voice on the other end.

"The longer you live, the more you discover that life is filled with receiving and dishing pain," I laconically replied.

"That's heavy, a heavy pile of bullshit! Are you on your way?" the voice on the other end barked.

"I said that I was coming," I countered.

"There has been a change of plans. Meet me at baseball field number four, twenty minutes from the airport," he replied.

"I'll be there," I said.

CLICK!

Out of the blue, I was surrounded by a large pack of TSA security guards. It felt like a hundred thousand milliseconds ran by my eyes before I realized they weren't coming for me. In fact, there was so much commotion that it was impossible to distinguish the good guys from the bad guys. Local and national news syndicates would later feature a story segment detailing how airport authorities arrested a well-dressed woman screaming obscenities while posing a threat to herself and others.

CHAPTER 2

Berlin

• • •

May 1, 2008, 2:15 p.m.

"THAT IS ALL I CAN remember, Dr. W.," I stated.

"Clint, you did an excellent job. How does your head feel?" he asked.

"It feels okay," I said with a cautious smile.

"How is your brain, is there any pain?" Dr. W. inquired.

"No," I said.

"Good, would you like to continue?" Dr. W. questioned.

"Yes, I would," I responded.

"Can you explain what happened when you met Berlin at the baseball field?" he asked after he glanced at his clipboard.

"Berlin, yes, I think so," I hesitantly replied.

"Okay, pickup right after you left the airport. Clint, it is very detrimental toward your recovery that you purge your brain of all your traumatic memories," Dr. Wiesenthal instructed.

I paused, then I closed my eyes before I spoke.

I was running about ten minutes behind schedule. The cause was a mandated detour to accommodate the overwhelming influx of roaring motorcyclists for a female biker convention. Berlin, the man I was meeting, happened to be my former best friend. We had known each other for over fifteen years; inseparable during college, now we barely spoke. The change in our relationship transpired after his senior year girlfriend's brutal car crash. Rain mixed with high winds and even higher speeds caused her foreign sedan to flip over. As she waited for help, she was trapped, suspended upside down as she was forced to watch her best friend choke to death on her own seat belt. Despite the hours of comprehensive-cognitive therapy, Berlin's girlfriend was never the same. In order to cope, she turned to illicit intoxicants as her comfort foods. One night, she was getting dolled up to go out with her friends.

Everyone on campus that was "in the know" knew that my products were premium. She called me, and I arrived with her order. After completing the transaction, we had a drink, and then I left. But as I exited her dorm room, I ran into members of Berlin's fraternity. This run-in only complicated matters, as my reputation, compounded with Berlin's girlfriend's social demons, quickly fertilized rumors that spread faster than syphilis at the Olympics. Clint + Berlin's girlfriend = SCANDAL. Even to this day, Berlin knows in his heart of hearts that nothing ever happened, but several talking heads within his frat kept pushing bugs in his ears. Tensions spawned, and our friendship no longer existed. In fact, after all these years, business was our only connection. Yes, I was a marijuana dealer. I suffered from GAD (general anxiety disorders), and marijuana was the only substance that helped me cope with my affliction. Most of my clients were people that suffered from numerous problems that marijuana could tame. My only connect was Berlin. Punctuality was a religion for Berlin, whereas I have no true religion with respect to time and space.

At quarter after two, I pulled into the parking lot. Once I got to the bleachers, his look was icy, and mine wasn't much warmer. Like a host gazing into the eyes of its leech, neither of us enjoyed the other, but there were mutual benefits for both parties in this fucked-up symbiotic relationship. The only reason we met was because he didn't believe in discussing business matters over the phone. He learned this when he handled some work for me during our college years. Berlin perpetually maintained that someone was always listening to every call. He said that there were two ways to verify if you were being federally monitored: one, if you heard echoes or clicking sounds whenever you dialed certain numbers; or two, and the most sure-fire way, if you stopped paying your cell-phone bill for three months and your phone isn't disconnected. Then you better get your bail money ready. Once the federals acquired enough information they would come busting through the door cuffing and stuffing—no questions, no debates. The plain truth is affidavits and warrants aren't printed without wiretapping, snitches, or both.

"How have you been?" I asked after ascending the aluminum bleachers. My right hand was extended in a gesture of respect. We shook.

"I have been busy. I am a businessman; I'm in the business of keeping busy," he replied.

"Did you hear about what happened last night?" I asked.

"Of course, I did," he tersely replied.

"All is well on your end?" I inquired.

"We wouldn't be here if it wasn't," he quipped.

Berlin's speech patterns were almost perfect except for the inescapable Boston accent. He often joked that during his next lifetime, he would like to be reincarnated as a New Yorker. Rugged in tone, his words were spoken with a rigid and measured purpose.

"So, which one of these boys is your nephew?" I asked.

After a pause, he finally responded, "The one wearing the blue Nike Sharks, playing catch with the redhead. His name is Madison. Like most of these kids, he is spoiled beyond fixing."

"Can he play?" I asked dryly. The inquisition about his nephew's athleticism was a potentially sensitive subject.

"He could if he pulled his head out of his ass," Berlin almost chuckled. "I mean, his father is never there, so that leaves my sister to teach him how to throw a slider. That's like trusting Paul Reubens around your grandmother's lotion," he quipped, and we both chuckled. For that brief glimpse, he was Berlin, the Berlin of old—that lasted all of about fifteen seconds, and it was back to rugged rigidity.

"I mean, were we that inept when we were that age?" he asked.

"Maybe we were, and we just didn't recognize it?" I theorized.

"The boy he's playing catch with is another class A jerk-off, an heir to a real-estate mogul. You should hear the stuff their generation talks about." Berlin shook his head as he spoke.

"Bring it in, guys!" yelled a man wearing a baseball cap, with a bushy mustache and a round midsection, as he leaned over the dugout fence and motioned for the team to come take a seat.

"You see, even the way he jogs is all wrong! Totally wrong, too much lateral arm flailing—wasted motion! I blame his damn father," he pounded his right fist onto his right knee. The increased volume of his voice drew attention. But his daunting size and intense snarl forced the nosey necks to return to minding their own business. Meanwhile, one of the parents of the opposing team sported an adult-sized replica of his child's baseball cap. That was his first mistake. His second occurred when he casually passed a twenty-dollar bill down the row among bitter rival parents to pay for his beverage. He couldn't have predicted what was about to happen. Not only did he not get the correct change, but someone drank half of his soda. Heated words were exchanged. Seeing that he faced insurmountable odds, he swallowed both his pride and whatever was left of his soda.

"Nerd!" Berlin shouted.

CROWD LAUGHTER

"This is mild. You should've seen what happened when the Tigers came to this ballpark," his voice was muffled between bites of the first of three hotdogs.

"So seriously, how's business? Are you still selling freezers?" I asked.

"Why not? That's where the money is; customers are thirsty. But things can change quickly. Soon associates become liabilities because they lie about their abilities. Then the mess comes. Promises go unfulfilled, and threats become fulfilled. You know how it is," Berlin's voice had become more serious. "Everybody is dirty these days: the cops, the judges, the politicians, the teachers, everybody."

As he spoke I was trying everything in my power to focus on his words and not the blood-red ketchup plopped onto and was now staining his shirt. My plan was to get the drugs from him "on the arm." This could be difficult. Trust was a dying dinosaur. Trust plus money was an entirely different monster. It was not like I didn't have the money. But when dealing with dirt, you sometimes need to have a little extra money on the side just in case you have to buy a shovel to dig yourself out of a hole. If I could convince Berlin to front me the money, then I could use the extra money to make additional moves on the side.

"I got the clientele," I added, to waylay any fears that he might have.

With a blank face, he silently passed me the two-remaining aluminum-wrapped foot longs. "Hold these. I gotta polish the porcelain," he rose and adjusted his drooping jeans as he repositioned his holstered firearm. I watched as he walked down the bleachers and off into the distance.

Minutes passed as I focused my attention on the baseball game. My cell phone rang, startling me. It rang twice before I was able to remove it from my right pocket.

"Hello," I said.

"I'm on the move. Look inside the hot dogs, and you'll find a door opener for a dirty white Buick sedan at the end of the lot. License plate *DLX12W.* Grab the product and toss the door opener under the driver's side seat. Money is due as usual," Berlin stated.

CLICK!

I opened both hot dogs. The one on the left was covered in relish and sauerkraut, and the other one was smothered in onions. Turning the right dog over, I jiggled it, and a cascade of onions fell off and revealed a black plastic car-door opener. On my way to the parking lot, I forcibly shoved the hot dogs into a dirty, dark nook between a red-and-white-striped popcorn box and a tray of chili cheese fries. Greasy door opener in hand, I continued to the expansive slate-gray parking lot that began exactly where the green grass stopped. For some odd reason, I rejected my initial idea of getting in my car and driving around the lot to look for the dirty white Buick. And I opted to pursue my "white whale" on foot. In this region, white Buicks were everywhere. Out of one hundred cars, forty of them were white. I finally found license plate *DLX12W.* I would have found it sooner if I had been looking for a cream-colored car and not a white one. Either Berlin was color blind, or I was the victim of his sick sense of humor. My bet was placed on the latter.

The opener unlocked the Buick, and I eased in behind the wheel. Gently closing the door, I slid my hand between my feet underneath the driver's seat and pulled out a chubby midsized hunter-green duffel bag. Locking the door from the inside, I placed the opener into its usual position and slammed the door shut. They say the quickest path between two points is a straight line, but I eschewed such dogma as my suede Pumas zigzagged around muddy puddles and unwelcome patches of dog excrement on the way back to my car. As I approached the parking lot, a black van with black tinted windows and a rear license plate frame that read *Saul Autos, Inc.* raced in the opposite direction of chasing police sirens. From my vantage point, I could barely see the numerous tar-black tire tracks tattooed into the street, but the smell of burning rubber was much more obvious as it wafted off the asphalt every time the van squealed to a stop. Rushed and frantic for freedom, the speedy driver repeatedly crashed into every police roadblock: east, west, north, and south. It was if they had been waiting for him, like a set-up or a speed trap. There were no sirens, just squad cars, so many squad cars that the black van's options were quickly erased. Desperate, the masked driver hurriedly jumped out of the van and fled from the scene. With officers and dogs in chase, he did not get far. In fact, the ordeal lasted no more than six minutes before the driver was apprehended. But his arrest was not without further incident as he cursed, kicked, and spat at the arresting officers.

"Motherfucker, do you know who I am! You and your family are going to be really sorry!" he repeatedly screamed before he was cuffed and then shoved into the rear of the last in a long line of unmarked vehicles. Still ranting and kicking even after the door was slammed shut, the prisoner's antics didn't dissuade the officers from joking and exchanging high fives as if they were celebrating a successful lion-sized kill. Before I left, I patiently watched and waited until every marked and unmarked car vacated the scene. Or so I thought.

Little did I know, though I got the story later, that parked within the same lot where I stood was a white van with red writing that read *HIGHz*. Inside, surrounded in darkness sat Officer Dansbury and Officer Douglas.

"Well, after six months, we finally got him," stated Douglas.

"Hell, yeah!" shouted Dansbury.

"Do you think he'll talk?" Douglas asked somberly.

"Talk? Give me forty-five minutes, and I'd get some answers!" Dansbury's nostrils flared.

"Like you do during most of your arrests?" Douglas questioned.

"And what is that supposed to mean!" Dansbury snarled.

Douglas calmly replied, "You know what I am talking about."

"Oh, that thing from last week? Why are you still hung up on something that happened a week ago?" Dansbury's voice maintained its normal amount of aggression.

"This isn't a discussion of time and space; it's a matter of integrity. Integrity has no expiration date," Douglas retorted.

"Why can't we just enjoy this victory? Our hard work is paying dividends, and you want to talk about last week. I apologized; it was a case of wrong time, wrong place, wrong vagina!" Dansbury's voice rose.

"You just don't get it! Has it been that long? I can't do this anymore; when we get back to the station, I'm filing for a new partner," Officer Douglas announced as he started the all-white *HIGHz* van.

CHAPTER 3

Damon

• • •

May 1, 2008, 3:15 p.m.

Across town, Melba, a caramel-complexioned woman in her early forties, was trying to talk to a man of Nordic-Ukrainian descent. Approximately thirty-five years of age, Damon had deep sunken eyes surrounded by hardened facial features. Though no matter how hard he tried—maybe he didn't try at all—his arrogance couldn't hide the dark, dirty secrets he possessed. In response to Melba's words, he turned and answered his cell phone.

"Yes, hello?" Damon said.

His conversation continued for well over a minute before he acknowledged that Melba still stood in his presence. "Wait!" Damon barked as he removed the phone from his left ear.

"Listen, Melba. Here's the deal; look the apartment over. If you like it, the contract is on the kitchen counter. Get this straight! Rent is due no later than the fifth of every month. Not at 12:01 a.m. on the sixth. This is nonnegotiable. Lateness will result in immediate eviction, and you and your daughter will be out on the street. If you're not interested, leave the keys and the contract on the counter, and close the door behind you," his eyes narrowed intensely.

"OK, where are the keys?" Melba asked.

Damon had become impatient with Melba. He dug into his coat pocket and produced a key chain. "Catch!" he yelled as he tossed the keys in Melba's direction. There was a brief moment of silence before his short-armed toss crashed onto the unforgiving pavement. "Don't worry; catching isn't part of the contract," he smirked as he turned, walked around the corner, and resumed his phone conversation.

"So, you're saying that you'll need some help with this job?" he asked the voice on the other end. "No, I haven't spoken to nor seen Rico. I waited at the airport for two hours, and that asshole never showed! Why do you think I'm talking to you?" Damon barked.

"Slow down; I can barely understand you! That won't be a problem; I can get what you need!" Damon exclaimed.

"Will two niggers be enough? That motherfucker owes me! Rico or no Rico, it's time to collect!" Damon violently emphasized each word.

"Did you hear me the last time? Fuck Nicky Nicotine and all those other so-called made men! I could give a dick about them. Their time is up! Be at the office tomorrow at eight, and we can go over the plan," Damon ended the call.

CLICK!

CHAPTER 4

Vinny, Vicki, and Me

• • •

May 1, 2008, 5:47 p.m.

ANYBODY WHO KNEW ANYBODY KNEW Vinny Del Negro (full name: Vinny Del Negro Vinzantinne). A middle-aged man with creased olive skin, he was a successful business proprietor; his latest venture, *EDIBLE GROOVES*, was a nightclub that dominated the city's affluent social scene.

"Good. So, you'll be here tonight?" Vinny asked.

"Yes, I got the message," I responded.

"Affirmative," Vinny retorted.

CLICK!

And with the click of that phone call, old business ties were suddenly reknotted. Time had passed since the last time Vinny and I had done business. Pressure applied by my foot revved the engine as I placed my cell phone in the black divots carved into my dashboard. An early-1970s vintage, charcoal gray *BMW 2002* was my car of choice. I had been driving it for about seven years, with all original parts, except for eight new tires, a paint job, and a new manual transmission. Authentic in nature, this car caught a glance or two.

My phone call with Vinny instantly rearranged the logistics of my evening. I needed to go home, shower, change, and package my product. It occurred to me that I hadn't eaten today. A sandwich-shop off Thirty-Second Street was a block over, but parking was always scarce in this city. To make matters worse, when I got there, a white van was double-parked.

Twenty minutes later, I scarfed down a honey-roasted turkey sandwich with smoked cheddar cheese, spicy mustard, and a generous piece of crisp romaine lettuce. I showered and changed into a pair of black, plain-front pants, a stiff white oxford, and a stylish yet modestly priced charcoal pin-striped blazer. I walked through the parking lot; my right hand carried my brown, weathered-suede briefcase. I placed it inside my car's rear-seat stash box. With contraband secured, I backed out of my parking spot, shifted into first gear, turned my headlights on, and veered right into the flow of traffic.

A maze of garden-variety yellow and red lights highlighted my drive. My meeting with Vinny was scheduled to begin in fifteen minutes. *EDIBILE GROOVES* was not the type of establishment that catered to the neohippie or the eco-friendly crowd. Money was the only green, and at this place plenty of it was required to have a good time. Vinny's portfolio revealed the profits he enjoyed as a businessman. The product didn't matter. Vinny could sell a forest fire to a park ranger.

Curiously, I missed this detail, but I should have taken note that only the fourth and fifth floors of Vinny's building were open to the public. Eventually, I would learn why such restricted access made sense. In an elevator destined for Vinny's office on the thirteenth floor, I watched the floor numbers light up *10, 11, 12*, and a large bead of paranoia glided down my back. It had been some time since Vinny and I had conducted business, and anyone with knowledge of Vinny's mercurial personality would understand my reservations.

Exiting the elevator, turning left, I walked down a dimly lit hallway encased in wood paneling. I passed two large men wearing dark suits as they escorted an older one wearing dark glasses. The mysterious trio stopped at the elevator. The heavier of the two suits pressed the button, and all three men were quickly swallowed up as the elevator's doors pressed together. Once they disappeared, I pushed a doorbell just under a dated picture of President Eisenhower.

BUZZ!

I turned the cold copper doorknob and walked into the foyer. To my surprise, a familiar face sat behind the reception desk. Victoria was her name.

"Hello, Clint," she still possessed a world-class smile.

"Salutations, Victoria," I said as we exchanged a brief embrace.

"Here, sit!" she motioned toward a plush, brown velvet chair.

"Thank you," I said as I undid the top button on my blazer before I sat down. My practice was to only button the top button, never both or just the bottom, only the top button.

"What have you been up to? Gosh it seems like it has been ages," she poured two tall glasses of water as she spoke.

"Yes, it has been a while," I said as I placed one hand on each of my thighs.

"It's a shame what happened," she said with a blank expression.

"What did they tell you?" I asked.

"I never got the whole story. You know my uncle," she answered.

"That was a strange time. Enough about the then, tell me about the now: boyfriend, husband, children, cat, hobby in your life?" I probed.

"No, to the boyfriend, husband, cat, and children, but I do have a new hobby. It's a great stress release," she smiled and blushed as she spoke.

"Oh really," I was intrigued.

"For the past few months, I have been going to the shooting range," her eyes brightened.

"Gun range—interesting. Are you taking over the family business?" I joked.

"No, silly! It's something a friend of mine turned me onto," she replied.

"Guns, really? I can think of several other ways to relieve stress," I said.

"Several ways? Tai chi, meditation, acupuncture? Maybe you could show me a couple of your techniques," she said, still smiling.

"That's a—" *BUZZ!* My words were interrupted.

"Send him in," Vinny's voice bellowed from a small black speaker with silver lettering that read *SONY* etched across its bottom border.

CLICK!

"Oh, denied by the buzzer," I said as I rose from my chair.

"Clint!" She grabbed my right arm with her left hand; we were face-to-face, and everything became silent. "It's good to have you back," she pulled me close; we embraced again, and this time both of us gripped each other a little tighter.

"Thanks, Vicki. It feels good to be back," I smiled just before heading toward Vinny's office.

I turned the knob and was astonished by its lavish nature. Calling it an office was an understatement. The square footage was more than the average single-family home. Its amenities included a sixty-five-inch plasma television and a marbled master bedroom suite, which featured a king-sized bed.

With a smile on his face and a freshly lit cigar poking out of his mouth, Vinny beckoned, "Welcome, Clint; take a seat!"

I placed my briefcase on his desk, inserted a tiny brown key into the jaws of its lock, turned the key, unlocked it, and slid the case in his direction.

"Is this a bomb?" he said as he put his left ear close to the closed case.

"Open it," I said.

He rubbed his hand against the case, making a sound like waves brushing back and forth against a brown shoreline. "This is a nice case. Where did you get it? I'll buy it from you! You should let me buy this case from you!" his hand was still rubbing.

"It's not for sale. I got it in Belgium from an Italian immigrant. He had a modest street-side shop in Brussels. His wife was named Millie, she had a beautiful smile but made disgusting pastries," I said as my face grimaced.

"Well, let's see if I want to buy anything else," he opened the case and produced a jeweler's loupe as he inspected a few samples from a few jars.

"Motherfucker! My clients will be pleased," he exclaimed.

"Same conditions as before?" I inquired.

"Your wares are impressive. But for the record, what happened last time would end considerably differently if it happened again," there was no hint or indication of humor in his eyes or the words he spoke.

"That was a case of miscommunication. Those days are in the past," I assured.

"Just remember what I just said," he reiterated.

"I hear you loud and clear. May I use your bathroom?" I asked, and he pointed in the direction past the wet bar.

"Brilliant terpenes! Sure, it passed the eye and nose tests. Now I am going to conduct a smoke test!" Vinny opened the upper right cabinet behind his desk and pulled out a glass bong.

About sixty-three seconds later, I returned from the bathroom.

"Ah, did you know that you had an Iranian prostitute with stomach cramps in your bathroom?" I asked, with a curious hint of sarcasm.

"Iranian? How do you know she's Iranian?" he reacted.

"She told me," I replied.

"How did you know she had cramps?" he inquired.

"Ah, refer to my previous response," I quipped.

"Well, I am through; you can have her," he said as he exhaled a marijuana cumulus cloud.

"I'm good. Herpes is transmittable at a fifty-fifty rate both vaginally and orally. I'm a betting man, just not with my penis," I replied.

CHAPTER 5

My Edible Grooves Gig

• • •

May 1, 2008, 9:20 p.m.

LEAVING VINNY'S OFFICE, I WALKED up a private flight of stairs that led to the fourteenth floor. Pausing, I scanned the dark hallway as I stood in front of a large, high-hinged mahogany door. Behind it was a designer sky lounge that had morphed into a Prohibition-style hash bar that I called *HAARLEM*. My job was to disseminate high-grade marijuana to the area's exclusive smokers. Here's how it worked: Special clients were given a personalized poker chip. Whenever *HAARLEM* was open, Special clients were instructed to knock on the door and then slide their personalized chip through the slot in the wall to the right of the entrance.

KNOCK-KNOCK!

Suddenly, a green poker chip rolled through the slot and produced a clanging sound as it fell into a metallic tray. Seconds later, two more green poker chips came sliding through the slot in the wall. Twisting the lock, I pulled the door open. Just like that, my gig had begun.

Weed is a simple substance. A plant sprouts from a seed that has been watered and nurtured. But for some strange reason, the government feels it is its right to allow us to smoke thousands of cigarettes a day, but then it becomes nosy once you unzip an oh-zee—all in the name of Reefer Madness. Propaganda at its finest.

In a matter of minutes, one by one, sometimes in twos like Noah's ark, customers filed inside of *HAARLEM*. Minutes later, the scent of marijuana generously wafted above the room as a popular jazz musician told a story he had heard while touring in Havana, Cuba.

"You see, there was this man who was happily married for five years. They were the consummate all-American couple. The husband had a demanding partnership at a respected law firm while the wife played the social butterfly. Nearly every Friday night they spent dining at the country club. One Friday night, before heading to dinner, the toilet in the powder room off the kitchen started to back up. The next day a plumber came to inspect the situation. The prognosis was a clogged septic system, too many flushed condoms. Rough calculations would estimate that there were 420 condoms of varied shapes, sizes, and colors. The plumber and his helpers smiled and applauded the husband's virility. Embarrassed, he hid his shame behind his pupils. Silently he stood, unworthy of their respect, because the condoms weren't his. Like a eunuch, three years ago a battle with prostate cancer had robbed him of his virility," stated the musician.

"Do you have his wife's number?" a voice echoed from the crowd. Then everyone began laughing. As if on cue EB & the Tweeters started their music set.

Four hours later, I waited for Vinny. I was a bit drained, but the night went quickly, and business was good—really good. I leaned over the sink, splashing water on my face, and looked up as Vinny walked through the door.

"What's up with the tailgating?" I sharply asked as I stood up. "Man, you could get into some serious trouble sneaking up on somebody like that in a public bathroom, or any bathroom for that matter!" I said.

"Great job tonight, Clint!" Vinny smiled with amazement.

"Yes, that's what I do," I responded.

"Do you have more of that same product? If so, would you like to work Fridays and Saturdays?" Vinny asked.

"Does a limp penis like to be licked?" I retorted.

"I'll take that as a yes. Come by the office next Friday. Here you go," he placed a brown envelope on the sink. "By the way, about last time, I did what I had to do. It's my business, and my business is personal. Next time, I won't be so polite!"

"Cool. I understand. Just remember what I said about sneaking up on people in bathrooms," my words followed him out the door.

As I counted the envelope's contents, my phone rang.

"Well, hello!" I was very surprised to hear the voice on the other end.

CHAPTER 6

Mysterious Screaming Woman

• • •

May 2, 2008, 4:32 a.m.

LATER THAT MORNING ACROSS TOWN, Lourdes, Melba's daughter, was comfortably nestled within her puffy, white, hypoallergenic blanket. While still cluttered, Lourdes's apartment was quaint; it offered vaulted ceilings, a pristine porcelain bathtub, and a natural wood-burning fireplace. Peace draped itself over her face.

A woman's screams jarred Lourdes from her sleep. Her new calico-colored kitten scooted across the apartment and found refuge behind a few stacks of unpacked boxes. Footsteps could be heard running down the hall toward her apartment.

Carrying only a dimly lit flashlight, wearing nothing more than a flimsy lace nightgown, Melba came running into Lourdes's room.

"What's wrong? Is everything all right? Were you having one of your nightmares?" she asked, exasperated and out of breath.

Lourdes clumsily reached for the light switch on the left side of her bed. With a flick of the wrist, a bluish light flooded the room. "I was going to ask you the same," she said as she rubbed morning matter out of the corners of her eyes.

Nervously, Melba quickly searched the room with her eyes. "Where's your baseball bat?" her voice cracked. "It sounds like someone is being murdered!" as she tiptoed toward the door, Melba turned and motioned to Lourdes. "Follow me," she whispered.

"Aren't we safer in here? Whatever is going on out there can stay out there!" Apparently, Lourdes wasn't as curious as Melba.

"You mean you're going to let me go out there alone?" Melba asked.

"Hey, I already saved one pussy this week, and unlike you, even that kitten knows it's time to hide," Lourdes responded.

"Shhhh!" Melba paused in her tracks. "Listen…" she paused. "The screams stopped!"

The screaming was replaced by an equally eerie silence. Painfully exhausted, the screaming woman was slumped over on the floor of her upstairs apartment as she slowly faded into unconsciousness.

"Look, either we call the police, or we don't do anything until we choke on the stench of her rotting corpse!" Melba sharply stated after debating for over five minutes.

Disgusted that she was missing sleep, Lourdes threw her blankets down past her feet and jumped out of bed. "OK, let's go!"

BANG! BANG!

Someone knocked on the main door of the apartment building. Melba and Lourdes crept out into the hall.

BANG! BANG!

"NYC Police, open the door!" the door rattled violently with each knock.

Melba and Lourdes could see a tall, dark silhouetted figure standing outside the glass-paned door.

"Ladies, hello; my name is Officer Douglas. I'm trying to respond to a 911 domestic disturbance call!"

"Let me see some ID!" Melba demanded.

"Here you go," he pressed his identification against the glass.

"Na-ah, that's not good enough! Slide it through the mail slot!" she insisted.

The officer bent over and funneled his ID through the mail slot, as instructed.

Lourdes and Melba examined the ID. Satisfied with its authenticity, the dead bolt was turned back, and the door was opened.

"Sorry, officer, but you can't be too careful these days," Melba grumbled.

"I understand." Looking around, he asked, "Are you two alone?" he inquired.

"Yes, it's just us. We live on this floor," Lourdes replied.

"We got an anonymous call from this address about a disturbance," Officer Douglas stated.

"Yes, there was somebody screaming, but we didn't make the call!" Melba snapped.

"I need to look around to make sure the building is secure," as he was about to walk up the stairs, static-based chatter came out of his shoulder radio.

Via POLICE RADIO: "Calling all units!" *CAA-SHHH!* "Be on the lookout for a tall Caucasian male wearing a long black T-shirt." *CA-SHHH!* "He's headed southbound on foot, armed and dangerous." *CA-SHHH!* "We have a possible one eighty-seven. Proceed with caution." *CA-SHHH!*

"Sorry, ladies, I have to go! Here's my card; call me if you have any problems!" he shouted as he ran out the front door.

Via POLICE RADIO: "Suspect was spotted with three others." *CA-SHHH!* "Possible gang affiliation." *CA-SHHH!* Again, suspect is armed and dangerous; proceed with caution." *CA-SHHH!* The glass-doors rattled as Officer Douglas exited the building.

CHAPTER 7

Talking Shit and the Art of the Escape

• • •

May 2, 2008, 6:37 a.m.

THE SUN BURNED THROUGH THE thin skin of my eyelids as its razor-sharp rays prevented them from opening. Still foggy from excessive brightness and the aftermath of too much alcohol, I violently shook my head as my partially shut eyes confirmed what I feared. There she lay as her alarm clock read 6:37 a.m. My only recourse was to quietly slip out of her bed and make my escape. The smallest nuance, a noisy bedspring or an unintentional tug on a stray blanket, could explode like a landmine, waking her up, leaving me naked and caught red-handed. It took some strategy, but I circumvented any possible commotion. With my shoes in hand, I stood emotionally motionless as I took one last look at Vicki's perfectly sculpted butt before rushing into her living room. Very little care was applied in shoving my legs into my pants, and even less care was employed as I put my shoes on. My oxford, unbuttoned, almost fell off my left shoulder as I hurriedly closed her townhouse door. The next sound was my car starting and the rev of its engine. Clutch, shift, gas, release, and I was in motion.

As I weaved my car through early morning traffic, twenty-five minutes later, I was inside my warehouse apartment. Minimalist at best, it contained a suede sofa, a glass-topped coffee table, a well-used, king-sized bed, and a fifty-inch flat-screen television. Thirsty, I grabbed a can of seltzer water off the table, cracked the tab, and sipped the warm, bubbly beverage. Providing my own soundscape, I hummed a popular car commercial jingle while I searched my barren refrigerator for something to eat. The lonely remains of a beef tenderloin caught my attention. Without heating it, I bit right into the cold cattle, before my cell phone rang. I answered. On the other end was Berlin's voice.

"Speak to me!" he echoed.

"My kids need more juice boxes," I replied.

"Chill! I am going to call you back from 917-555-1834," he reported.

CLICK!

A stained issue of *Furniture Creators* rested on top of a mounting stack of junk mail as I gnawed on the tenderloin. When my cell phone rang again, thinking it was Berlin, I blindly answered.

"Hello," I spoke sheepishly, before Vicki's voice surprised me.

"Hello! What happened to you? Why did you leave without saying good-bye?" she asked. I needed to change gears and repave the situation.

"I apologize. But my stomach was bothering me. I thought it was best for the three of us if I just left," I replied.

"The three of us?" she asked cautiously.

"You, me, and your innocent bathroom!" I replied with the coyness of a wolf in any coop.

"Your stomach was bothering you? Oh, I thought it was something I did!" I could hear the smile in her voice as she spoke. At that moment, the momentum of the conversation shifted from confrontation to sympathy. Everything was trouble-free, until she made her next statement: "I must tell you that last night was everything I remembered," she gushed.

Truthfully, I also enjoyed last night, but I knew that my actions could yield some unfavorable consequences.

"We did enjoy a degree of seminal success," I replied.

"That's soooo nasty!" she had a habit of stretching out her *o*'s when she said "so." "Sooooo, when am I going to see you again?" she asked.

Just then *917-555-1834* flashed across my cell-phone screen. It was Berlin.

"I'm sorry, but I have to take this call. Is it OK if I call you later?" I asked.

"Yes, I'll be here for the rest of the morning," she responded.

"OK, cool," I said and clicked over to Berlin.

CLICK!

"Speak!" he barked.

"I want the same juice boxes I got last time, but I need much more. There's a planned field trip for my nephew and all of his third-grade friends," I stated.

"How much more? Are we talking two, three, or more?" he inquired.

"More like five to six. His friends really liked the Blueberry Blast and the Sour Orange juice boxes," I replied.

"I'll have it in two days. Just make sure you're ready to settle up from our last meeting!" He said just before he hung up. The deal was arranged. In two days, I would acquire enough weight to classify for charges under fed statutes. Therefore, I was officially "*taking risks and prospering,*" and just like that, I was trapped. Exhausted, I passed out to the televised sounds of an NPR debate on legalization.

CHAPTER 8

Saul's Invitation

• • •

May 2, 2008, 6:37 p.m.

MUCH LATER THAT SAME DAY, I was still in bed. The room had become dark as dusk, and I hadn't been awake for more than ten minutes when my phone rang. The person on the other end was my longtime friend Saul. Extremely heavyset, his license said his age was twenty-nine, but his waistline stretched into the mid-forties. A life-long entrepreneur, he owned car dealerships and other business ventures throughout the city. Before I'd left for the West Coast, we'd met at least once a month; now back on the East Coast, I was looking forward to reconnecting. A typical night out with Saul featured more than a few beers and a whole lot of laughs.

Always robust in voice, Saul could sound demanding even while whispering. "Are we still on for tonight; you know the fight's on?" he retorted.

"Is that tonight?" I inquired. Not only was my vision blurred from sleeping too long, but I also found it difficult to gather my thoughts.

"Fuck you! No, it's exactly three weeks from tonight! Don't try to back out on me, man! I've already ordered pay-per-view and bought enough booze to drown half of Ireland. The fight is tonight, and your ass better be here!" he demanded.

"Gambling?" I asked.

"Definitely—fuhgeddaboudit!" he replied.

"Easy greasy, I'm not backing out. I would never skip the chance to take your money. I might even be there early," I responded.

"You, early?" he quipped.

"Droll, you slay me," I responded.

"Ha-ha. Hey, I've got somebody you might be interested in meeting," he added that last bit of information as if it was an extra incentive.

As soon as he told me that, I initially feared that he was trying to hook me up with one of his wife's girlfriends. Hook-ups in the blind are a lot like the flop in Texas hold 'em poker. Sometimes they're successful, but most of the time it was a thin intersection between minimal luck and grand disappointment.

"Not another one of your she's-got-a-great-personality chicks?" I asked. "If she's got a big inseam, then chances are she has a low self-esteem," I knew that my words were edgy.

Saul was fully aware that my idea of a good night did not include spending quality time all hugged up with a big mama. Like my aversion to MRI exams, it was a long story for another time. But I'd once dated a plus-sized woman, and I really liked her. But she needed too much attention, and that made me socially claustrophobic.

"Saul, read my lips: no big women! I mean that, Saul. Man, I'm serious!" I voiced this as bluntly as possible.

"What about thick women?" Saul joked.

"Thick? What's your definition of *thick*? In my opinion, Serena Williams is thick. Drew Barrymore is thick. Anything larger than a thirty-two-inch waist is probably too large for me," I chuckled, listening to my own insanity.

"Did you know that fat chicks give good head?" Saul added.

"Oh, really! I guess that makes you an expert in such matters?" I joked.

"Ooh. That's harsh! Even if a woman is built like a castle, you should still treat her like a princess," he added.

"You sound like a big man who's married to an even bigger woman—oops!" I playfully proclaimed.

"Man, if you weren't my best friend, I'd have to shoot you!" the car dealer said.

"Yeah right, man. You'd shoot me with what gun...a Twinkie?" I asked.

"Whatever, just get here!" he giggled like a kid on his birthday.

"I'll be there around nine," I said.

"By the way, are you interested in making some money?" he asked.

"All the time. As long as it doesn't compromise my freedom," I stipulated.

"It's sensitive; we'll talk at the party," he concluded.

"Understood," I replied.

CLICK!

Oddly, he cut the call short. Saul, 99 percent of the time, had to be talked into getting off the phone. I usually knew what Saul was talking about, but his last words this time were different. During all the years that I'd known Saul, he'd never offered to include me in any of his business ventures.

CHAPTER 9

The Best Parties End in a Bang!

• • •

May 2, 2008, 9:25 p.m.

IN BUSINESS TERMS, MY ARRIVAL time would have been undoubtedly late, but in party terms, I was right on time. I approached Saul's house and rang the doorbell. Swinging the door open, Saul grabbed me like I had just returned from the war. He wore a green velvet smoker's jacket that partially covered a T-shirt that read, *Anorexia Nervosa*.

"It's nine twenty-five; you are always late!" He bellowed as his head flung back.

"It's not even nine thirty," I exclaimed.

"Man, it's good to see you; it's been too long!" he smiled as if I'd brought dessert.

"Not long enough for you to have gotten to a gym, I see," I said while looking him up and down. "*Anorexia Nervosa*, ha-ha, fat shirt," I said.

"Thanks, man, I picked it at—"

Before he could finish his comment, I hit him with another insult.

"No really, fat shirt, what is that size? Extra huge! When are you going to lose some weight, man? It should say *Massive Mammary Glands* or just *Big Titties*! I know this dude at a gym that would hook you up with a very cheap initiation fee." I teased. To the outsider, I could've been seen as a jerk, but this was our normal give-and-take.

"Don't be a wiseass, son! How many times must I tell you that I'm not paying to go to a place that promotes sweating? The only two times that I want to sweat are during a summertime barbecue and at a whorehouse!" he snorted.

"Hey, man, it's your heart," I added.

Out of the blue, a curvaceous brunette came around the corner. Wearing a spaghetti-strapped dress, she looked like the type of girl that you see at a casino, not necessarily a "working girl," but not necessarily a "nonworking girl." She made her presence known as she put her left arm around Saul's waist.

"Saul, are you going to introduce me to your handsome friend?" she asked as our eyes locked.

"I'm sorry; I almost forgot," Saul playfully replied.

The last thing a married man wants to hear is that he's married. And for Saul to introduce me to an attractive woman caused serious waves of suspicion to run through me. I immediately started to examine the size of her hands, the shape and width of her shoulders.

"Clint, meet Morgan; Morgan, this is Clint," Saul said.

"It is a pleasure to meet you," I replied with a smile and a suggestive handshake.

"Nice to meet you as well," she said, still smiling. I didn't know if she was smiling because of my appearance or because of the rather tall glass of dark liquor in her left hand. Nonetheless, I was fairly certain that she could tell that I was at least partially curious about her aura.

"Listen, later for all that *Vibe* magazine meet *People* magazine bullshit! Morgan will be here watching the fight, and so will you; there will be time for her. Let's get to the real task at hand," he said as he pulled out a bankroll so thick it caused his left hand to look like capital *C* clenching the bills. This was Saul's way of saying it was time to concentrate on making some money and spending less time focusing on trying to get laid.

"Just like a fake-ass high roller to bring his mortgage payment to a poker table. Did you get Kelly's permission to play with that type of money?" I asked.

"Permission!" he said defensively. "The only woman I answer to is my mother. This is my money. Shit! Kelly's money is my money. I don't need any motherfucker's permission to spend my motherfucking money!"

"Ha-ha! Oh, now you're Mr. Big Tough Guy. Where's Kelly? Let's see what she has to say. I bet dollars to doughnuts she isn't even here. Is she? Kelly!" I yelled.

"Ah, no! Don't waste your breath; she's on a Bible cruise with her sorority. Let's go play cards," he responded while slapping his heavy right hand on the left side of my back.

We left Morgan in the living room, as Saul led me through a pantheon of rooms that boasted dual marbled fireplaces and bad overpriced art. We turned down a long narrow hallway that spilled into a room located in the back of his home. This room contained a group of well-dressed men sitting at a green felt card table. To my surprise, some of the faces were familiar.

I leaned into Saul and whispered, "What's the action on this table?"

"The buy-in is five hundred dollars, and we charge an extra hundred dollars for any calls. Don't worry; if you need me, I can spot you. You can put your car up for collateral," he joked.

"Ha-ha! No sale, but with your money and my skills, we could do some damage," I retorted.

"Be careful; you won't hear their bark but make no mistake; their bite is fatal," as he spoke, his playful demeanor quickly evaporated.

"I got you. I promise not to let you down, sensei," I retorted.

As we waded deeper into the room, my eyes encountered more glances. The muscular Asian male was curiously named Carlos; he was also a business proprietor. Some people referred to him as "Felix the Cat" because he'd brushed against both death and the law, and every time he came away unscathed. His connections ran deep, so deep that his connected connections had connected connections. I'd taken him for thirteen grand about a year ago.

"Carlos, my friend, long time no see. You're traveling alone? You usually travel with a *Miss Manhattan* or a *Dairy Queen* recipient. If my memory serves me correctly, last time our paths crossed, you also left a few grand lighter," I smiled while I said this.

"Not so fast, my friend, I don't think that lady luck will have the same smile for you this evening," he added with an evil smile of his own.

"On the contrary, I just met lady luck a few moments ago, and she told me that all systems are go for this evening. So, as always, I'm feeling quite positive." The mind-games had begun.

"Tough talk for a man whose face is as soft as a baby's asshole." At this point, Carlos brandished a platinum-plated handgun; pausing, he admired its craftsmanship as the low-hanging light brilliantly reflected off its barrel.

"Oops, I take that back, it appears that you did bring one of your bitches with you," I deadpanned.

"Are you talking to me?" he asked, while he and the third eye of his handgun looked me dead in my eyes.

I looked at Saul to see if he had any nonverbal advice. His expression was blank. I hadn't been this close to a gun that size in quite some time. My head started to pound, and my heart became heavy with adrenaline. But that didn't stifle my genetic predisposition for being a wiseass, so I uttered the first words that came to my mind.

"Am I talking to you? Of course, I am talking to you, you fake Larry Wong! Fuck you and your loud-ass yellow shirt!" I snapped.

The room became silent. I had made my move, and everyone waited to see what was going to be the Asian PED user's countermove. It didn't take long for him to stand up and start walking around the card table in my direction. I quickly took notice that he still had the gun clutched in his hand. My fingers clenched on their own. Questions swirled in my head as an ominous sensation crept down my spine. Each step brought him painfully closer to me; his stature was much larger standing than sitting. Mirrors in cars always report that *objects are closer than they appear*; well, I wished that I was in a car right now so that I could run his six-foot-five-inch frame over. When his steps came to a halt, the gun was less than a yard from my face.

"Any last words before I send you to the hereafter?" he spoke with a deep gravelly voice.

"I'm cool. At least my death won't be a mystery. You couldn't possibly have enough bullets to absolutely kill everybody in this room," was all I could muster.

The room was once again hushed with silence. I couldn't hear anything except for an incessantly high-pitched ringing sound. My eyes darted between his eyes and into the ominous dark hole at the end of his gun's barrel. I waited to see the final flash of light and feel the silence-shattering *bang*! His eyes were hazel green and clear, so clear that I could see my own death. Suddenly, out of the blue, Saul's voice rang loudly.

"That's enough; both of you fools, sit down! Especially you, Carlos!" Saul shouted.

With the gun still cocked in my face, Carlos started laughing. His mouth was agape, and his head reared back enough so that I could see his teeth had several fillings. Still laughing, he never put the gun away as he continued to keep me in his sights long after he returned to his seat.

"Put the fucking gun away!" Saul forcefully reiterated.

Finally obliging, Carlos put it on the table.

"Carlos, I told you to put it away! And where the hell is Rico?" Saul was agitated.

"Who's Rico?" I thought. The more I looked around, I realized that practically all of these faces minus Saul's were familiar because I had seen them in news editorials, highlighting their "alleged" behavior.

"Patience. Trust me; he will be here. I don't know when, but he will be here. When's the last time you spoke with him?" Carlos asked as he sipped his drink.

"About two hours ago," Saul responded.

"You seem to be in deep thought; what's on your mind?" Carlos bellowed in my direction.

"On my mind? A guy points a firearm the size of Cambodia in my face, and—what? —I am expected to be Joe Cool about it?" My sarcasm was biting.

As I spoke, Carlos's probing eyes were pointed at me, but this time, without the gun. He seemed to be looking through me. I mentally cursed myself for agreeing to attend this party.

Finally, he broke his trancelike state. "Gun, what gun?" Carlos responded. "Not so fast, my friend; this isn't a firearm!" he exclaimed.

Much to my chagrin, Carlos started pulling back what appeared to be a wrapper off the gun. He held it up to show me, and he started eating what I initially believed to be a killing machine, but it was a candy .357 Magnum. The sight of this imposing figure taking enormous bites of chocolate without impunity (the portions were so large that melted chocolate started to collect around the corners of his mouth) quickly erased what I perceived to be calamitous as the situation morphed into comedic irony. Like fans doing the wave at a baseball game, laughter in the room jumped from mouth to mouth. Even Saul laughed uncontrollably. There's nothing worse than being the brunt of a joke unless it's being the brunt of a joke in a room full of deviants. My margin of reciprocity was minimal. In hindsight, I had already dodged one bullet, so being laughed at was a more favorable alternative.

"Funny, very funny, gentlemen," I replied augmented by a cynical golf-style clap.

"I tell you one thing, Clint; I have to hand it to you; you've got moxie," Carlos had stopped laughing and resumed eyeballing me.

"Let's see how well you hold it together while I'm taking your money during this card game," I responded.

"Well, hell, let's play ball!" Saul shouted.

The table was set; we arranged the limits and the buy-in amounts. I was sitting two chairs away from Carlos, who sat across from Saul. We had played five hands. During the last hand, I bet heavy and bluffed Carlos into folding.

"What were you holding?" he asked.

"Whoa, Carlos, if I told you, then I would have to shoot you!" The room filled with laughter. As Carlos's eyes glared that all-too-similar stare in my direction.

KNOCK-KNOCK!

The door opened. It was Morgan, and she had three female friends with her.

"I hate to interrupt this Illuminati meeting, but the fight is about to start!" Looking at me, she added, "My friends and I wanted to know if you and Saul could join us in the bathroom?" she tapped her right nostril with her right index finger as she cracked a devilish smile.

"Ahh! Ladies your arrival is right on time. Clint and I were just about to send these gentleman home—to get their shoe boxes!" Saul exclaimed. Their interruption signaled an end to the poker game.

As soon as I stood up, Morgan rushed to my side. I don't know how many drinks she'd had, but she split her breasts with my arm as she pressed her chest against my right triceps.

"You come with me; I might need you to hold my hand; I'm not good with violence," she said playfully.

"I think I can accommodate your needs," I added, smiling as we walked out of the room.

"I think I've heard enough of your bullshit!" Carlos barked as he walked right past me, not close enough to touch me, yet still close enough that I could see that the fabric in his houndstooth blazer was poorly stitched.

"What was that all about?" Morgan queried.

I merely dismissed his actions with a mild shrug of the shoulders. "Maybe he has gas," I hypothesized.

Just as I turned to leave the room with Morgan, Saul grabbed my left arm and whispered in my ear, "We'll talk about what I mentioned over the phone later."

"OK, cool," I said and nodded in agreement.

Suddenly, the doorbell chimed. Saul had a super expensive multimedia audiovisual system, and his doorbell, which someone just pressed, chimed throughout the house.

"I'll grab the door," Saul announced, as he was last to exit the room.

In the living room, a small clutch of partygoers sat around a man with long dreadlocks, while he played the piano. Saul walked past this spectacle into the foyer and opened the door.

Expecting someone else, Saul said, "Cheese, what's up! Man, I'm glad you could make it."

"Whatever! The only reason I was invited was because I told you I would pick up some ice cream," Cheese said as he playfully pushed the bag into Saul's robust midsection. "Wait a minute! Did I miss the fight?" he asked.

"Cheese, why are you so late? You know you barely made the guest list, and you show up at this hour?" Saul queried while shaking his head in disbelief that Cheese actually came.

"I'm here! I think I'll grab myself a brew and go mingle with a lovely lady," Cheese said.

"You do that, Cheese! Go and do whatever it is that you do," Saul said, still shaking his head. "Hey, Cheese; thanks, man," Saul said as he patted the bag and walked back to the viewing room.

Before he could even claim a seat, Carlos bellowed, "Is Rico finally here?"

"No, but Cheese is," Saul responded.

"Who the fuck is Cheese?" Carlos snarled.

"Cheese? Who ordered pizza? I'll take a slice!" a faceless voice from the crowd yelled.

"Clint, you remember Cheese, don't you? Wait a minute; I think you had already left for the other coast at that point," Saul said.

"Nah, bruh, I don't know any Cheeses," I responded.

"He's a different type of dude," Saul retorted.

HDTV is good, but HDTV is exceptional when it is in conjunction with a special-edition 250-inch flat screen projection television. Images are crisper; sounds are more audible. Quality TV can make life more enjoyable. The fight was about to begin as excitement rose within the group of viewers. Television fight prognosticators predicted this would be the bloodiest fight of the year. After months of buildup, finally, the opening bell rang. As we leaned back among the sofa's cushions, Morgan placed her left hand on the inside of my right thigh. I saw, while everyone else was focused on the fight, Carlos and Saul walk toward the kitchen. Little did I know, I would later discover what happened during their private business meeting.

Inside of the kitchen, after the kitchen door swung closed, Carlos said, "Can this guy be trusted? I don't want you telling me this dude can swim, and before things get deep, he's gurgling for a life jacket."

"I trust him; I've known him for years," Saul added.

"I hope you are right because this could get very hairy, and I don't like to find hair in my food!" Carlos voiced.

"I haven't discussed anything with him. He has no idea of our plans," Saul added.

Their conversation continued through the heavy cheering that came from the viewing room. On several occasions, Saul's guests jumped to their feet as the heavyweights waged a brutal war of attrition. First the champion, a crowd favorite, imposed his will only to be rebuked by the scrappy and equally gainful challenger. As the sixth round began, the combatants had increased the brutality. Vicious blows were exchanged, as each gave as good as he got. Then boom! The ending occurred faster and stranger than anyone could've anticipated. Both fighters threw earth-shattering blows after they met in the center of the ring. Fists flailed as they landed shots that sounded like baseball bats slamming against raw meat. Before anyone could blink, the challenger, who had absorbed a seemingly insurmountable level of punishment, connected a left uppercut that sent the champion crashing facedown into the canvas, breaking his nose, which shoved its bridge directly into his brain. There was so much blood. Unfortunately, the exhausted challenger's punch momentum caused him to lose his balance, and he tripped over the fallen champion and fell through the ropes before he crashed cranium first onto the ringside bell. His body flapped around and convulsed on the scorer's table right in front of the ringside judges and reporters. Initially, the referee was confused when presented with such a quandary. Diplomatically, he offered a general ten count that received no response from either fighter as medics and various types of security personnel rushed into the ring. By then, it was too late; the champion died before they could turn his body over. The official decision was a draw. Everyone was in a state of shock at the gruesome spectacle. Commentators, ringside fight experts, and other spectators were all shaken and had no precedent to relate to regarding what had just happened. Raw with emotion, a majority of Saul's guests laconically walked outside to the heated pool for a change of scenery and some much-needed fresh air.

Morgan led me to a gazebo several feet away from the rest of the patio furniture. Long shadows cast by tiki torches created a tribal motif around the yard's perimeter. But the automaticity of the chemistry between Morgan and me wasn't shadowed. Our interaction graduated from playful kisses into full-blown making out. Similarly, Saul and one of Morgan's friends, a petite, brunette named Albany, were sprawled out on a plush lawn sofa. Meanwhile, the guy everyone referred to as Cheese was obviously drunk, complaining, almost whining about the unsatisfying nature of his life. As he spoke, he stumbled and almost tripped over his own ego. He even interrupted our conversation. Morgan flashed a compassionate smile as she engaged Cheese.

"Why do they call you Cheese, Cheese?" Morgan asked.

His speech pattern was long beyond slurred at this point. "When-n-n...I was younger, my parents were very poor, and we always ate cheese sandwiches for lunch and dinner. Eventually I became clinically constipated. I was so embarrassed, so I never said anything. I guess silence didn't help my situation. But people at school teased me. So, I scraped together any amount of money and bought bubble gum and gave it to my classmates, so they would like me. I figured if people were chewing, then they would be less likely to say anything to or about me—or the fact that I smelled like cheese," he blurted.

I could barely contain my laughter. "Do you still suffer from constipation?" I asked.

"No!" he responded succinctly.

"I thought they called you Cheese because you always smiled," I added to make him feel better.

"Maybe it's twofold; he's always smiling because he's no longer constipated!" Saul comically shouted, as a small group started to laugh.

Morgan whispered something into my ear. I don't remember what she said, but I do remember that it made me smile. I turned to her, I nodded my head, and we stood up.

"None of that matters because one day I might not be famous, but I will be rich. Then people will give me the respect I deserve!" Cheese now spoke with shades of defiance filtered through his voice. He swayed side to side, as he clutched a half-empty Grey Goose bottle in his left hand.

"Cheese, real respect is earned, not bought. I've seen plenty of guys that became rich. But even after getting money, people still treated them as if they were still broke. Always invest faith in yourself, not your money," I advised.

"Hey, Saul, we're going to take off," Morgan announced.

Saul rose from his lawn sofa. "You're leaving?" he asked.

"Yeah, man, is everything OK?" I asked.

"Everything is cool," Saul replied. "My pleasure, glad you showed up. Clint, I'll call you tomorrow."

"Cool," I said as we fist bumped.

"You aren't coming, Saul?" Morgan asked quizzically.

"No, but I'm sure Clint will at some point tonight!" he laughed.

"Hey, I'm not that easy!" Morgan protested.

"Thanks again, Saul. It's too bad we can't help you clean up, but Cheese is still here. I think he just got in the hot tub," I added as we walked away.

"Cheese? In my hot tub? Damn, I hope he isn't rubbing one out again! No one's in the mood for egg-drop soup!" Saul's face was covered in disgust.

"Yuck!" Morgan blurted.

"If that cocksucker is doing what I think he's doing, then somebody's in a lot of trouble!" Saul rambled as he said his good-byes again and rushed toward his precious hot tub as fast as his fleshy legs could carry him.

Morgan and I walked around the west side of the house to my car. The path we traversed was brick and lined with lavender and well-manicured flowers. I opened the door for her; she smiled as I closed it. Then I walked around. To my surprise, she reached over and unlocked my door. Once inside, we started joking about some of the people we'd met during the evening.

"Did you see that woman who was so drunk that she started kissing everyone in sight?" Morgan asked with an extended chuckle.

"That was sad. I was told that she inherited millions of dollars after her parents died in a plane crash. Since the tragedy, she's been sleeping with every guy or girl she could get her hands on," I reported. "But enough about them! Let's talk about what we're doing for the rest of the evening," I deadpanned.

"I know of a place that you'll really enjoy," she said with a sly smile.

"Your place?" I asked.

"Slow down, Hank Moody! I at least deserve a few drinks and the offer of a meal. If you met some random woman in a bar, you would spring for at least a couple drinks. Besides, this place is a lot of fun. Part restaurant, part postmodern club—it's called *IDEAL*. Have you ever been there?" I noticed whenever she tried to be persuasive, she had a way of tossing her long, beautiful hair over her shoulders.

"The way you were talking earlier had my mind spinning," I confessed.

"Trust me; everyone will be happy once the night is all over," she said and smiled.

"Just lead the way; what's our ETA?" I asked.

"About twenty minutes," she replied.

Random night, here I was, driving my car with a woman that I'd just met a few hours earlier, and now we were headed to some unknown club. My mind wandered back to Saul; I wondered how his evening turned out. As if on cue, like she was reading my mind, Morgan started playing with the hem of her dress.

"Would this dress have a different effect if it was shorter?" she made this inquiry as if she hadn't noticed that her current hemline receded well beyond the middle of her thighs and even further from her knees. My mind and all its previous thoughts were now focused on one thought and one thought alone.

"I think there's always room for improvement," I retorted.

"Well, how about this?" she hiked it up just enough to increase the tease.

"Now we're getting somewhere!" I announced.

In the meantime, unbeknownst to me, back at Saul's place, a business discussion had encountered a few wrinkles and several unsolved scenarios that were causing Carlos to become angry. Saul's bullmastiff puppy started barking.

"Would you calm down! I mean, what worked the last time might not be suitable for this situation. And all the extra window dressing—is this a Macy's Day Christmas sale?" Saul tried to get Carlos to understand his point of view.

"Listen, you fat fucker! If not this way, then how would you propose we do it? Tell me why I shouldn't mop the floor with you! I'm curious as to what brilliant ideas are going to be shared by a fat-assed, idiot car salesman!" Running on red, Carlos clearly favored confrontation, whereas Saul was attempting to peacefully resolve matters.

"First of all, the name calling isn't necessary! You ignorant immigrant from some Third World nation, fuck you! I don't care how it gets done. Vinny assured me that we were all equal partners. Wait until Rico gets here; he'll tell you the same! Everyone is going to eat; there's enough food at the table. When I eat, I like to chew my food slowly. I just want to make sure it goes down, and when it goes down, I want it to go down smoothly. Indigestion is not an option! Indigestion that lasts for ten to fifteen years isn't GTI, it's a *prison sentence*!" Saul shouted.

Hearing enough rhetoric, Carlos pounded his fist on the granite countertop. "You don't have to tell me about jail. There's a reason it's called a *penal* facility! I've seen the biggest dudes go in as hardened mercenaries only to come out with their shirts tied above their belly buttons, switching and twitching, acting like the littlest bitches!" Carlos yelled.

"Whatever, little man, I can roll my sleeves up with the best of them; you keep popping off like that and you're about to find out!" Saul was getting his second wind and talked tough.

"What are you saying? Are you looking to get dirty?" barked Carlos.

"Dirty!" Saul chimed sarcastically. "I'm saying if you're feeling froggy, then leap, motherfucker—leap!" Saul raged.

Walking to the island counter in the middle of the kitchen, Carlos pulled one of its drawers open and produced a shiny, real handgun. "I don't have time for a fist fight, but I can aim!" he screamed as he pointed his gun at Saul.

Saul, on the other hand, spoke in the coolest way possible, but his voice still cracked. "You have two lips and one tongue, right?" Saul quizzed.

"What's that supposed to mean?" Carlos inquired.

"That means you can suck my dick!" Saul retorted.

The kitchen door quickly swung open. Like in a John Wayne movie, out of the shadows and through the door stepped Rico, a reputed member of the underworld, a vicious, cold executioner, generally devoid of loyalty apart from one man and one man only. Rico had killed before and would kill for the rest of his days.

"What's all this noise? Where's the stuff?" Rico demanded.

"Call the police; this SOB is crazy!" Saul urged.

"Where is the motherfucking stuff? Your time is up," Carlos said in a matter-of-fact manner.

"I told you that Vinny has the stuff!" exhorted Saul.

"Well, if Saul doesn't have the product, then, Carlos, what are you waiting for? I thought that this would have been done by now!" Rico shouted as he flashed a gun of his own. "Where's the shit? Who's got the shit?" Rico screamed like a psychoactive psycho.

"I put it in the oven!" Saul yelled, and Rico walked over to inspect the gas stove.

"What? Don't tell me this is a set-up!" Shocked and exasperated, Saul couldn't believe what was transpiring.

"Where's the rest? This bag is light!" Rico unzipped the bag, examined its contents, turned, and walked directly to Carlos.

"So many chances and yet so many screw-ups! You're like half short. What type of games are you two playing?" Rico now directed his questions to Saul and Carlos.

"Look, I can make things right. I just need more time! I can pay you double whatever he's paying you!" Saul pleaded.

"Sorry, Charlie, time's long overdue. I've been waiting for the moment to kill you ever since you opened your first dealership. John Smith, the man who you bought out back in 1996, was a decent man with a good

American upbringing. His family was born and bred in this country. I went to school with his sister, but your greedy, mongrel money forced him and his family out onto the street!" Rico turned to Carlos and yelled, "The sooner you off this fucker, the better!"

"Looks like tonight isn't your night, fat boy!" Carlos said with an evil smirk as he put the business end of the revolver against Saul's forehead.

"Any last words?" Rico asked.

"If it's the money you need, then I can get it for you," Saul's tone had changed dramatically—it was almost as if he was whimpering. "Carlos, you and I have made a lot of money together; that has to count for something—right?" Saul continued to plead.

"I just can't risk another situation like the one I had about ten years ago. The story goes something like this: Around four in the morning, I was on a backwater dirt road, just finished a situation, and out of nowhere, a hog ran in front of my car. It slammed its left hindquarter against the grill, spun around, and disappeared into the underbrush. I stopped my car, pulled out a flashlight and searched the darkness looking for that beast. Eventually, I gave up. Early the next morning, a cop was at my door asking questions about a pig that I allegedly hit. Caught dead to right. I came to one conclusion and one conclusion only. The pig told on me; he was the only one that could've squealed. Get it? He squealed! Ha-ha!" Rico was the sole voice of laughter. "Oh, for Christ's sake!"

Without hesitation Rico pulled another gun from his rear holster and squeezed both triggers until the clips had been bled empty. The sounds of shell casings fell to the ground as violence rang throughout the kitchen. Blood from both Saul and Carlos splattered over Rico's face. It looked as if he had contracted a severe case of chicken pox.

"Fuck, what did you do that for?" Carlos screamed as he collapsed, stunned and disabled.

"You took too long! I gave you an order and you hesitated. Real killers kill! They don't try to figure out the square root of pi. They just point and squeeze. Remember that during your next life," Rico admonished as he bent down and grabbed Carlos's wallet and car keys.

Having shot everyone in the room, including the hapless puppy, Rico was careful not to leave any evidence. He snatched a towel off a rack in the powder room and wiped down the gun, the doorknobs, cabinets, counters, the bodies, and everything else. Using the same towel, he turned the faucet on and washed the blood from his face. Then he found a large, black trash bag and stuffed it with his bloody shirt, Carlos's and Saul's keys, wallets, and cell phones, and the cleanup towel. His eyes assessed the room as he stepped over a puddle of blood oozing from both corpses. Bags in hand, murders committed, he vacated the premises through the back door just off the kitchen.

CHAPTER 10

Nips and Tucks

• • •

May 3, 2008, 2:17 a.m.

WE FINALLY MADE IT TO the club. And it only took about fifty minutes, I thought sardonically. A detour allowed us enough privacy to be able to inhale a few blasts from her bat and dugout. Morgan's weed was more than serviceable; it just wasn't on par with my stuff.

We finally reached *IDEAL*. The menu was cleverly designed as a plastic lightbulb; the waitress screwed it into a tableside socket, and it cast the menu in the form of a 3-D hologram. As my body sank into the leather booth; we ordered four cocktails and three appetizers, and my mind began to drift.

"So, what do you think? Nice isn't it?" she said as a passive-deliberate way of redirecting my attention back on her.

Realizing that I wasn't much company, I pretended to give her my full attention. I smiled and placed my right hand on Morgan's thigh.

"Very mellow, I think I could get real comfortable in a place like this," I responded.

Our server was named Carin "with a *C*," a young coed, maybe twenty, no more than twenty-five. Her nipples were perky and so was her smile. "Have you seen our dessert specials? The kitchen will be open for another forty-five minutes. Can I get you anything else?" Carin questioned.

"I'll take a club soda, and the lady will have—"

"I'll have a chocolate martini." Morgan smiled as she interrupted me.

"Will the drinks complete your order, or will you be ordering any desserts?" Carin asked.

"I'll have a large slice of pecan pie with whipped cream on the side in a to-go box," I requested.

"OK, well, I will be back shortly with your order." She was all business, and as she spoke, she turned and bounced toward the bar.

IDEAL offered a dance floor and bass-heavy, frantic music. I knew that Morgan was about to ask what I hoped she wouldn't.

"Do you dance?" she asked.

"I do, but I have been diagnosed as being technophobic," I replied.

"So, what are you saying? You're allergic to techno music?" she inquired.

"Yeah, but not just techno, you could say that my body has a disdain for most forms of dance. I was diagnosed eight years ago," I added.

"Pity, I enjoy working up a sweat on the dance floor," she said, "Well, if you'll excuse me, I'm going to use the restroom. When I get back, we'll see if I can't change your mind about techno—or at least the prospect of some form of dance."

As Morgan disappeared into the crowd of dancers, I suddenly had a bad vibe. My grandmother once told me that I had a gift of connecting past events to the present, as well as an acute penchant for identifying premonitions. I always wrote it off as older-generation hocus-pocus. But this sensation was so strong that it forced me to grab my phone, and I dialed Saul.

"Greetings, you have reached Saul Automotive Industries, Incorporated, please leave a detailed message including your name, number, purpose for calling, and someone will get back to you in a timely manner. I thank you for your call, have a nice day." The recording ended with the usual beep.

My consternation stemmed from my knowledge that Saul was never one to wait to say anything, especially if it involved the prospect of making or spending money. His exact quote—"We'll talk about what I mentioned over the phone later"—troubled me. I started to break down the events of the evening until two excruciatingly loud women sitting four booths down kidnapped my thoughts. One of the women, a natural blonde, wore black jeans and a matching denim jacket as she shoved pasta into her mouth while donning dark sunglasses, and the tackiest costume jewelry dangled from both ears. The second woman was dressed in a dark green maternity gown with a pair of crisp white tennis shoes. The two women grew louder as they continued to argue.

Morgan returned from the bathroom amid the chaos and confusion. "What the hell is going on?" she frantically asked.

"Apparently, the pregnant woman was having an affair with the other woman's husband, and before she could fully confront her, the pregnant woman's water broke, and all law and order was lost after that," I succinctly summarized.

"Are you serious?" Morgan asked.

"I don't understand how people get themselves in situations like that. I mean, just be honest about what you are doing, and the truth will set you free. There are about one and a half billion available women in the world; some dudes make it so difficult," I said.

"Church! This much is true. I'm not looking for a wedding engagement, just a good time. Guys and girls put up this elaborate facade when we all just want the same," she acknowledged.

"What's that...to be held?" I asked.

"No, to fuck!" she vehemently uttered.

"Oh really, just like that?" I responded.

"Without a doubt, the confusion enters when the guy or girl knowingly only enjoyed the act of sex, and as they continue to enjoy the sex, one person starts developing feelings while the other person enjoys the lust. Vulnerability becomes intimate, but once the spark goes out that's when the luster walks out. Then, the jilted shifts from a casual stalker to a full-blown sociopath. So much wasted time and resources when it should have been a simple situation with a simple solution," she said with sincerity and confidence.

"Really? What kind of jive are you slinging? A former friend of mine always said that a woman that just wants an orgasm and no relationship is like a good-looking woman that cooks and cleans—they just don't exist," I said. "I personally don't feel that way. But I would say that it's rare to find a sexual partnership in which at least one participant doesn't develop feelings."

"You don't think it exists; I'll prove it to you," she said as she looked me square in the eyes. "I think you've been running among the wrong women. There is a diverse collection of women that feel just as I do," she replied with conviction.

"Hey, I'll take your word. Maybe you could be my Ponce de Leon?" I quipped.

"Well, let me be the first to initiate you to the other NWA: *Neo-Women's Association*. Are you ready for directions to my place?" she asked as she grabbed my hand and slid it down to what her underwear once covered.

Carin returned at an inopportune time.

"How much for the drinks?" I asked with my hand still planted inside Morgan's thigh.

Startled, Carin paused and said, "Thirty-two seventy-five."

"Here's fifty. Can you deliver our drinks to the baby-mama-drama table? I think they need them more than we do," I replied as I took Morgan's left hand and we stood up to leave.

Exiting past two oversized doormen, we were free from the rabid-paced techno scene. Feeling mentally sluggish, my mind could not and would not exorcise my daunting premonitions. If Saul would just answer his damn phone, then the rest of this evening would take care of itself.

Out of nowhere, a siren screamed at all decibels as a cherry-red ambulance bounced down the boulevard with its lights flashing spastically. The alarmed paramedic jumped out of the truck, his medium frame sported a left arm that was completely covered in tattoos. "Is this 3617 *IDEAL*, the spot of the pregnancy?"

I nodded.

As we walked to the car, I knew that I should be engaging Morgan in some kind of conversation, but I was engulfed in my own thoughts.

"Hey, cosmonaut, I'm over here," she said, waving her hands in a mocking manner as if she was a drowning swimmer desperately trying to grab a lifeguard's lifeline.

"Apologies, I promise from this point forward, you will have my undivided attention," I replied.

"This might bring you back to earth. Want to hear a crazy story?" she was so excited; there was no way I could say no.

"Sure, shoot," I responded.

"My mother once traced our family tree back to the nineteenth century, a string of upper-class women, who were so sexually inhibited that they instructed their doctors to surgically remove their clitoris, so they wouldn't have to deal with the embarrassment of libido." Her hair fell over her eyes as she spoke

"Did you and your mother get clipped as well?" I asked, almost laughing at my own foolishness.

"Hell no! But you might if you don't give me the attention I deserve. Did you see all of those men in the club checking me out?" she protested.

"Yes, I did," I said, but we both knew that most of the men at *IDEAL* weren't interested in her clitoris or anyone else's.

"Attention is still attention," she exclaimed.

"Sure, so what do you want me to do?" I inquired.

"If I let you spend the night, you have to promise to focus on *me*," she playfully grabbed my right cheek as she said this.

"I can do that; just tell me where's home," I said.

Three hours had passed since we left Saul's party, and just thirty minutes after we arrived at her house, I was discovering Morgan's clitoris and all its magical wonders.

Meanwhile, somewhere across town, three bodies were cooking in Saul's kitchen. A neighbor had called the police. It took authorities about five minutes to respond. Forensics personnel snapped pictures and collected evidence as Officer Dansbury spoke on his cell phone with the chief.

"So, we have one seriously injured man, one dead man and one dead puppy. It's a shame what they did to that dog," Dansbury said as he walked around the dead.

"Yes, the scene has been properly secured and the coroner just arrived," Dansbury confirmed.

"Do you think these murders are connected to the guy we caught two days ago?" Dansbury asked.

"I agree," Dansbury replied.

"No, I haven't, but I will check with the *EDIBLE GROOVES* surveillance team. Hopefully, they have discovered more information," Dansbury stated.

"Yes, the CI has been activated and everything is running smoothly," Danbury responded.

"Affirmative, I will call you when I get there," Dansbury confirmed.

CLICK!

CHAPTER 11

Putrefaction

• • •

May 3, 2008, 8:31 a.m.

"Good morning, sleepyhead," she said, smiling.

Confusion impaired my vision. Still straining to focus, I rubbed my eyes until I could see straight. There she stood, presenting buxom breasts and taut buttocks, with only a suede-trimmed bra and matching panties separating her from absolute nakedness.

"*Me gusta tu leche*," were the words she spoke.

Before I could resist, she mounted me and playfully started to choke my abdominal core between her powerful thighs. Her cell phone vibrated, and she answered the call.

"Hello. Yes, I'm fine. How did everything go on your end? That's too bad. Yeah, I met someone," she giggled. "OK, I'll tell you all about it while we're shopping this afternoon. Good-bye," Morgan said.

CLICK!

"Now that your conference call is finished, how about some breakfast? You aren't so evolved that you've transcended the art of hospitality?" I joked.

"What about some coffee?" she inquired.

"Some people drink coffee. Me, I usually wake up with a shower. But since you're making it, I'll try it. What kind do you have?" I questioned.

"A friend just came back from Negril. I have an excellent Jamaican blend. Do you take cream and sugar?" she flicked her dark hair back as she spoke.

"Black with seven sugars and a splash of cream would be hip," I said with a wink.

She returned minutes later with a copy of the morning's newspaper in her left hand and a steaming cup of java in the other. Surrounded by a collection of multicolored throw pillows clustered against the headboard, my head rested as I fumbled through black print typed against recycled paper. The newspaper pages crumpled like leaves as I thumbed through the *METRO, BUSINESS,* and *STYLE* sections. I had a penchant for starting with the sports section before gradually reading my way into the "real world." To my dismay, during my initial search, the *SPORTS* section wasn't present, but I was instantly mortified at what I stumbled upon on the front page of the *SOCIETY* section. I felt like I'd been given a swift kick to my heart. I was so overwhelmed that the paper-thin article nearly became too heavy for me to hold. The title said it all:

SOCIETY

Local Automobile Mogul
Found Slain in His Home

-By Charles Taylor

Mount Vernon—Saul Briggs was found slain inside his palatial estate early Sunday morning. An unidentified body and canine corpse were also at the scene. Neighbors said that they heard what they believed to be fireworks coming from his home, but that the noises weren't anything out of the ordinary.

"He was always throwing some type of party or social event," reported an unidentified source. Mr. Briggs was notorious for his wealth, which was generated through his family's automobile business, but he was just as famous for the elaborate parties he and his wife would host. Another neighbor who also chose to remain anonymous stated: "Saul was a respected member of our community and his generous contributions will be missed." Saul Briggs leaves behind his second wife Kelly Charese Briggs. Authorities have not released information pertaining to any leads regarding the investigation.

Realizing a New Vision for the City's Port

Octocan—District developers have formed a financial consortium with a Los Angeles

I didn't need to read the rest of the article.

"What's the matter?" Morgan asked.

The grim look on my face startled her. "I'm sorry, but I have to go," I mumbled.

"Why? Did I do something wrong?" she queried.

"No, it's just that I…" Instead of trying to explain, I simply passed her the article.

"What's the matter?" Morgan asked.

"Saul's dead," I quietly announced.

"What! We just partied with him last night. What happened?" she was confused.

I later learned that she and Saul had known each other for years, dating back to the opening of his first dealership. She was one of his original showroom girls. They had become quite close; he was somewhat of a mentor.

"I can't believe it!" she spoke in utter shock.

Considering the situation, I felt it was necessary for me to leave. As I started to corral my clothes, Morgan tried to grab my hand.

"Where are you going? Don't you think we should do something—anything? Should we call the authorities?" she asked while trying to pull me closer.

"The cops! I don't trust the cops," I abruptly responded as I resisted her efforts.

"Well, if not the police, then who?" she inquired.

"Morgan, I don't think there's anything that we can do at this point. I really just need to leave; I hope that you understand," I moved my lips and these words limped out of my mouth.

Bending over the right side of her bed, I dragged my T-shirt over my head and then slid on my jeans. Chugging hot coffee isn't always advisable, but my numbness embraced the scald. Morgan was adamant that I stay. But I had to absorb, process, and react. I thanked her for her hospitality. She walked me to the door. I opened it and walked out. Still undressed, she peeked around her door and watched as I stepped down five steps and walked down the driveway. I can't recall if I said good-bye. I can recall, there was an exchange of words, a brief embrace, and maybe a kiss. Honestly, all of those details are fuzzy. Once I drove off, unbeknownst to me, Morgan picked up her phone and dialed.

"He just left. Yeah, he was shaken, not stirred," she said to the voice on the other end as she chuckled.

"We exchanged numbers. Don't worry; I know how to play this," she stated.

CLICK!

I was five miles away from Morgan's house when I pulled my car to the side of the road, turned it off, and unzipped the passenger-side headrest. I had it hollowed out to conceal my emergency revolver. I removed my gun and put it under my seat, restarted my car, shifted gears, and drove off. I was still trying to make Saul's death a reality.

Damn! I knew he straddled the line, but I thought he spent more time stepping with the good guys than the miscreants. I had question after question, but not one answer. Where should I begin? I didn't know whom to ask, let alone trust.

Traffic was a static-lull, as cars barely advanced. I took the opportunity to rewind the faces and conversations as I tried to deduce who was the author of Saul's murder. Of course, Carlos was the first person that came to mind. I had other suspicions—like, who was Rico, and did he kill Saul? I knew that I could be doing more, but what? Should I contact the police? Am I one of the suspects? These questions flooded my mind until my head hurt. Heavyhearted and heavy minded, the reality of Saul's death continued to hammer me in the chest, harsh cold nail after harsh cold nail.

My brainstorm: During every turn and twist, Saul had been there for me, even during a rough patch out West. They say that the good die young. I'm not necessarily saying that Saul was good; Lord knows his womanizing ways could alone condemn him to Hades. But judging him strictly as a man's man, there weren't many men better than Saul. His generosity was well documented; he was the life of every party, affable, and made people of all shapes, sizes, and personalities feel comfortable. And here I sat, trapped, a prisoner of my own thoughts, paralyzed by my own fears.

CHAPTER 12

This Ain't No Love Seat

• • •

May 5, 2008, 11:35 a.m.

IT WAS LATE MORNING. No, it was actually closer to early afternoon. Damon slowly climbed the stairs of the complex until he stood outside of the mysterious screaming woman's apartment door. Her apartment was the only apartment on the fifth floor, and this was the only home she could afford. Facing foreclosure, finances forced her to move. The last few days had been sheer hell. Under her lumpy bed, in a shoe box, was a shabby photo album filled with tattered pictures, pictures of happier times. In one of them, her son was blowing out his birthday candles. Everything had changed after her husband died thirty years ago.

The old woman was a Ukrainian immigrant; her American name was Martha (Mar-tah). Formerly smooth as ivory, now her skin sported deep creases. But her face was too wrinkled to be mistaken for laugh lines. Shit, she hadn't laughed since 1972. Five presidents later, and Martha was still suffering. Once a respected housewife, she now lived in constant fear of her firstborn son as he took delight in littering her small frame with bright ruby bruises that resembled the red-clouded eye of Jupiter. Mother-and-son conversations were now heard and spoken with his fists. Her life was as miserable and dry as thirteen-day-old meatloaf. She lived only because living was all that she knew. Today was one of those days. If Jack could feel the tremble of the Giant's footsteps, then Martha definitely heard Damon's footsteps coming up the stairs. Panic-stricken, she quickly ran into her bathroom and locked the door. Quivering in fear, she leaned every ounce of her weight against the door, and her heart rate elevated as keys clanged outside her door. Seething, Damon walked into her apartment.

"You skanky, dirty two-timing cunt! Who the fuck have you been talking to?" he ripped the phone out of the wall as he yelled. Then Damon used the receiver as a knocker and banged it against his mother's bathroom door.

"You called the police, didn't you? Has it really come to this! I told you what would happen if you stepped out of line!" Martha's weight was ignored as Damon shoved himself into the apartment's only bathroom, and his force sent her sprawling backward onto the floor. Then he slammed the door shut and turned the hot water on. In horror, Martha crouched in the corner, while he stared stoically into the mirror until it fogged up. Eyes closed, he bowed his head until his chin rested on his chest. And without saying a word, Damon walked over to his mother and violently beat her like she was a stranger. Martha ate blow after blow until the total exceeded double figures. For good measure, Damon kicked her in her abdomen. The third and final kick knocked her dentures out of her mouth and across the floor. He ignored the blood, sweat, and tears that dripped off his left hand as he continued to abuse her.

"What did I tell you about the importance of silence!" he shouted as his eyes and ears delighted at the sights and sounds of his mother as she sobbed in pain.

Eventually, Martha clutched her chest as her head drooped and her breathing became labored. Damon had cracked her sternum. In grave pain, she meekly squawked like a pale white turkey. Now there was only one thing left to do. Damon plugged in an old transistor radio to muffle Martha's moans as he slid a plastic bag over her face. Death couldn't come quick enough. She offered little resistance as she gagged on her own carbon dioxide. A dark smile crawled over Damon's face as she suffocated on her last breaths. Martha was dead within a few brief minutes.

He stepped over his mother's body as he picked up his cell phone and dialed. As the phone rang, the floor creaked while Damon paced back and forth over one of its many dead spots.

"I need you to come pick-up some furniture!" he said before he walked back into the bathroom and stared at himself in the mirror as his mother lay dead on the cold grout.

Forty-five minutes had passed, and Damon was still staring at himself in the mirror. Grabbing his phone again, he had grown impatient. "You're where!" he barked.

"You have no fucking idea of where you're going!" Damon screamed.

"Do know what a brownstone looks like? You're a fucking defect! What are you, Niggarican? If you don't hurry up and get here, I'm going to slap you and give the job to someone else!" Damon abruptly hung-up.

CLICK!

Next, Damon casually placed a bedspread over the corpse. Grabbing his tool belt and a piece of bread from the cupboard, he lit a cigarette and calmly walked out of the apartment and down the stairs.

KNOCK-KNOCK!

Sunlight flooded the foyer as he opened the door; there stood Alphonso. Alphonso was a pudgy, peanut-shaped man. He survived off of odd jobs and his old lady's pension.

"Alphonso! Where the fuck have you been? You've been out boozing, haven't you? Look at your eyes; you're shit faced!" Damon's was beyond annoyed.

SMACK!

Startled, Alphonso rubbed his stinging right cheek and decided it was best if he kept quiet.

"I've got some work to finish upstairs. While I'm doing that, you can start knocking this wall out and then pull up this carpeting!" Damon demanded.

"Hey, man, you think I could bum a smoke?" Alphonso asked.

"Sure!" Damon took a deep drag and blew it in his face. "Now you've had your smoke; get the fuck to work!" Damon turned and went upstairs.

While Alphonso started the demolition project, Damon began the gruesome task of disposing of his mother's body. She'd died from internal bleeding, so the resulting cleanup was minimal. But Damon had not planned on killing his mother…today. It was purely an impulse killing; therefore, he was taking care of the disposal on the fly. He concluded that he should shove her frail frame between the mattresses of her old living-room sofa bed. Damon covered his mother with heavy-duty black garbage bags. Then he tossed his mother, fully wrapped and duct-taped, on the sofa bed and walked toward the foot of the bed and proceeded to neatly fold the crevices of the sofa bed over her seventy-pound body. For added security, with Martha's body compressed inside the mattress, he wrapped additional tape around the bed's metallic handle and looped it under and over the sofa, taping it together like an accordion. He lit another cigarette, inhaled deeply, and expelled an impressive cloud. Damon had not felt this relaxed since he got his first blow job. With his mother all cleaned up, he pulled out his cell phone and dialed. Then he opened the apartment door and yelled downstairs.

"Hey, Alphonso! Stop what you're doing and come on upstairs! I need help throwing this old love seat away!"

CHAPTER 13

If You Can't Stand the Heat

● ● ●

May 5, 2008, 9:25 a.m.

THAT SAME MORNING, THE RUSH had gotten frantically busy at *LETTUCE EAT*. This restaurant was filled with coeds, business personnel, a few artists, and hipsters. Today, a customer had informed the manager of a problem with the bathroom. Short on staff, orders started to pile up. To her displeasure, Lourdes was the only server working, because the other server named Lorraine, a rumored crackhead, never showed up. But her job was secure because of the efficiency she demonstrated when sucking the owner's penis. The only other employee present was the dishwasher, and he wasn't any help because he only spoke Portuguese.

"OK, I'll get right on it!" the owner told the unsatisfied customer. "Lourdes, we have a problem in the bathroom!" he yelled.

LETTUCE EAT was extremely small. The entire restaurant consisted of a phone-booth-sized janitor's closet and a tiny, single commode bathroom. Today, the toilet was dirty and covered in greenish-brown shit stains. A gray, dim light offered hints of wall graffiti, and the small, dead rat that had slipped into the bowl and drowned overnight. Sick to her stomach, Lourdes bravely held her nose and attempted to resolve the problem by flushing the toilet. Unfortunately, the handle slipped off and crashed to the floor. Fed up and overworked, Lourdes was at her wit's end.

"Pick up, Lourdes, pick up!" the owner continued to snap.

Visibly annoyed, she sharply said, "Coming!"

As she leaned over to pick up a cold order of French toast, two people in a booth by the front door suddenly got up and ran out the front door without paying their bill.

"Fire, fire!" vehemently shouted the owner.

"Stop, please, stop!" Lourdes shouted as the two thieves sprinted around the corner and out of sight. She gave chase for about two hundred yards, but her efforts were fruitless.

Dejected, as her respiratory system burned, Lourdes bent over and tried to catch what was left of her fleeting breath. Smoking cigarettes had clearly become a problem. Lourdes slowly lifted her head toward the sun and turned to walk in the direction of *LETTUCE EAT*. Before she was even halfway back, she could see her disapproving boss standing in the front door. Furious, he wildly waved his arms and then shook his left fist in her direction.

Before he could assault her with one of his infamous verbal barrages, Lourdes took her apron off, the one with the faded green *LETTUCE EAT* logo, and yelled, "Let me save you the trouble; I quit!" she screamed.

"What! You can't leave me shorthanded!" he demanded.

"Yes, I can! Keep your eyes open and watch it all unfold in front of your face! First, I will throw this apron to you. Then, I will turn my back and walk to my car. See—it is all so very simple! Have a nice life!" she yelled over her right shoulder.

"You can't be serious! Six months ago, I gave you a job when you didn't have one! And now you're leaving?" he shouted.

"And as of now, I still don't have a job! By the way that mess in the bathroom is going to require more than a plunger. I suggest you call the cops; tell them to bring a tiny body bag!" she snapped.

"Don't ever come back! Your job won't be here for you!" her boss screamed at the top of his lungs.

Taking a deep breath, she released a loud sigh. "You hear that? It's me not holding my breath! You are a horrible boss and a terrible person!" Lourdes reported loudly.

She pulled out her cell phone and started to dial. But before she could press *SEND*, her friend Maki's number popped onto her screen. Lourdes immediately answered.

"That's so weird; I was just going to call you! Girl, do I have a story to tell you!" Lourdes exclaimed.

"Well, I just walked out on my boss!" Lourdes countered.

"Yes, I now exist with the other six-point seven percent of America that's unemployed," Lourdes lamented.

"Oh, really?" asked Lourdes.

"Let's meet for drinks, and you can tell me your crazy story!" Lourdes suggested.

"Yeah, I know it's a Monday morning; what's your point?" Lourdes questioned.

"Martinis at the *SLIPPERY OLIVE* sounds good! I'll be there in ten minutes. First round is on you!" Lourdes exclaimed.

"Hey, I'm unemployed—remember?" Lourdes stated before she hung up. *CLICK!*

Exactly twenty-one minutes later, Lourdes entered the *SLIPPERY OLIVE*. By that point, Maki had already finished half of her meal and her first cocktail. The *SLIPPERY OLIVE* was a twenty-four-hour martini bar that served light fare and boasted over one hundred types of martinis. The waiter took Lourdes's order; then Maki dove right into her story.

"Let me tell you about the date my cousin went on last evening. This guy got her pregnant, and he had been blowing marriage smoke up her ass. I mean, he appeared to have everything: nice car, nice job, nice house, and a not-so-nice secret wife of three years that followed him and my cousin to the restaurant. All was calm, until the wife stepped into the restaurant; then foolishness erupted! The wife yelled at my cousin, my cousin yelled at her, and then my cousin's water broke!" Maki reported.

"What did she do?" Lourdes asked.

"What could she do? She had the baby right there in the booth. The baby is named Carin, with a *C*, after the name of their waitress. I think she's the person that called the paramedics," Maki said.

"You're kidding me! Tell me you're kidding me!" Lourdes responded with an increased level of interest.

"No, I'm not," Maki deadpanned as she adjusted the brim on her heather-gray fedora that intentionally matched her black-and-white Gucci open-toed shoes.

"So how are you and your man doing?" Lourdes asked.

"I was thinking about leaving him, but when I hear stories like that, I think maybe I should stop watching talk shows and figure out the intricacies of a forty-six defense!" Maki giggled as she spoke.

"That sounds pathetic. It's your life. Hey, are you going to eat your hash browns?" Lourdes asked.

"Knock yourself out!" Maki sipped from her drink. "What do you mean pathetic? Have you decided what you are going to do now that you are unemployed?" Maki quipped.

"It's only been half an hour since I had my last job. Let's allow the dust to settle and have a moment of silence. My emotions are still raw," she laughed. "I was thinking this might be an opportunity for me to pursue my music full-time. I just need to schedule some gigs," Lourdes said.

Maki waved her hand to get the waiter's attention. The *SLIPPERY OLIVE* was relatively empty. If you counted the waiter, the morning manager, Maki, Lourdes, and the old buzzing twenty-one-inch television behind the bar, then there were only four people in the entire restaurant.

"What about the Peace Corps? Have you heard back from them?" Maki asked.

"No, but I am expecting an answer within the next week or so," Lourdes responded.

"What happens if they say yes and you get accepted?" Maki asked.

"That's a tough one. I guess I will deal with that once I hear back from them," Lourdes replied as she briefly stared out of the window into the morning bustle.

"I have to be honest, Dez; I am not feeling your passion for the corps," Maki divulged.

"I agree. I woke up this morning and decided that singing is what I really want to do. Singing is my passion. I can no longer bottle up the pursuit of my dream. Like the adage says: if a girl can sing but she never sings in public, can she really sing sort of situation?" Lourdes chuckled as she waxed poetically.

Maki ordered them another round of drinks. "Exactly, everyone is just one simple break from success," she said as she slowly chewed the last olive of her latest martini.

"Yes, but finding that break or that break finding me is the hard part," Lourdes said while she used her small, plastic olive sword to pick between her two front teeth.

"Have you tried that place, *EDIBLE GROOVES*?" Maki questioned.

"No, I haven't, but someone was just mentioning that place the other day. What's it all about?" Lourdes inquired.

"Good food, eclectic musical acts. I saw The Eclipse there last week. You should try it; they are always looking for quality acts," Maki urged.

"I just want to put down the cornbread and sing! Where's it located? I'll call them now." Lourdes's tone had perked up.

"Grab a *City Paper*; look under the *PERSONALS* section. The ad might say: 'Looking for a good blow job?'" Maki chuckled, almost choking on her drink.

"Ha-ha! Cool, thanks for the tip." Lourdes gestured with her right thumb up.

"What's the story with your new apartment?" Maki paused and checked her watch. "Is it OK if we ask for the check? I have an appointment across town," she stated.

"Everything's fine, except the woman upstairs was screaming at the top of her lungs in the middle of the night."

"What?" Maki asked.

"Yes, you heard me correctly. Our first night, she screamed at full volume for the better part of forty-five seconds without taking a break. Happily, she didn't scream this morning. Look, I'm going to go outside and grab a *City Paper*," Lourdes said.

"No problem, I'll settle the tab," Maki said as she unzipped her Saint Laurent clutch to get her wallet.

Half a block down, Lourdes dodged traffic as she walked through the chalk-white crosswalk toward a yellow metal newspaper cabinet to grab a free issue of the *CITY PAPER*. She instantly turned to the last page, found the ad she sought, and immediately dialed *EDIBLE GROOVES*. Before the call ended, she had a 3:30 p.m. appointment for tomorrow.

In an effort to celebrate Lourdes's interview, Maki decided they should have one more drink.

Zeik for Hire

• • •

May 5, 2008, 4:25 p.m.

On the south side of town, Damon entered a business complex, one of those new industrial complexes that housed many different types of warehouses and manufacturing plants. Seconds after opening the door, he quickly disarmed the alarm, picked up the office phone, and dialed. Still no contact from Rico. Damon became increasingly perturbed, borderline maniacal.

He screamed into the receiver, "Where the fuck is he?" Damon asked just before his cell phone rang.

"Where are you?" Damon snarled.

The man on the other side of the conversation was named Zeik. "Bizee," Zeik flatly replied.

"Listen, the maid is out of town, and I need someone to clean up. Meet me at *Tike's Tiny Raceway* in twenty minutes," Damon instructed.

Zeik was one of Damon's most reliable associates. If Damon ever encountered a problem that required "special attention," Zeik would be one of three people he could call.

Damon left the complex fifteen minutes before four o'clock; it took him twenty-seven minutes to get to *Tike's Tiny Raceway*. Tike's lobby boasted purple carpeting and an extensive collection of arcade games, including an upright *Galaga* console, as well as the still popular *Ms. Pac-Man* cocktail table. Thirty-two steps inside, Damon approached a large desk with a small woman wearing an even smaller blouse. Her name was Patricia; her back was to him. As she filed her nails, she spoke on the phone. Showing more patience than normal, Damon waited for Patricia to notice him. Several moments later, still engaged in conversation, she turned around.

"Oh shit! You scared me!" her left breast beat harder than her right breast as her eyebrows arched.

"Tell Zeik I am here," Damon said.

"And who are you?" she asked as she regained her composure.

"I am here," Damon grunted.

Rolling her eyes, she said, "OK, let me page him," as she picked up the hard, black plastic telephone, dialed an extension, and suddenly her voice blared over the loudspeaker.

"Zeik, he's here," Patricia reported.

"Hafe him meet me in da' garage," Zeik responded.

Zeik's mother had died when he was just fourteen; as a child he was very awkward and large for his age. Possessing the temper of a lion and huge in stature, Zeik was a very dangerous thirty-three-year-old child. Damon called him "the perfect blend of brutal violence and unquestioned loyalty." Zeik's priors over the last twenty years read: armed robbery, assault, aggravated assault, breaking and entering, misdemeanor possession, and felony possession with the intent to distribute.

The garage was at the far end of the building. Dirty and poorly ventilated, it had authentic-style bay doors that were raised and lowered via rope and pulley. Zeik wore navy-blue overalls that were smattered with stains, while part of a red bandanna brimmed out of its right rear pocket. Zeik didn't talk much; his speech pathology was practically incomprehensible. When he saw Damon approaching, he spat a large chunk of brown tobacco juice to the right of his feet and pulled the bandanna out of his pocket and wiped his hands.

"Was good?" Zeik asked in the most southern of southern accents as he extended his hand.

They shook. Then Damon cut right to business. "For twelve and a half, how would you feel about taking a baseball bat to some shmuck's skull? But the bat has to be specific. I'll give you the address where you can get it," Damon assured.

"In howse or outhowse?" Zeik replied with his undying twang.

"In," Damon replied.

"Whin you reckon ya' wanner dun?" Zeik asked.

"The sooner the better," Damon replied. "Hell, I'll even make it twenty-five large if you can do it within the next seventy-two hours!" Damon proclaimed.

"Sheat, dat somabitch wetback pult three hundred grand per dinger las' season, an ya' gonna' pay me twenty-five to mash in a skull. Leas I don't have ta' hit a curvy ball. In da' hi skool I ain't neva' coulda' hit ta' curvy ball!" Zeik chuckled at the thought of all that money.

"You'll take the job?" Damon asked.

"Hell yeah! Now, ah reckon, I ca' bye tieres an a nu' tramission' fer ma' hemi. Gawd-fuckin'-blessamerica!"

"Gawd-fuckin'-blessamerica!" Damon shouted.

"Once dat monee in me hands, dey'll be so muct dang bluud his oun mama' wont kno who da' boy is," Zeik assured.

"Nice, very graphic," Damon replied.

"Who da' sumabitch?" Zeik asked.

"I'll let you know, but I am going to pay you half right now," Damon said as he handed Zeik a brown envelope.

"Hu-huh, o dis' guud!" Zeik responded.

Using his left hand, Damon motioned for Zeik to come closer. Once he and Zeik were close enough, Damon whispered the name and the "delicate" circumstances that this situation demanded.

"You still have that mask, right?" Damon asked.

"O' couse!" replied Zeik.

CHAPTER 15

Death Threat

● ● ●

May 5, 2008, 3:37 p.m.

LOURDES DIDN'T MAKE A LOT of money, and this was the reason she wasn't able to spend a lot of money. This morning she forgot that she needed at least one gallon of gas to drive to *EDIBLE GROOVES*. But Lourdes didn't have enough cash to pay the $2.27 required to buy her low-grade gas. Being cash poor, her credit card was her only option. Lourdes was the classic charge-card owner, one who repetitively charged her financial future deeper into a pile of debt. Exhausted, Lourdes skipped the project of getting a gallon of gas and "swiped" herself a cab. Thirty-three minutes later, the orange and black car dropped her off in front of *EDIBLE GROOVES*.

After checking the list, one of two doormen escorted her into a waiting room that was painted every imaginable shade of brown. Even the baseboards looked like they were semi-glossed in brown-crimson-gold. Waiting, she sat on a velvet sofa flanked by two armed chairs of the same cloth drenched in chocolate. Twenty minutes later, a restless Lourdes decided to do something.

"Hello?" she cautiously called as she entered another room that sported palm-tree-green walls and a pool table. Suddenly, an upstairs toilet flushed, and Lourdes walked toward the base of the stairwell.

Unexpectedly, Vicki came from around the corner. "May I help you?" she asked with a kind smile.

Startled, Lourdes whipped around to address Vicki. "Yes, I have an appointment with Mr. Vinzantinne," she replied.

"Are you Lourdes?" Vicki inquired.

"Yes, yes, I am," Lourdes nodded as she spoke.

"Here, take a seat; I'll announce your arrival. Would you like something to drink?" Vicki asked.

"No thank you. How long has this place been open?" Lourdes inquired for the purpose of initiating small talk.

"It will be six months next month," Vicki answered.

"I like the brown," Lourdes said, trying not to laugh.

"Yeah, sure! Sit tight and fill out this application. Vinny will be with you shortly." Vicki stood up as she spoke. "I'll be in the office around the corner. Let me know if you need anything." She walked around the back of the velvet sofa and past a window with a long, flowing brown curtain. She knocked on Vinny's office door.

"Hello!" Vinny growled, as a trail of heavy smoke seeped out from underneath his office door.

"Your next appointment"—*COUGH!*—"is here." Vicki spoke hurriedly as she quickly stuck her head into her uncle's office.

"What are you doing to me?" Vinny asked. "Come here and give your favorite uncle a hug!"

"Who said you were my favorite uncle?" Vicki asked, embarrassed.

"I did!" he deadpanned. "I also happen to be the same uncle who pays you thirty dollars per hour to make coffee and answer phone calls!"

"Oh yeah, right, you are my favorite! How could I forget?" Vicki turned and embraced her uncle.

"So, how ugly is she?" Vinny asked.

"On the contrary, she's quite attractive," Vicki added.

"Does she have nice tits?" Vinny had no verbal censor. He spoke when he wanted and consequently said whatever he wanted to say.

"I really wasn't looking." Vicki quickly grew tired of her uncle's anti-feminist line of questioning, and she turned and attempted to walk toward the door.

"Where are you going?" he bellowed.

"May I please leave; this smoke is killing me." Coughing, she continued to advance to the door.

"Wait!" Vicki stopped, as Vinny rose and met her ten steps from his desk. Without warning, he leaned in and started sniffing his niece's hands. "I smell cocoa butter!" he was immediately stimulated.

"I don't get it! You're so racist, and yet you sleep with all types of women. What gives?" Vicky asked out of confusion.

"I'll tell you loud and clear. Throughout history, my ancestors—*your* ancestors—fucked everybody's ancestors! Centuries later, some of them are now wearing Gucci, Louis Vuitton, Prada, and achieving PhDs. And those lustful asses…It's almost as if those women are listening to rap music and pounding out deep leg squat after deep leg squat. Just like some woman enjoy fellatio; other women enjoy sodomy. If you think about it, by sodomizing certain women throughout history, it's ironically the reason for all those fat assess that you see and envy today. That's a part of American history that is less publicized. If you ask me, it is all within my birthright! I am the shit, and I don't give a pussy ass fuck about who has a problem with it!" Vinny's voice rose.

"I don't envy anybody's ass!" Vicki asserted.

"Watch your tone, young lady!" Vinny admonished.

"What about Clint?" she blurted. Vicki knew she had made a grave mistake even before the words had completely exited her mouth.

"Clint! Why are you bringing him up? Don't even think about it; you're my only niece, but I wouldn't hesitate to kill *you* and *him*. That's what gives—I swear to it!" He didn't flinch as he spoke; his eyes and voice maintained the same level of intensity.

She had seen her uncle mad before, but this was the first time she ever saw him mad with her. Trying not to stoke the fire, Vicki delivered him one of her award-winning smiles.

"Enjoy your interview," she said as she turned to leave his office.

"Fuck you; just send the bitch in!" he tersely responded.

CHAPTER 16

Berlin Falls Down

• • •

May 6, 2008, 7:13 p.m.

SLEEP BECAME A STRANGER AS insomnia and I started to bond. Saul was killed four days ago, and I was trying to stay sane. My business had been put on hold. I locked myself inside my apartment as the events from Saturday night continued to bang around in my head. Faces—there were too many faces. The more I tried to reason with the truth, the more the truth seemed false. Saul was dead, and I had no idea who, why, or how. The funeral was ten days from today. I was undecided about attending. The whole story still made zero sense.

My meeting with Berlin was for eight o'clock p.m. I barely made it on time. We decided it was easier to meet in his car in a dark corner of a parking lot across from a nondescript bar. Nothing made sense; maybe it was my marijuana habit, or perhaps it was the inane story that Berlin was pushing into my ears. The sole reason I agreed to meet with him was his product. Money aside, my sense and sensibilities were derailed by his mindless yapping about some erotic reoccurring dream.

"So, I'm in hell, and I am desperately trying to get laid. Do you know how hard it is to get laid in hell?" he kept repeating this for what seemed forever.

"Hey, are you paying attention?" he barked, annoyed that I was ignoring him.

"Yeah, I'm following you. I mean, you would think that it's pretty easy. But then again it is hell. Hell is for suffering. Suffering means no attractive women—period. That type of pleasure would happen in a bizarro-type heaven. I'd imagine hell being full of ugly women with hairy legs, dressed in dirty, oversized muumuus," I added.

"On the contrary! In my dream, all the women were hot. I mean, the female roster in hell is a list of seminal all-stars: Pamela Anderson (before her second breast job), Jennifer Aniston, Britney, Aguilera, and Lil' Kim. Cher is the events coordinator. Everyone's mad that the Olsen twins haven't arrived yet. I guess they're still virgins. But here's the catch: Satan is Heffner, and of course he's the only one fucking! In this dream, I made out with Martha Stewart. She smelled like lilacs in the spring, and she was a great kisser. The action got hot and heavy. Her panties were sopping wet. Just as I was about to give her the shaft, Monica Lewinsky barged in with six security guards. One was Mr. T from the *A-Team*, and another one strongly resembled Donald Trump. Monica ranted and raved about some legal injunction that allowed her to have a chastity belt placed on me pending the outcome of the paternal suit she'd filed against me!" Berlin howled.

"What happened next?" I asked.

"That's when I woke up. Weird, huh?" he questioned.

"You can say that again," I stole a quick glance at my watch as I spoke.

A weird pause followed, and then he spoke, "I know that I have asked you many times, but I have to ask one more time. Look me in the eyes and tell me that you didn't fuck her!" He implored, clearly still not over that college situation.

"How many times do I have to defend myself! I told you that chick was about as faithful as a convicted atheist. Remember, I introduced you to that girl! Look, she came onto me, and I refused her advances—end of story! What more do you want from me?" I snapped back.

Berlin's face bent in many different angles, until he resembled a madman. His words were spoken with the sharpness of an exotic blade. "Faith is the antithesis of proof. I don't have any proof to think that you didn't sleep with her. Don't feel guilty. Guilt is for the weak. Are you guilty or just weak?" he ranted.

"I am neither weak nor guilty. I didn't sleep with her. I might've been one of the few that didn't, but I didn't," I replied succinctly.

"Always a smartass! I bet you get that a lot. And in case you don't, hey, you're a fucking smartass! There, what do you think about that?" he was nearing full-tilt.

"Are you through? Because I don't care who you choose to trust. I am here to discuss money; discussing money makes money, and making money makes sense. Either we do business, or I'm out. It's a done deal!" I threatened.

"Whoa, I didn't drive to this shit stain for nothing!" he yelled. The more he spoke, the more erratic his demeanor became. He kept pressing his left index finger into the left side of his left nostril and sniffing. As he leaned forward, the light from a nearby lamppost highlighted his face, and his nose was noticeably redder than the rest of his face. I also noticed that his eyes were bloodshot and incredibly glassy. I was starting to get concerned. Cocaine was my immediate theory. Berlin was back to snorting. If true, that could create several problems. My history with cocaine was the reason I'd stopped dealing with cocaine. It was an unstable chemical, and Berlin, with his personality and psyche, shouldn't be snorting anything: stable or unstable.

"Yes, money is why we're here. Here's the keys; the product is in the trunk. Use this key and grab the duffel bags. We can settle up later at our usual spot," he said as he turned to exit the car.

"Where are you going?" I asked.

"Inside the bar to use the shitter and to grab a drink. Is that OK with you?" He yelled as he forcefully patted me on my shoulder and opened the car door. But his seat belt slowly retracted and tripped him as he got out of the car. He stumbled forward until he regained his balance, stood upright, and then went into the bar.

Something wasn't right, but my nine-millimeter tucked into the right side of my belt under my untucked, collared shirt gave me a false sense of protection. I sat there and waited, after I watched him enter the bar via the rear exit.

One minute turned into several.

Little did I know, inside the bar's bathroom, Berlin was bent over a toilet, violently puking up anything and everything. He lost his balance and fell. The left side of his head collided with the toilet, and he blacked out upon contact. Powder-white circles traced his nostrils and lips.

"Where the hell is this guy?" I thought. Ten minutes passed as I sat in this parking lot with my dick in one hand and my firearm in the other, just waiting to get fucked by the NYPD. Eventually, the wait became too much. Something told me to go into the bar and check on him, but another voice told me to grab the drugs and leave. I chose the latter. I opened the car's trunk, spotted two green-duffel bags, grabbed both of them, and drove off in Berlin's sedan: my destination, a nearby garage close to where my car was parked. After loading my stash boxes, I started my car and drove away. As I drove, a voice in my head directed me to drive to Vicki's place.

CHAPTER 17

When It Rains, It Pours

● ● ●

May 6, 2008, 10:11 p.m.

I HID IN THE SHADOWS outside of Vicki's apartment like OJ. The adrenaline rushed through my veins and augmented my paranoia. If anything happened to Berlin, Vicki would be one of the first persons notified. She'd sounded cheerful when we spoke on the phone, but that was nearly forty minutes ago. Anything could have transpired during the time it took me to get here. I dug into my right pocket, pulled out my cell phone, and dialed her number. It rang and rang, but there was no answer. Had she taken delivery of any news? Was she alone? I walked out of the shadows and approached her front door. Promptly, an oversized, black SUV slowly drove up her street. I retreated, back into the shadows, and stayed there until the SUV vanished. Finally, I approached her door. Before I knocked, I pressed my left ear against the door. What I heard was the muffled sounds of a woman crying. Taking two deep breaths, I knocked.

She opened the door, but the face I saw wasn't the one I hoped to see. Vicki greeted me, but her face was sad, and her mascara blurred her cheeks. Without a moment's notice, she grabbed me and tightly wrapped both of her arms around me as she sobbed uncontrollably.

With her head buried into my chest, all I could muster was, "What's wrong? Are you OK?"

Vicki stepped back, rubbed her eyes with both hands, and said through sobs, "Something...terrible...happened to my cousin!" she couldn't stop herself from sobbing.

"What! Calm down. What's wrong with your cousin?" I rubbed her back as I tried to coax the story from her.

"I just got a call from Saint Agnes," she continued through more sobbing. "They said…that Berlin is in a coma!" she wailed inconsolably.

Her words sent a tingle down my spine as if I had just experienced a lumbar puncture.

"What happened? What are the doctors saying? Is he going to be OK?" I asked.

"They won't say! Uncle Vinny…is at the hospital. He said he'll keep me posted," she slowly started to regain her normal speech patterns.

"I am going to stay with you. We'll get through this together," I consoled as I hugged her.

Hearing that Berlin was still alive was a relief and a downer. With him alive, I didn't have to worry about being implicated for manslaughter. But if he came out of his coma dazed and confused, mumbling my name, then I was as good as dead. I needed to get my mind off everything.

Vicki disappeared into another room. She returned with a small, orange vial in her right hand.

"What do you have there?" I asked.

"Valium," she replied.

"You can't trust modern medicine. Why pop pills when we could share a little of this?" I showed her my plastic, orange vial.

"Ahh, good idea!" she exclaimed.

I rolled enough for two. Placing the joint in my mouth, I lit it and inhaled deeply. After two or three more hits, I passed it to Vicki. She barely inhaled.

"What was that? Are you smoking? Or are you trying to convince yourself that you're smoking?" I cajoled.

"OK, let me try it again," she said as she sniffled.

Many tokes later, we sat on her sofa, high as the price of gold, staring blankly at the ceiling.

"I have an idea," I said.

"Oh really?" she quizzed.

"Yes, here, give me your hand," I said as I led her into her bedroom. I took off my shirt and kissed her. Then I slowly removed her shirt as our eyes connected. Soon, we were both naked, except for the silver key that dangled between her breasts on a platinum necklace.

"Oh, my!" she responded.

Forgoing foreplay, she straddled me as she grabbed her headboard. I pulled her waist harder against my midsection. Minutes later, we shifted our position to doggy style. Still burning, I took the joint, inhaled, and passed it to her. As she inhaled and exhaled, a lonely candle cast our shadows against the far wall.

"Look at us!" she exclaimed at the sight.

Our breathing became more boisterous. Just before the climax, her phone rang. Gasping for air, she franticly searched through her sheets to find her ringing phone. The display read: *UNCLE VINNY.*

"Shhhh," she whispered with her left index finger over her lips. She closed her eyes, said a quick prayer, and then answered the phone.

"Hello, Uncle!" she said.

"Am I interrupting something? What are you doing? Are you being dirty?" he sternly inquired.

"Of course not, Uncle! I was trying to do some Pilates," was her response.

"Oh really? Pilates at this hour? What—*va fangul!*" he growled.

"Is Berlin OK?" she asked.

"You can stop worrying and start crying! Berlin was pronounced dead ten minutes ago," he said before abruptly hanging up.

CLICK!

The phone slipped out of her hand as she almost fell off the edge of her bed. Vicki's reaction told the whole story. She cried hysterically. I could breathe easier knowing that Berlin was deceased. But Vicki was a wreck. Her whole body shook as she tried to catch her breath between multiplying sobs and tears. I slid next to her and tried to comfort her.

"Oh shit!" she groaned as she jumped up. The dirty, dark-red Rorschach stain on her white satin sheets made her next declaration somewhat academic. "I just got my period!"

"Jeez! When it rains, it pours," I thought.

CHAPTER 18

Crook and Juice

• • •

May 7, 2008, 9:11 a.m.

ANOTHER SHARED JOINT AND TEN milligrams of Valium sent Vicki to La-La-Land. I left a few hours after I tucked her into bed. Today, I needed to make a few deliveries to satisfy some of my most trusted clients. If I could sell ten pounds to these two guys, that deal alone would yield a very sizable profit. Today I was in "Skateboard-P" mode. Disguised as skateboarder I donned: a pair of black-and-white Vans, a graphic T-shirt, semi-tattered jeans, a skateboard, and a backpack. It had been some time, but once I balanced my weight on the board and swung my right foot against the asphalt, the process came back as I easily rolled in and out of traffic. Several blocks later, I arrived at my destination. I only hoped these cats were ready to do big business because I wasn't pulling out a hand-held scale and breaking down ounces today, not even if my own mother was buying. Since college, I hadn't sold anything less than a quarter pound. My attitude was "buy big or I go home."

I walked to their apartment building's front door, found their apartment number, and pressed a decrepit, faded yellow button. I was very thorough. I always used gloves during the breakdown and packaging process. As an extra precaution, I vapor sealed every package and used an antiseptic cloth to erase any stray prints. When it came time for the exchange, I never gave product or accepted any money directly from my clients. All monies had to be put in an envelope and placed on an inanimate object, like a table for instance. That way, I could always say on oath that I never took delivery of any money.

As for the nature of this deal, I could only hope for the best. The button on the intercom appeared to be jammed; it never felt like it was actually ringing. I heard nothing on my end, but in actuality, five quick rings were heard in apartment *34C*.

In less than three seconds, a female voice responded from the intercom labeled *34C*. "Take it eeeeazeee on the buzzer, man!"

The entrance buzzer buzzed, and I walked through one heavy wooden door into a minimal foyer. The door slammed shut, as two kids chased a tennis ball that bounced behind me. I eschewed the elevator because it was broken, and I decided to climb the requisite four flights of stairs. Minutes later, hunched over, battling smoker's lung, I labored to catch my breath. Apartment *34C* was on the left, approximately twenty paces from the stairwell landing.

With my lungs refurbished by the inhalation of oxygen, I stood on the outside of *34C* looking in. Before I knocked on any perspective buyer's door, I often took a few seconds to eavesdrop before I announced my presence. If the vibe did not feel or sound right, then I would leave and live free to deal another day. Without pressing my ear to the door, I could hear Crook's voice. His name was an absolute misnomer because his silver-spoon upbringing ensured that he didn't need to steal anything. Next, Juice's voice announced his presence. Juice was Crook's best friend and business partner. A tall, thin-framed man, he was called Juice because he was drunk eight days out of seven. In addition to his alcohol dependency, he was born with a slightly crooked left foot that caused complications in his gait. As my ears strained, I could hear them debating the benefits of smoking blunts versus joints. While they jostled, I programed my cell phone's alarm to go off approximately three minutes after entering their apartment. If things weren't copasetic, then the alarm would be my excuse for my rapid departure.

"Blunts provide a stronger and longer high," Juice said.

"Yes, true, but joints allow you to taste the quality of the weed," Crook retorted.

I knocked on the door. A waifish chick with curly blond hair opened the door, and I followed her inside.

"How straight are you living, Crook? Juice?" I asked.

"What took you so long?" Juice challenged.

"Like Benicio Del Toro, I was in traffic," I fired back.

"Hey, Clint, before I forget, do you remember Michelle Green?" Crook asked.

"Of course! Nice body, cute face," I detailed.

"Juice told me that he 69'd with Michelle Green!" Crook exclaimed as I glanced at Juice in a quizzical manner.

"Yes, I did! Michelle Green! Michelle definitely fucking Green!" Juice shouted.

"Maybe in a wet dream, but from a reality standpoint, he's lying. I know Michelle, and he's lying," I said.

"Fuck both of you! I did fuck her!" Juice barked.

"OK, when?" I asked.

"Last year, right around the holidays," Juice said.

"Oh, during last year? When she lived in that Manhattan apartment?" I questioned.

"Exactly! You know what I am talking about!" Juice responded.

"Yes, I do, and I am calling bullshit!" my voice rose slightly.

"What?" Juice asked.

"I know for a fact that Michelle hasn't lived in that apartment for over two years. So, as I said, bullshit!" I repeated.

"I knew you were lying! I can't believe anything you say!" Crook yelled.

"Prune Juice is what we should call him! Even if he ripped his spinal cord out of his body, he would still have trouble getting his dick sucked!" I retorted.

Everyone laughed.

"Is that what you bring with you to my door? Stale jokes and even staler weed!" Juice said, as he shifted in his chair.

"Stale, huh? Then stop smoking it between your burned lips. I'm sure you have your cool days, but truth be told, the only reason I deal with you is because of Crook. Juice, your lips are so black they look like two spoiled-ass bananas," I cracked.

Everyone laughed.

"My lips *are* fucked up. I need to stop smoking all those Black and Mild cigars," Juice said.

"You need to smoke bleach!" I snapped back as Crook laughed heartily. "Hardly, more like Julia Childs! That's right; you have old pussy lips. Your lips are so ragged they look like you've been trying to stop your car with your mouth. Get a brake job and some olive oil, you cheap bastard!" I mockingly made screeching sounds with my mouth.

Everyone laughed.

"Fuck you!" was all he could say as he pointed his middle finger at me.

"This dude's tires are so bald you can't even read the sidewalls. Tires look like shredded wheat. And somebody please pay me before I talk about his nine-eleven teeth!"

Everyone laughed.

"Crook, are we straight?" I asked as Juice stewed in anger.

"Yes, follow me," Crook directed.

We went into his bedroom and closed the door. He opened his safe and started counting money.

"Clint, you're really getting out of the game?" he asked.

"Yes, that's the plan. I had my fun and made some money on the way. Now is the time for me to make my exit. I gave you half Blueberry Crush and half Jamaican Blind-Eyed. Both are A++ grades—high grade. For example, if you had the time and patience, you could make a killing by breaking that package down and sell eighty-five-dollar eighths or hundred-fifty-five quarters, all day, every day," I instructed.

"I got you, bro, but my half will be for personal use. Juice is talking about entering the game. But that's not for me," Crook said.

"Heaven help us all! Juice in the game is an apocalyptical sign that it was in deed time for me to get out ASAP. You be careful, bro! Ten pounds is weight. And with weight comes a whole different type of heat. Don't keep a lot of cash in your crib. Absolutely zero paraphernalia should be present in your home. And never ever, never sell from where you lay your head!" I vehemently shared a portion of C. Wallace's "Ten Crack Commandments" with him. Crook paid me.

"All these years, and you've never counted in front of me," he said.

"You've always been a straight shooter. If I have to count your money, then I have really been in the game far too long," I replied.

"I got you, bro," he said as we started to walk back into the living room.

I paused. "Keep an eye on your boy. I don't trust him," I whispered.

"Really, why?" asked Crook.

"It rests in his eyes. Jealousy can be hidden for only so long, but like vinegar mixed with baking soda, jealousy will always bubble up and surface in the eyes. There's simply no hiding it, like a woman's period," I shared.

We finished our exchange and reemerged into the living room.

Juice was still sulking. I couldn't help but further agitate his feelings.

"Juice, life is filled with all kinds of killjoys. This isn't Senior Week. Don't crack if you don't expect to get cracked. Get hip or shut your lip." I picked up a pen from their coffee table. "Here, take this pen and use it to write down something funny; draw a cartoon or something. Maybe next time you'll be better prepared. See you later," I said before I left their apartment.

As soon as I closed the door, I could hear Juice talking behind my back.

"I have always hated that pug-nosed pretty boy. Somebody should do something about that guy," Juice snarled.

"Why are you so angry with that guy? I have known him almost as long as I have known you. He's always been cool to me. You're just jealous because he has been with all the women you wanted. He smokes good weed; he's funny. What do you have? Your game's weak. When women see you, they wince like they're on PMS and you are their creepy gynecologist!" Crook had picked up where I left off.

Downstairs, as I was exiting the apartment building, a confluence of people approached from the east and the west. I didn't know this, but Cheese was mixed in this group. Once the crowd cleared, he followed three college students through the front door of the apartment building. To his dismay, the elevator was broken. So, he had to walk the stairs. Winded, he knocked on Crook and Juice's door.

"Are you expecting any more visitors?" Juice asked while staring at Crook.

"All my visitors are trained to call first," Crook responded. "You, on the other hand—we've lived here for over three months, and the only gash that you've had here was your mom when she put up our drapes!" Crook was still giving Juice a heavy dose of verbal jabs.

Cheese knocked again.

"Hold on! Who is it?" Juice asked.

"It's me, Cheese."

The door swung open, and its doorknob almost smacked the blonde in the butt. Cheese was red in the face and frantic in his movements.

"Yo, Cheese, what's going on?" Cheese was more Juice's friend than Crook's.

"Today was hectic. I felt like I was breathing stress. You dudes get the…" He whistled.

"Whistling isn't the code for weed; whistling is for coke, you fake mobster! How many fingers did you break today?" Crook was on a roll.

"I was going to break your mama's, until she agreed to make me a sandwich!"

Everyone Laughed

At that point, Crook lit a joint and inhaled. After a few puffs, Crook passed the joint to Cheese. "Go ahead and hit that Memphis Bleek." Crook and Juice started laughing.

"Don't you start laughing, Juice! You grimy motherfucker, it's because of you we invented the term ménage a trois mothers!" Crook joked.

"What's that?" asked Cheese.

"Juice only dates pregnant women that are having girls, just so that he can be the mother's last and the daughter's first. How sick is that? Yuck!" Crook exclaimed.

"Yeah, that's not kosher at all," Cheese replied.

"How many of these sleepovers have you entertained?" Crook asked.

"Only a few," Juice responded weakly.

"Bullshit!" Crook shouted with conviction.

"When we go out to certain clubs, this fool has been seen both waltzing and freaking pregnant mothers. I've seen him bring back at least a half dozen. And I've been splitting time at my girlfriend's place," Crook said.

"What's worse for a fetus? Inhaling secondhand smoke firsthand or enduring the trauma of Juice's slimy body bouncing on her mother's mound?" Cheese queried.

"No wonder today's children are so fucked up! I'm sorry, Cancer Society, but knowing Juice the way I do, lymphoma doesn't sound all that bad!" Crook added to his already mounting list of cracks against Juice.

"Fuck you!" Juice articulated before he started coughing.

"So, Cheese, how have the ladies been treating you?" Crook inquired.

"I've been doing that Internet thing," Cheese responded.

"The Internet! I read somewhere that Internet dating was designed for men and women with AIDS and other STDs!" Juice joked.

"Cheese, don't tell me you've been humping those HIV chicks?" Crook queried.

"Naw, I just started. This one is different. It's a Christian online dating service," Cheese retorted.

"Christian? What do you want from those Holy Rollers? The last time that you were in church was the summer of 1984. I remember, because I was there," Juice replied.

"Wait a minute, Juice; the kid might be onto something. Religious women are supposed to be really frisky. Go ahead, Cheese, a clean-cut square like yourself is probably knocking them dead!" Crook said.

"Gee, thanks for your approval, but I know what I'm doing. This is good green. Where did you get it?" Cheese asked.

Crook got up off of his chair. "I'll get you his card; it might take me a little bit. Oh, here it is!" he passed my card to Cheese.

"Why are the cards so fucking small?" Cheese countered.

GO GREEN
800-420-2734
Ask for Ralph Nader

"I asked him, what's with the stamp-size cards? He replied, chicks groove on small cards; they like them almost as much as they like big—" Crook reported.

"But don't worry; I might have a better connect. I'll let you know in a few days," Juice replied.

"Hey, Cheese, how's your cousin doing? The one that's playing pro ball?" asked Juice.

"He got kicked out of the league six weeks ago. They caught him snorting," Cheese replied.

"Cocaine?" Crook and Juice chimed in at the same time.

"No, the third-base line!" Cheese deadpanned.

"What's he got, Lyme disease?" Crook chuckled first; then everyone else followed.

CHAPTER 19

Showtime

• • •

May 7, 2008, 7:15 p.m.

I HATED HAND-TO-HAND DELIVERIES. AFTER the drama with Berlin's girl-friend and then the fallout with my West Coast partner, I found the concept loathsome. To be frank, apart from having a car, party favors, or appliances brought to my door, I had no interest in delivery service. As I rolled my skateboard away from Crook's apartment, I officially declared that delivery to be my last and final delivery. Once I got back to my apartment, I took a long nap; then I showered and changed before I headed to *EDIBLE GROOVES*. This was the first Friday of the month. I wanted to get to the club earlier than normal.

In my car, traffic was much lighter. I arrived at quarter after seven. My inclination was to park inside the garage, until a tiny voice in my head instructed me to park on a side street a few blocks south of the club's entrance. Suede briefcase in hand, I walked toward *EDIBLE GROOVES*. It was twenty minutes till eight by the time I entered the garage elevator. Just as I reached to press the button, I caught a glimpse of a large procession of black, military-style SUVs right before the elevator doors came together. As I exited the elevator, I entered *HAARLEM* and started getting ready. Meanwhile, within the confines of his office, Vinny and Vicki were having a conversation.

"Do you have anything that you want to tell me?" Vinny had a tendency to frown when he attempted to peek into a person's soul.

"What's with the questioning? I thought I was your favorite niece?" Vicki responded.

"You are, and there's still hope, provided you tell me the truth!" his eyes continued to press her eyes for answers.

"I always tell you the truth, Uncle. I have nothing to hide," Vicki replied.

"Is that so?" Vinny replied sardonically.

Suddenly, the office door opened, and two large Afros stood in the doorway. Vinny clenched his chin, leaned back in his chair, and smiled.

"Listen, Vicki, why don't you get me a sandwich, and come back in twenty minutes," he instructed.

"How about I have your food sent to you by one of our supremely capable waitresses?" Vicki suggested.

"Because I don't need to have an important conversation with my employees. I reserve the important conversations for when I am firing one of them; you, on the other hand, are a totally different animal. Get me a New York strip, on a Kaiser roll, extra bloody, with a side of less lip! By the way, after you bring the steak sandwich, you should take the rest of the night off!" he snapped.

Before Vicki could protest, Vinny turned, stood up, and ushered her onto the other side of his closed office door. He motioned for the Afros to take a seat as he grabbed his cell phone and dialed. "Tell me what you know!" he told the voice on the other end.

"Oh really!" Vinny exclaimed.

"Look, we have a new plan. Make sure you don't leave my side tonight, or you'll never get paid," Vinny ordered and hung up.

CLICK!

Vinny turned to the two Afro-sporting men. "Are you guys as good as he said you are?" Vinny asked.

"We wouldn't be here if we weren't," said the more muscular of the two.

"Just what I wanted to hear! OK, here's the new plan!" Vinny said.

Downstairs, inside the club, people started to fill table after table, booth after booth. Three separate groups of underworld figures walked into *EDIBLE GROOVES* and headed straight to the front-row tables; they sat ignoring the RESERVED signs. Nicky Nicotine, or NN, headed one group. He was a classic type A personality, who always wore dark sunglasses. Whenever he smoked, Nicky smoked two cigs at the same time, one in each corner of his mouth. Other times, he would stack two cigarettes on top of each other. Reports may vary, but Nicky was directly and indirectly responsible for at least thirty-five murders in the last five years. A nicotine driven murderer, his MO was to place the gun barrel directly into the mouths of his victims before he pulled the trigger. Through the years, any witnesses against him had either been assassinated or had disappeared without a trace. At the table next to Nicky sat a self-proclaimed gentleman; the police called him Bobby Bobbing for Bodies or Bobby Boldface. Ten years ago, he claimed he was robbed at knifepoint and his assailant cut him just under the left side of his jaw. Strong rumors later surfaced that the scar actually appeared because he'd had liposuction to eliminate a double chin. Since that incident, he had been referred to as Bobby Boldface, as in bold-faced lie. But like NN, Bobby was just another cold-blooded killer with a cosmetically altered face. At the third table to the far left sat the Black Dome and his entourage. The Black Dome had a big shaved head. Not much was known about him except he always wore a turtleneck no matter the weather.

The three bosses drank booze and schmoozed with scantily clad women as the large men in dark suits encircled them. Later, the three bosses planned to have a very expensive "business discussion" with Vinny.

The first entertainer, a comedian, was just finishing his set.

"How many people like ice cream? Raise your hands!" the comedian shouted.

"OK, wow, that's damn near everybody in this room, shit!" he exclaimed.

"What are your favorite brands? Let me guess, Baskin-Robbins, Breyers, Carvel, Häagen-Daz?! Yes, this looks like a Häagen-Daz crowd!"

"Wait a minute; what about you? Yes, you miss! No, not you! I was talking to your girlfriend, the one with her nipples and titties bulging out! Looking like she supplies for Ben and Jerry's new Butter Pecan Breastmilk flavor!"

AUDIENCE LAUGHTER

"Miss, I'm just playing; what type do you like?" the comedian asked.

"Godiva or Mövenpick...It's Swiss," she replied.

"Y'all hear that? 'It's Swiss,' she said." He pantomimed the busty audience member tossing her hair back. "Well, excuse me, but if I'm not sucking on them, I don't care how big your chest is! Fuck you and all the other ice-cream lovers! Why?! Because I hate ice cream! I hate the cows that supply the milk! I hate the grass that they eat! I hate the fucking milk farmers! And I absolutely hate that stupid ice-cream truck jingle!"

AUDIENCE LAUGHTER

"Some of you might think I am allergic or lactose intolerant. Nope, I just despise ice cream. And here's why. I once traveled to a Third World country with a homeboy that hadn't had sex in over a year. We were in Costa Rica, and my homeboy, a guy that I had known over fifteen years, met a woman in an alley the first night. Let that sink in. He met her in an alley! Not at a stoplight, not even on a street corner! They met in an alley. We arrived on a Tuesday, and by Saturday, dude was in love—in an alley. They did all sorts of nasty stuff, the type of stuff you reserve for birthdays and welcome-home-from-jail parties."

AUDIENCE LAUGHTER

"Full buffet service! Forget à la carte! I'm talking cunnilingus before, during, and after menstruation! His tongue was even inside of her rectum! Yeah, he's one of those types. Initially, I had my doubts. But she was so freaking ugly there was no way she was a prostitute! But after my homeboy went days without showering, dude had our apartment smelling like spoiled cold cuts. And this woman still sucked his penis! That's when my *punta* alarm started ringing! In fact, within eight days he was on the phone introducing her to his parents. I am serious! Within two more days, he discussed going to the embassy to fly her to the states. By week two she had keys to our place, and that's when all hell broke loose! This chick convinced him that she could convert American money into pesos at a ninety-six percent rate of exchange. The national bank only offered eighty-five percent, but she convinced him that she could guarantee a ninety-six percent return rate. He and I decided to take our last seven hundred fifty dollars, and he would escort her to the exchange spot. I knew something was awry when she said she needed to speak with him privately. Meanwhile, I went onto the balcony and smoked a cigar. If only I could have been a fly on the wall in his room. Little did I know, while I smoked she put her lips on his tiny wiener and verbally extracted all sense and sensibility out of his brain. She was definitely ahead of her class—a real valesucktorian!"

AUDIENCE LAUGHTER

"By the time she was done, she convinced him that he didn't have to go with her, and she would return with our money. Well, boys and girls, that was the last time we saw her or our money!"

AUDIENCE LAUGHTER

"No call, no show! Check this out! We even went by her house and discovered that she never really lived there! Six hours later, her phone was turned off! And there we were: sober, somber, and flat-ass broke! With two full weeks left, we only had fifty dollars between us, and half of that was to pay for our exit visas. So, the only thing we could afford was ice cream. For twenty-five cents you could get an ice-cream sandwich: chocolate, vanilla, strawberry, or Monte Carlo, and I'm still not sure what the heck that Monte Carlo flavor was! For two weeks, I ate three to four ice-cream sandwiches a day. Do you have any idea how disgusting Costa Rican ice cream tastes after thirty-six sandwiches! By my fiftieth sandwich, I was just eating so I could get out of bed! I was so sick when we boarded the airplane they gave me a seat in the bathroom!"

AUDIENCE LAUGHTER

"And, since then I have been like fuck ice scream, you scream, we all scream for ice cream!"

AUDIENCE LAUGHTER AND APPLAUSE

"Thank you! Thank you! Thank you! Thank you! You've been a great audience; don't forget to tip your waitresses!" he said as he bowed and walked off the stage.

Master of ceremony: "Give another round of applause for *That Kid from Brooklyn!*"

AUDIENCE APPLAUSE

"I told you that man had issues! We were friends, but I had to stop messing with him! Jesus is taking notes! And it's going to be nearly impossible for me to get into heaven on my own. The last thing I need is his foolishness!" the Master of Ceremony joked.

AUDIENCE LAUGHTER

"Our next performance is by a group; I want to say they're soul; I want to say R & B, but I don't know what to call them. But I heard their demo, and they got *it*, whatever it is; they got it! Please give a warm *EDIBLE GROOVES* welcome for Lourdes and her band *Ladybug Sodomy!*"

AUDIENCE APPLAUSE

The stage curtain was drawn. Lourdes and her group instantly ripped into the first song of the evening. As if she was born with a microphone in her hands, Lourdes's vocals were robustly captivating. Approximately three minutes into her performance, everything flowed smoothly until Nicky Nicotine and his crew stood up and walked away from their table. Seconds later, an unidentified person produced a semiautomatic weapon and opened fire on everyone and everything.

DAKKA-TAKKA-DAKKA!!!

A riotous frenzy erupted. For every gun blast, more blood splattered. Women and men shrieked while food and furniture crashed to the floor as people trampled people. Lourdes and her band members ran offstage through a back door and down a skinny alley. Once I heard the gunshots, I grabbed my product, the cash, and dashed. Outside of the club, expensive cars of every make, size, and model raced into the street. By the time the police arrived, the only bodies to interview were corpses.

CHAPTER 20

No Shooter

• • •

May 8, 2008, 10:33 a.m.

A MEDIA FRENZY SPAWNED IN response to last night's shooting at *EDIBLE GROOVES*. City dignitaries, politicians, and other prominent community members demanded answers. First Saul Briggs and now this. The boiler room intensified as questions continued to mount while solutions were not available. Police presence throughout the city instantly became more visible. Less than six hours had elapsed, and press reports leaked that authorities had collected crime scene evidence: fingerprints, DNA, and GSR residue. Everyone wanted to know if rumors of an apprehended suspect were true.

Forensic specialists Pau and Miranda were assigned to this bloodbath. This former twosome had their own checkered past stemming from a botched Radiohead concert. Pau had an unusually sharp nose; it resembled a beak as he leaned over and peered into the high-definition microscope until a baffled look dominated his face.

"Less than five percent!" he blurted.

"What are you talking about?" Miranda wrinkled her pretty face before she responded incredulously.

"Here, take a look for yourself," he replied as Miranda peered into the microscope.

"Pau, you're correct! These readings show less than a five percent chance that the fingerprint found on the chair matches with the suspect they have detained upstairs!" Miranda exclaimed.

"Then take it one step further, when you reevaluate the ballistics models in conjunction with the maître d's table-setting map. All of these factors suggest that the alleged suspect's table location wasn't optimal; also, his documented disability made it highly improbable that he could wage such elaborate gun violence," Pau added.

"Additionally, there isn't one iota of GSR on this suspect. You'd think if a person fired a Rambo-style semiautomatic weapon into a crowded club, then there would be traces of gunshot residue in his hair, on his hands, or somewhere! I ran a background check; in addition to his handicap, this man was there for an anniversary celebration. He's not a killer. He doesn't even have any outstanding parking tickets. If this feeble suspect is the best that the authorities can do, then we are all in trouble. Ostensibly, they just grabbed anyone to reduce the press's pressure. I'll make the call," Pau stated.

"Wait—look at this firearm retrieved from the scene!" Miranda chimed.

Blessed with a generous donation from a widow whose son was murdered in the line of duty, their forensics lab was one of the most advanced ones in the North Atlantic Region.

"Pau, hold off on the call. I have a hunch. It's just a hunch, but we've known for some time that there are some serious holes in security protocol at this station. I think this gun is smoking, and it might lead us somewhere. I hope my hunch is wrong. If it comes up blank, then make your call," she advised.

Minutes later, Miranda's speculation was given a breath of reality. Her findings were shocking; a conspiracy of this magnitude would send typhoon-like ripples throughout the entire precinct.

"Pau, we have a serious problem; this gun belongs to Officer Dansbury!" she gulped as she passed him the results.

He evaluated her findings. "We can't release this. We might have to sit on something this serious. There's no telling how many lies live within this spider web!" he was just as shaken as she was, but he wasn't ready to put both of their lives in grave danger. They both knew Dansbury and were well aware of his reputation.

"Well, how do we proceed?" Miranda queried.

"I suggest we proceed with our first plan. Release the results about the innocent man in detention. Once he's free, we'll figure the rest out. I have a guy that might be able to assist us," Pau said.

Reluctantly, Miranda agreed to this plan. Pau decided he would be the one to make the call.

There was only one phone in the lab; it had been painted red with a red magic marker by a former OCD-afflicted technician. They called the phone Alpha One, or *Alph*. Pau walked past a gurney with a semi-exposed female corpse lying belly-up; he reached across two canisters of vapor-locked formaldehyde and picked up *Alph*. While dialing the four-digit extension, he knew that this type of news would be poorly received.

"Hello, Chief; it's Pau in forensics. I've got some bad news."

"There's less than a five percent match," Pau reported.

"Bottom line, your suspect is not—I repeat—is not the shooter. But, in regard to that nine-millimeter you brought in a few hours ago, the prints are so faint; we're waiting for proof-positive results. We might have to run a firearm discharge test," he added.

"OK, thanks, Chief," Pau said.

CLICK!

The chief and Officer Dansbury sat upstairs, above the forensics lab, in the chief's office as the call came from forensics.

"I take it we didn't get him?" queried Dansbury.

The chief was visibly irritated. "Which part of the story do you want first? Heads or ass-fucking tails? I swear, it seems like someone in our department is fucking with evidence, because shit has been coming up short! Remember that bullshit behind the Deshazo case. Bullshit, pure bullshit. Once again, we're getting fucked backward. And by the way, what were you thinking? That arrest was horrible police work! Some real third-grade shit!" the chief yelled as he pounded his right fist against the whiteboard on the near wall.

"I don't know about you, but I'm raring to go in there! Give me ten minutes. Turn the cameras off, and I can get our confession!" Dansbury insisted.

"Did you hear anything I just said? That arrest was senseless, pointless, exactly the type of stuff that brings Internal Affairs to my desk! I already received one direct initiative stating that any more complaints against us will result in serious repercussions. We're at the point that if we breathe on a suspect too hard, heads could roll. It's code red, and you're playing Mr. Majestic! What the fuck were you thinking!" shouted the chief as the extra weight in his midsection jiggled.

"How so? We needed an arrest to take the heat off. Mission accomplished. In the interim, don't forget that we caught Carlos 'Felix the Cat' Sanchez!" Dansbury quickly pointed out.

"Correction! We stumbled upon Carlos. Who's barely alive I might add! And we got him? We got who? What are you talking about? That man we have in custody is squeaky clean! We'll be lucky not to hear from his lawyer!" the chief fired back.

"And you're talking about letting him walk; we can detain him for a few more hours!" Dansbury shouted.

"Half a print and no body! No witnesses that saw him pull the trigger, not even a junkie jury would believe our accusations. No GSR! We got nothing. He was at that nightclub on a date. The roses and chocolates he bought were found inside his car with a card that read, 'I had a good time tonight and hope that these red-faced friends remind you of me every time you look at them xoxo.' The only gun he was planning on using that night was between his legs. This case could turn into a lawsuit! Process him, apologize, and let him know we are extremely sorry for any inconvenience this may have caused. Hell, if he asks you to blow him, then you blow him!" The chief's voice continued to rise.

"Slow down, Chief! Look, Carlos was found at Saul's place. We know that he had been drinking that night, and we know that he's the bookie that's been carrying Saul's seven-hundred-fifty-grand gambling debt. Everybody knows that there has always been bad blood between him and Saul. Evidence shows that Saul and Carlos exchanged blows that evening. Preliminary data revealed that the unknown assailant shot both Saul and Carlos several times. Saul died, and Carlos slipped into a coma," Dansbury said.

"I have a different perspective; this was either a very bad assassination attempt or the shooter wanted someone else to take the fall. Either way, all we have is a comatose suspect. Something about this reeks to high heaven, but I just can't put my finger on it!" said the chief. His heavyset cheeks resembled those of a British bulldog.

"So, what if forensics only retrieved part of a fingerprint? OK, so I made an error in judgment with the other arrest, but we bagged Carlos. That has to account for something!" Dansbury's pulse beat even harder.

"Provided he doesn't die on the operating table! If he doesn't wake up, then we're back to square one, and then what do we have?" the chief retorted.

Detective Dansbury had already rolled up his sleeves; his face was becoming red, and a thick vein bulged from beneath his left eye. "Martyr? Carlos? That piece of shit ain't no martyr; that sumabitch is going to fry! I'm going to see to it!" he yelled. Angrily, he shot out of his chair and headed for the door, but Officer Douglas stepped into his path.

"Dansbury, you heard the chief; cut the detainee loose. He gave you a direct order!" Officer Douglas said with a face filled with seriousness.

"Hey, it's super-cop! Officer Douglas to the rescue. Anything you say, sir! I am on my way to processing; then I'll check in on Carlos, just to see if he needs anything," Dansbury replied with a smirk.

"Remember, all roses and smiles when you cut that guy loose. You really messed up. Next time, this goes on your jacket!" the chief threatened.

"OK, I got you, Chief," Dansbury continued to smirk.

Officer Douglas approached the chief as Dansbury exited.

"Chief, I wanted to talk to you about any files we have on Damon Nemo," Officer Douglas said.

"Sure, I'll order whatever we have," the chief replied. Officer Douglas was a consummate professional. This city was his home; he wasn't afraid to interact with citizens of all neighborhoods. He conducted police work like it had been done during earlier, more civilized times, when police officers were viewed as problem solvers and not the problem.

"What's itching you, Douglas?" the chief queried.

"Come follow me to my desk; there's something that I've been working on that you should see," Douglas said.

The chief sat back in a black, industry-standard, faux-black-leather swivel chair as Officer Douglas produced a folder from a locked desk drawer. Inside was the following:

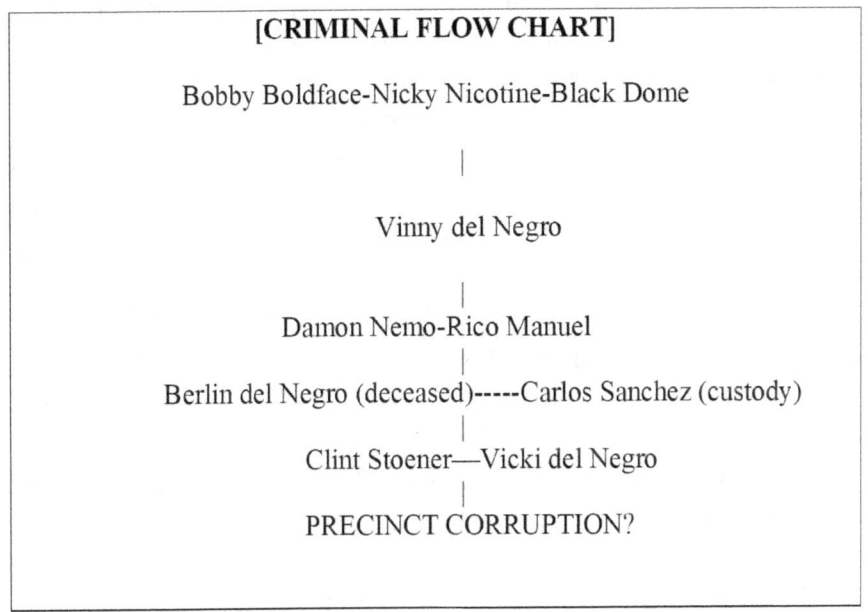

[CRIMINAL FLOW CHART]

Bobby Boldface-Nicky Nicotine-Black Dome

|

Vinny del Negro

|

Damon Nemo-Rico Manuel
|
Berlin del Negro (deceased)-----Carlos Sanchez (custody)
|
Clint Stoener—Vicki del Negro
|
PRECINCT CORRUPTION?

The chief squinted and then pulled his reading glasses out of his breast pocket and examined the documents. Dismayed, the chief lifted his head. "How long have you been pecking away at this?" he asked.

"Not long," Officer Douglas replied.

"Have you shown this to anyone else?" the chief queried.

"No, only you. There is a curious way in which business is conducted around here, and I have very few options regarding sharing such information, especially when I am certain there's a rat working here right under our noses. This wasn't my original focus, but as events started unfolding, pieces made themselves available, and soon the obvious became too difficult to ignore. For example, according to my CI, Clint Stoener has minor drug-trafficking connections to Mr. Vinzantinne. Mr. Stoener transacted marijuana sales in an upstairs hash bar inside *EDIBLE GROOVES*. Sources also reveal that Mr. Stoener was definitely working the night of the shooting spree. After I ran the previously referenced Damon Nemo's files, I came up with a sealed juvenile record, but since 1983 he's been clean. But here's the kicker: the other day I caught a ten-sixteen off the airways, an anonymous tip phoned in about a possible domestic disturbance involving an old woman. But before I could question her, I was called to another emergency. Since then, I called a few times, but the number has been disconnected. The old woman's address matches the last known address for Damon Nemo. Nemo is on record for renting vans, among other transactions from Saul Briggs, the car salesman that was murdered," Douglas reported.

"Bingo!" yelled the chief. "Look, I'll get Detective Ricks to pick up Stoener. You follow up on this Nemo character. Now I need to find Dansbury before he breaks every Geneva Code known to the civilized world!" the chief exclaimed.

"I'm on it, Chief! I have one lead to follow up, and then I'll swing by Nemo's address," Officer Douglas added.

Outside, the sky turned an ominous gray. Officer Douglas gathered his belongings; then, as he approached the main exit, he paused to make a phone call, just before he left the precinct. By the time he was firmly planted behind the steering wheel, heavy raindrops plopped on the hood.

CHAPTER 21

Rotten Cheese

• • •

May 8, 2008, 5:30 p.m.

THE RAINS HAD STOPPED, AND the temperature warmed up considerably, so warm that the concrete reeked of the sweat that collectively rolled off the backs of strangers. Cheese stood outside of Damon's office between a phone booth and a large, dirty puddle. He smoked part of a joint as he talked with Damon over the phone, while Vinny sat inside. Following the nightclub shooting, not only the police, but the criminals were also on edge. Cheese finished his phone call with Damon and then walked inside.

"Damon, is that you?" Vinny beckoned.

"Nah, it's me, Cheese," he said as he eyeballed Vinny.

Vinny always traveled with a supremely large bodyguard, and today was no exception.

"What the hell is going on? Where's Damon? I thought he was coming." Damon's last-minute absence created suspicion, and Vinny didn't enjoy suspicion.

"Be cool! Damon stepped out; he should be back real soon," Cheese replied.

"Did you see that mess that went down at the club? People are still buzzing about it!" Vinny's words conveyed his level of concern.

"See it? I was standing two feet from a woman when her guts exploded!" Cheese replied. "Shit happens! Last night, shit just happened to happen at your club!"

"Cut the history lesson! Who the fuck do you think you guys are?" Vinny might have been nervous, but that didn't hide his displeasure. He was accustomed to being in charge, but over the past twelve to twenty-four hours, he'd felt control slipping away. Secretly, he believed that Damon set up the massacre at his club. Was it to send some type of message? He wasn't sure.

"Us? You're the problem! You could've prevented all that bloodshed if you weren't so stubborn! But no, you had to do it your way!" Cheese's words got louder.

"I've already paid my debt! What do you want now?" Vinny questioned.

"Where's the package? What did you tell the cops about last night?" Cheese's voice grew louder as he rapidly fired off questions.

"Nothing! I didn't tell them anything! They've been calling, but I haven't spoken with them!" The more Vinny spoke, the more he sounded like a liability. "Look, I can come back at a better time. As for the package, tell Damon it's right where it's been for the last five years. I haven't done anything with it." Vinny stood up, but he never made it to the door.

"Bullshit, you're a liar! How long have you been working as an informant for the police?" Cheese inquired.

Vinny's face dropped as he turned around to face Cheese. "What do you mean by that? Are you calling me a rat?" Aggression simmered on both sides of the conversation.

"Yeah, you heard me correctly! How long has it been?" Cheese screamed.

"Those are serious accusations; you better think wisely about the words that follow!" As Vinny shouted, his bodyguard was put on sudden alert.

"Because dirt recognizes dirt! I know all about you. That was your own stubborn bad luck. That shooting cannot and will not come back on my head! Your fuckup can't be my fuckup. I didn't have anything to do with your present misfortune, but I can affect your future. You see, Vin, lightning is like AIDS. If you don't have a rubber on when either of them strikes, then you're dead!" With the precision of a trained marksman,

Cheese drew his gun and shot it four times: twice into Vinny's face, a third one into the bodyguard's chest, followed by a headshot to blast his fate. Quickly, two men wearing hazmat suits walked in from one of the back rooms.

"Clean him up; make it resemble a suicide or something!" Cheese ordered.

"But you shot him multiple times; no coroner could miss that detail!" the huskier of the two suits said.

Cheese drew his gun and fired at close range.

BANG!

The huskier hazmat worker fell facedown, dead.

"Hey, you! Better make it a triple suicide, or I'll turn it into a quadruple homicide!" Cheese threatened as he pointed his gun at the last remaining hazmat worker.

"Yes, sir!" he blurted.

"When you've finished arranging the bodies, pull the teeth, cut the hands and feet off, douse them, and then light a match. And make sure this place burns quickly. Remember, any job worth doing is a job worth being done correctly. Here, give me your hand!" Cheese took a pen and wrote the number on the *HAZMAT* worker's hand. "Call this number when the job is done," Cheese said.

With business completed, Cheese returned to his apartment. He was in his car, on the phone, talking to a "female business associate." She was harping upon the integrity of the deal they struck, fearful that Cheese was not going to honor his end.

"You'll get paid! I have two small ends to tie up, and you can come get your money!" he fumed.

"Fine, woman, meet me here in about two hours!" he hung up the phone.

CLICK!

She arrived sixty-seven minutes later, wearing a cheap plastic pair of stilettos and a rayon skirt to the middle of her thighs. Their greeting was bland. It was obvious she could not stand him, but he was paying, and she was in need of some quick cash. Time for talk ended, and they fucked. Afterwards, Cheese tried to negotiate a cheaper price.

"A discount! What do you mean you weren't satisfied? I knew it; your type is always looking for a cheap-out!" she fretted.

"It's just that I should have called you three weeks ago," Cheese responded.

"Three weeks ago? Why three weeks ago?" she asked.

"Because your vagina would have been fresher. I should've gotten drunk! The entire time, all I smelled was rotten oysters and sweat. And as far as taste, you tasted terrible!" he added.

"Yet you persevered. Aw! You poor bastard! A hundred dollars to have me milk sperm from your tiny dick!" she jeered.

"Hey, if I'm paying, I want to get my money's worth. Website said you were a wholesome Christian girl, not some holy-roller prostitute," he said.

"Yeah, and I thought that you were an architect. So, we're even!" she snapped.

"Hey! Hear this, hotshot! You mean to tell me that over the past twenty-four hours, the thought of a shower never crossed your mind? How about a vaginal wipe? C'mon!"

"My job is hard enough! Eff you! I could do without the abuse. If you can tell me that you didn't come, then I'll just charge you whatever you have on you," she conceded.

"You have a lot of mileage on you," Cheese proclaimed as he probed the contents of his pockets. "Uh, ten ones and six quarters," he mumbled.

"Eleven bucks! Not no, but hell no! You need more money!" she shouted.

Suddenly, his phone rang.

"What time is it?" he queried.

"A little after eight thirty—why?" she asked as she wiped the left corner of her mouth.

"Fuck you, I need to answer this," he barked.

Cheese answered the phone and responded, "Proceed as planned." *CLICK!*

"Whore! You almost cost me." He paused, shook his head, and thought about what he'd just said to the person on the other end. "Shouldn't fuck with them," he paused and then chuckled, "But I seemingly can't fuck without them!" he continued.

"Uhhh…can we get my money now?" she implored.

"Whatever," Cheese said before he opened and closed his apartment door as he and his prostitute left.

CHAPTER 22

Connecting the Dots

• • •

May 9, 2008, 10:05 a.m.

TWO DAYS AFTER THE BULLET-RIDDLED event at *EDIBLE GROOVES*, the police spent most of the morning dragging Vinny Vinzantinne's car out of the reservoir. "Never put your nose on the ground for the cops. You can be anything in this world. No matter how bad things get, never put your nose on the ground for a cop!" Vinny would repeat this over and over, whether on holidays, at christenings, or during wedding speeches. Yet in the wake of his death, rumors could not help but spread about him being nosy for the feds.

Over the past forty-eight hours, lots of blood had spilled, yet no suspects had been apprehended. Authorities had interviewed anyone that was available and present that night. Today, Vicki had been called to the station to identify Vinny's body. With Berlin dead, she was his next of kin. She confirmed it was Vinny's corpse, signed some documents, took possession of his belongings, and started to leave. But before she could exit the precinct, Detective Dansbury yelled her name: "Victoria Vinzantinne!"

Apparently, she hadn't heard his first attempt.

"Stop!" Dansbury shouted.

Vicki turned around, face flushed. Her breathing was labored. It felt like her heart was beating inside of her tongue. "Yes," she replied weakly.

"Victoria Vinzantinne, my name is Detective Dansbury. Come back inside; I need to talk to you," he waved his right arm as he spoke.

Stunned, she followed his instructions as two tears dripped from both eyes. He held the door for her and then led her into a stuffy interrogation room.

"Here, take a seat," he said, and she obliged.

"It's a shame that you have to find out like this, but I can confirm that your uncle was working for us, and yes, it is true that you could serve jail time if you don't openly cooperate with our investigation," Dansbury said in an uncharacteristically calm manner.

"What? My uncle was working for you?" her moist face was overwhelmed with shock.

"Yes, I know it's hard to believe. He was a very useful CI until his murder." Dansbury's words quickly became callous.

"But how am I involved in all of this?" Vicki asked.

"Are you kidding me? You're kidding, right?" he laughed. "That's funny! You worked at *EDIBLE GROOVES*, and if my records are correct, you were responsible for bookkeeping at the club, right?" he asked.

"Yes, yes, I was," she replied.

"Well, you were either blind, deaf, dumb, or just stupid. How could you not have noticed suspicious monies being funneled in and out of that place?" he questioned.

"What? I didn't do anything illegal. I just handled deposit slips, answered calls, and made coffee," she sniffled as she searched her purse for a tissue.

"Hey, Vicki, how many fingers am I holding up?" asked Dansbury as he raised the index and ring fingers on his right hand.

"Two," Vicki responded.

"Well, at least we know you aren't blind or deaf. So, it must be stupid!" his voice got louder, and his eyes looked like they were strung out on too many coffees with extra cream plus extra sugar. "Cooperate, and I could become your best friend. Double-cross me, and you could be looking at five hard years for obstruction of justice. Just how long do you think a pretty, privileged, tender morsel such as yourself would get treated inside the joint? You'd be licking gash before breakfast!" Dansbury spoke with crass conviction.

"Do I need to have my lawyer present?" Vicki sobbed and then sniffled.

Keeping with the classic "Good Cop Bad Cop" methodology, at that very moment, another officer walked into the office carrying a box of Kleenex and a mug of steaming hot coffee.

"This is for you," he gave her the mug and placed the box of tissues on the table next to her. "That will be all, Officer Dansbury. I am hereby relieving you of your duties, and furthermore, I am considering placing you under investigation for witness harassment."

Detective Dansbury jumped to his feet and shouted, "This is bullshit!" he jolted the door shut behind him as the new officer turned to Vicki.

"Thank goodness that's over! Hello, my name is Special Agent Detective Ricks. Let me be the first to offer my condolences to you and your family. I'm the leader of a Special Forces team that has been tracking racketeering and other nefarious behavior within the city. I just need you to answer a few questions; I promise this will be gentle, and we will only discuss what you feel comfortable with discussing. Deal?" Special Agent Rick's voice and demeanor were a welcome contrast to Dansbury's.

She nodded in acceptance of his offer.

"Have you ever seen this man?" he asked, holding up a photo.

She blew into the cup before sipping from the piping-hot mug while blankly staring at the black-and-white photo featuring her uncle and a man of Asian descent. "No," she replied, "I have never seen him before."

"Not ever?" Ricks asked.

"Never," she replied.

"Well, we believe that this man was a conspirator in a lottery, or *bolita*, a Cuban numbers game that produced large profits for a notorious Cosa Nostra leader. This man right here"—he held up another picture—"Romero Marquez, and the other man in the photo ran the lottery and other multimillion-dollar operations until he was found on a park bench covered in newspaper outside of a brothel. His head was bashed in, and his throat had been slit," Ricks reported.

"Maybe I missed something; how does my uncle fit into all of this?" Vicki questioned.

"I'll tell you. Four nights ago, there was a raid as part of another case at an undisclosed office on the other side of town. Among the cash and drugs recovered by my agents, they also found an 'ice list.' This ice list was a compilation of money records that dealt with illegal transactions. Your uncle's name was listed various times. Also, Mr. Rico Manuel's name was repeatedly seen as one of your uncle's business associates," Ricks stated.

"Well, why don't you call him in and ask for answers?" Vicki insisted.

"I would, but as the story goes, when the last lottery numbers came out, there was an unusually high number of winners. Suspicions quickly rose, and we have reasonable cause to believe Mr. Manuel rigged one of the lotteries for his own gain. Your uncle hired an *eraser* to rub out Mr. Manuel. And before that, in 1998, Mr. Manuel and your uncle along with this man"—he held up another black-and-white photo—"Nestor Ukamara, were apprehended by Interpol and local authorities during a traffic stop as they attempted to drive out of Havana. Your uncle was acquitted. But Mr. Manuel and Mr. Ukamara escaped before conviction. Since then, those two have been on the DEA's Most Wanted for the last ten years. The ten-year anniversary was four days ago, which coincided with the same day as the nightclub shooting. Now that your uncle is dead, you shouldn't need a wizard to guess who he wants to talk to next?" he paused. "My guess is *you*. In case you're wondering what type of deranged person we're dealing with, he was a major player during the OxyContin and cocaine crush. It's alleged that he was also part of a group that recently imported nearly a hundred twenty-five kilograms of pure, uncut cocaine, several hundred pounds of pharmaceuticals, and countless tons of marijuana in a semi-trailer that made deliveries across the country," Ricks continued.

"But I still don't understand what all of this has to do with me," her eyes swelled with tears.

"Are you sure?" he chuckled as he replied. "We have IRS reports that show you filed taxes disclosing your uncle made two hundred fifty thousand dollars a year from the club alone. But you and I are fully aware of the fact that your uncle makes—excuse me, made—much more money than that, some of it clean but most of it dirty. All money is dirty until laundered," he laughed. "Excuse me, that's a running department joke. Shortly following reports of your uncle's murder, we procured a warrant and investigated several of his properties and discovered a myriad of 'legal' front businesses that shadowed other activities. For every seemingly legitimate enterprise, we found equally questionable operations, like Del Negro Dumping and V & V Construction and Contracting. In fact, the deeper we searched, the more dirt we found. In one west-side residence, we confiscated two-point-eight million dollars in large bills and five hundred fifty thousand in jewelry, several high-end vehicles, and countless deeds to prime real estate both in and out of state. In addition to the lottery and drug activities, your uncle spent time as a human sex-slave trafficker. Once that venture was dumped, your uncle focused on restaurants and clubs. But according to our CI, marijuana was a substance that your uncle used recreationally as well as distributed for profit. Additional CI reports shed light upon an alleged upstairs hash bar above *EDIBLE GROOVES*. Ms. Vinzantinne—may I call you Vicki? Are these allegations true? Sources say this man"—he showed her a black-and-white picture—"is Clint Stoener. We have reason to believe that he was the mastermind behind the hash bar operation. The night of the shooting spree, we intended to raid your uncle's club, a raid so thorough that it would have surely resulted in all of your arrests, including you and your associate Mr. Stoener. He is an associate, is he not?" Ricks probed.

"Yes, I have known Clint for a few years," she sniffled as she spoke.

"OK, seven days ago on the northeast side of town, a car salesman was shot to death in his home after a fight party. It just so happens that we have knowledge that Clint left that party with a very attractive brunette. He and Saul, the car salesman, were much more than just associates. Oh, by the way, here's a picture of Clint's brunette lady friend," he showed her the photo of a woman. "You're pretty, but this woman? Hmm, I'd leave my wife for her," Ricks stated.

Shocked to see the photo of this other woman, Vicki's heart ached. "What do you need from me?" she asked.

"I think when we find Mr. Stoener, then we might be able to find your uncle's killer," he articulated.

"I know of Mr. Stoener; I just don't know him as well as you think I do," she said.

His tone changed sharply. "Liar! Telephone records show that you and Mr. Stoener have been in communication. A maximum of twelve hours is how long you two have gone without talking. We have records that show you know him better than you say you do. Did you fuck him? You fucked, didn't you? Why did the two of you stop talking for over six months? What happened? Lovers' spat? Did you see him at the club two nights ago?"

Special Agent Detective Ricks asked a lot of questions but received very few concrete answers. Vicki was overstimulated and overwhelmed. "I have only seen him a handful of times in my uncle's office. Yes, we've talked a few times. I was curious, but it never led to anything serious; he has a girlfriend...I guess the girl in the photo." Vicki was lying, but she wanted so desperately to keep Clint clean.

"Years ago, something happened. Can you explain why Mr. Stoener stopped working for your uncle?" he inquired.

"I can't answer that. Whatever happened—that's between my uncle and Clint," she snapped.

"I guess I'll just have to ask Mr. Stoener when we catch up with him! But if I find out that you're lying...Oh, I just hope that you aren't!" he barked.

"OK! I have had enough. That's enough questioning," she protested.

"Fine, if not today, not tomorrow, you know that I'll come calling!" he admonished.

"And what if I don't answer that call, Special Agent Detective Ricks?" she fired back as tears rolled down the contours of her cheeks.

"You'll be arrested and charged for obstruction of justice, money laundering, conspiracy, and anything else I can come up with! Do us all a favor, and make sure you answer my call," advised Special Agent Detective Ricks.

"I will, if I'm by the phone; good day, Detective," she responded curtly and stormed out of the station.

Finally, out of the police station, she contained herself until she got to her car. Once she opened the door, she plopped into her seat and fully cried. Her uncle's death with Clint's perceived infidelity and Special Agent Ricks proved to be too much for her to handle.

To further her demise, while in the precinct, someone placed a GPS tracker on the underbelly of her car. Ten minutes later, she called me from a pay phone.

"Vicki, I thought the plan was for us to meet here at two? Why the change in schedule?" I questioned.

"Long story. Did you smarten up and decide to stay at a motel?" she asked.

"Yes," I replied.

"Look, whatever you do, don't go back to your apartment! Meet me in one of the booths at the pool hall on Thirty-Third Street. Do you know where that is?" she spoke with guarded words, as if she knew something that I didn't.

"I'll find it," I responded, very wary of the situation.

It took me twenty-three minutes to find the pool hall. A fat man whose belt screamed for fewer carbohydrates as his stomach continually thirsted for more beer sat just inside the door on a tiny stool. Behind him, thick, stale smoke rolled around in the air like fog hugging a mountain. Just about everyone in the joint smoked and drank all sorts of cheap intoxicants. Before this place was a pool hall, it had been a tanning salon, but once reverse gentrification occurred, the neighborhood changed. The new faces had zero need for tanning beds. Once the property was sold, proprietors replaced the beds with garden-green felt tables and multicolored balls. Seconds after I stepped in, I spotted her. She sat in the booth closest to the door. I approached.

"Hello, Vicki," I smiled as I spoke.

"Hello; take a seat, Clint," she looked tired and visibly shaken.

I sat down, and she ordered two beers. Nervously, she lit a menthol cigarette. I immediately noticed that something wasn't right. I just couldn't put my finger on it. Then it hit me. Vicki never—I mean never—covered up her cleavage. (And she never smoked cigarettes, except for an occasional American Spirit.) She didn't have much to start with—cleavage, that is—but she was determined to flaunt whatever she had at all times. Today, her cleavage wasn't present. I didn't know what was going on, but I had a feeling that things were going to get very interesting.

"Damn, girl, it's early to be drinking!"

As I spoke, her face became flushed. "Vinny's dead," she sobbed mightily as she spoke. "He was shot. They found him in his car parked at the bottom of the Hinckley Reservoir." Additional tears began to well up in her eyes. I thought she was strong, so I was so surprised at how easily she'd lost it.

"Vicki, I'm sorry to hear that; when did you find this out?" I consoled.

"Right before I called you. When you left, the cops called me so that I could identify the body. Then I had to answer questions with a special agent named Ricks," she reported.

"Really, what type of leads do they have?" I inquired as paranoid brain cells multiplied in my mind.

"They are looking for someone so that they can question him," she replied.

"And who might that be?" I asked, with the eerie feeling that I knew their suspect personally.

"I'm speaking to him right now!" she blurted.

"Me! What do they want with me?" Based on everything that had transpired, I wasn't surprised by her words.

"They didn't say, but they did say a lot. They know about my uncle's business, and they also know about *HAARLEM*."

I could tell she was emotionally spent. For a majority of her early years, her uncle had raised her as his daughter. He'd even financed her forty-thousand-dollar-a-year college tuition.

"That explains it!" I exclaimed.

"What?" she asked.

"I've been feeling like I've been followed the past few days. Remember when you picked me up on Friday? Well, I parked my car in a random lot. When I came out of one of the strip-mall stores, a suspicious man was inspecting it," I reported.

"Clint, your car is a classic; maybe the man was just admiring it; you know those car freaks," her rationale seemed flaccid.

"Not a chance. This guy was walking with a cane and a seeing-eye dog. How can a blind man admire a car without touching it? I doubled back later and picked it up. Fortunately, no one was there. Hey, were you followed?" I asked.

"Where's your car now?" she inquired.

"It's safe. So, the cops said that they were casing the club? Everyone knew your uncle was into more then he let on. What kind of questions did they ask about me?" I probed further.

"The usual. Did I know where you were? Are we lovers? Stuff like that," she shared.

"And how did you answer?" I wondered if they had photographs.

"I didn't say anything. I was real vague. I told them that I knew you, but I didn't *know you* know you. You know? And that your girlfriend was the reason we weren't together," she added.

"Girlfriend? I don't have a girlfriend," I protested.

"Ummm, that's not what the picture said," her eyes drowned in tears again.

"Pictures!" I exclaimed.

"Yes, some pretty-faced brunette. When were you going to tell me about her?"

"I don't know who you're talking about!" I replied.

"Really? You didn't meet a woman at Saul's party?" her demeanor changed as she spoke.

"Oh, that girl? She was just some girl that Saul introduced me to at his party," I replied casually.

"Oh, yes, that girl! Now I guess you're going to tell me that you didn't fuck her!" Her words and countenance became quite animated.

I looked dead into her eyes and lied unflinchingly: "No, I didn't!"

"Clint, I don't know what to believe!" she exclaimed.

"You have to believe me! You're the only woman I have been with since I returned back east!"

Her eyes probed mine as my eyes probed hers.

Seconds later, she paused, shook her head, and closed her eyes. She desperately wanted to believe me.

"Vicki, you have to believe me!" I corralled her left hand between both of my hands and pressed it dearly to my right cheek.

Sighing, she said, "Clint, I believe you! I'm sorry; between my uncle's murder and those asshole detectives, my head is spinning," she replied.

"Well, thank you! I understand what you're going through, but I need a favor. I want you to take a deep breath and try to remember everything that you and the detectives discussed. Can you do that for me?"

"OK, I can try," she exhaled, and I began my own questioning.

"Did they say that they were going to try to pin your uncle's murder on me?" I asked.

"I didn't get that impression. But I think you should just go down and cooperate with them. Answer their questions and get past this," she said those words with such nonchalance, as if I was going to a job interview at the Gap.

"Well, with my past, there's no telling what they'll try to do. When I was in college, I was called in for questioning regarding an alleged assault case. A man had fingered me as the person that jumped him the night before Halloween. Luckily, I had an alibi. Plus, my hair was much longer, and when the actual assailant was caught, I was shocked because we looked nothing alike. He wore glasses and sported a bald head. Based on that experience, I thought the best thing for me is to lay lower than a snake's belly until it is absolutely necessary to show my face. Anyways, thanks for the heads-up on the motel; if I hadn't paid by cash, then I would have left a serious paper trail. But I wish you had told me about your meeting with the cops earlier," I said.

"And why?" she probed.

"Because I wouldn't have met with you," I curtly replied.

"Honestly, Clint!" she exclaimed.

"Of course, they might be following you. Duuuh!" I retorted.

"Not possible. I took two cabs and a bus to get over here."

Vicki was obviously lying. She hated public transportation. It hurt me to find that she had possibly turned against me. The way I saw it, if she would lie about a bus ride, then what else would she lie about? Her actions forced me to view her as a potential threat to my freedom. For all I knew the boys in blue could be waiting outside, ready to put me in bracelets.

"Good," I said as I rose from the table.

"Where are you going?" She was startled at my movements. "Aren't you going to have a drink with me?" she almost pleaded.

"I'm putting myself into my own witness protection. Sorry about your uncle; I'll keep in contact. Vicki, whatever you do, don't call me via my cell phone," I implored, as I briskly headed for the exit.

With a little more pep in my stride, I exited the pool hall. As I walked, my eyes caught a tag board littered with a cornucopia of pamphlets, advertisements for things on sale and any other clutter that people felt necessary to post to the public. One item in particular caught my eyes; the paper was pink and covered with very demonstrative print. I pulled one off and scanned the title: *Encountering Police—Survive the Unexpected*. Still striding, I folded the paper and walked out into the sunshine. I hadn't taken more than three steps outside when I heard an authoritative male voice calling me by my last name.

"Mr. Stoener! Mr. Clint Stoener! I need to talk to you!" the voice shouted.

Instinctively, I wanted to run, but I deferred to my sense of rationale and slowly turned around to face my questioner. Before I could blink, a dark, late-model Lincoln Continental pulled up in front of me, and three men jumped out, guns drawn: two uniformed officers and one suit. The suit did all of the talking.

"What's this all about? I haven't done anything wrong!" I protested as one of the uniforms proceeded to cuff me.

"Mr. Stoener, my name is Special Agent Detective Ricks. I just want to ask you a few questions about your involvement with an establishment named *EDIBLE GROOVES*. We come in peace and for your own protection. I will only take a few minutes of your time," he stated with the slither of a serpent's tongue.

"My own protection? Then why the cuffs or the guns?" I growled.

"Look, I'll take the cuffs off so that you can be comfortable, but you will be taking a ride with us!" he retorted.

"Am I under arrest?" I asked.

"No, but if you refuse to cooperate, then I could arrest you!" Detective Ricks snapped.

"On what grounds?" I inquired.

"Suspicion of marijuana trafficking, conspiracy to commit murder, resisting arrest—should I go on?" he asked. Most of those alleged charges were bullshit; he knew it, and I knew it, but he was the one with the gun.

"You have no evidence to those charges!" I vehemently responded.

"Mr. Stoener, do you play poker?" Detective Ricks inquired.

"Occasionally, why do you ask?" I questioned.

"The beauty of poker stems from the art of speculation. For example, maybe my hand is a dud, and I'm bluffing, or my hand could contain a full house of information. Therefore, it's up to you to speculate as to what I am holding. What would you say if I told you that I know you served more than just drinks at *EDIBLE GROOVES*? Or if I told you that the man you worked for was found shot dead, illegally parked at the bottom of a local reservoir? What about Berlin Vinzantinne? Does that serve notice? Your rap sheet reads like a Biggie Smalls record: two years of probation for possession of a firearm, six days in juvie for joyriding. It says here that you were also expelled from college for some undisclosed reason," he smiled that cocky cop smile as he spoke.

"I've made a few mistakes. Are you squeaky clean, Detective? Have you ever bent the rules or broken an arm to make a point?" I almost started to crack a smile of my own. I loved to debate, and here we were at the precipice of verbal banter, a classic battle pitting an MS in street knowledge versus a suit with a gun and a badge.

"The Bible tells us that no man is pure. Read John chapter three, verse sixteen. I was young, but I quickly learned that I had to play the game by the rules, or the game was going to play me! Do you understand what I am talking about?" he asked as he took out a generic lollipop. What can you tell me about Vinzantinne?" Detective Ricks started to unwrap the colorful, circular candy perched on a stick.

"What do I know about Vinny? Well, for starters I think he was a Gemini with potential anger issues. Other than that, he was your average business owner," I responded.

"Business owner! Malarkey, his fingernails were dirtier than a three-year-old with ringworm. Mr. Vinzantinne was well known in all the wrong circles. You don't get that type of notoriety in this city for serving holiday lunches to the poor and elderly. Tell me about *HAARLEM*, the upstairs marijuana bar that you ran," Ricks smiled and then placed the pop in his chops.

I was tripping. This so-called Special Agent Ricks had showed all of his cards. Soon there would be no need to go downtown; he had just asked me every pertinent question outside a seedy pool hall.

"Don't you mean *alleged* marijuana bar, Detective Ricks?" I retorted.

"OK, *alleged* marijuana bar," Ricks sardonically responded.

"Ha-ha, there was no marijuana bar in that club. Maybe in Amsterdam, but not in *EDIBLE GROOVES*. It seems that you have your information confused," I knew I was lying, and he did too, but until he presented physical evidence to corroborate his charge, then that was my story, and I intended to stick to it.

"Not so, I have my information correct! I already interviewed his niece; she told me who was who and what was what. Just honestly answer my questions, and we all can sleep in our own beds tonight," Ricks replied with that cocky smile spawning from the left corner of his mouth, as he bit the lollipop.

CRUNCH!

"His niece? Who's his niece?" I continued the idiot-savant role.

"C'mon, stop being an asshole! Just truthfully answer the fucking question! She goes by the name of Victoria, but you call her Vicki. You know, that pretty little thing you just met in that pool hall. Are you fucking her?" he asked as he pointed to the building behind me.

I immediately began to poke holes into his hot-air-balloon theories before he could pull out any of his black-and-white peepshow photos.

"Detective, I randomly run into all types of people all the time. You really shouldn't believe everything that you—"

He angrily grabbed me by the shirt. "Admit it. You know Santo, the downtown investment banker with the hot Brazilian wife! Let me guess, he always ordered Purple Haze! Are you surprised? Yeah, he and I go way back. Cut the crap; stop the diarrhea of the mouth and tell me what I want to hear! You're an intelligent boy; you were accepted to USC. Wise up and talk. Cooperation can be a good thing," sensing momentum, he wore a full-fledged smile across his smug mug.

"First of all, get your hands off me! Maybe I did; maybe I didn't. You have no proof whatsoever! When you picked me up, did you find any paraphernalia? Do you have a receipt of purchases connecting me to this Santo or any of your allegations, for that matter? Everyone knows the drug industry is a cash-and-carry industry. So where is your evidence? Bring Santo down here so that we can sort this out! Oh, that's right; you can't! Because Santo is dead! Allegedly, he was killed during the nightclub shooting. See, Detective, you have nothing; for all I know, that shooting at the club was done by your soldiers. Am I under arrest? Either take me to the station or let me go!" I demanded.

"Humph!" was his only reply.

The squad car pulled up just a few paces in front of where we stood.

"Oh, we're taking you to the station. Your problem is that you aren't a team player. Problems can be overcome with teamwork. You help me, and maybe I can help you. Teamwork makes the dream work!" he spoke as he motioned for one of the uniformed officers to place me in the backseat.

"Me helping the cops is like a Steinbrenner working for the Red Sox. I have nothing to say. Tennis isn't a team sport, so show me some love and let me go!" I stated.

"Well, digest this: if you pass the residue test, then you're free to go. But if your results come back dirty, then you've got yourself a whole different ballgame," Detective Ricks retorted. He was grasping at straws, but I figured I'd play along. The faster I got to the station, the faster I could get out of dodge, theoretically.

We went to the station, and I used my complimentary phone call to contact Sasha. She was in a meeting and wasn't able to come until it ended. Fuck it, I had nothing to hide, so I took and passed their test. Two hours later, I was in the backseat of the same unmarked car as we departed the station. This whole thing was an overdramatized ruse. I was being chauffeured around like a mark. Typical bullshit. The ride was very quiet, until the car rolled to a stop in front of the same pool hall where they'd picked me up.

"Well, Clint, before you take off and start running like a Kenyan, keep this little tidbit in mind: there are six-point-nine million people incarcerated in jails throughout this country, a hundred thirty-one thousand more than last year; that's three-point-two percent of the population, or one in every thirty-two. Twenty-five percent of them are locked up on some sort of drug charge. If I find out that you lied to me, I will make you into number one hundred thirty-one thousand and one. Then you'll be just another sad, sorry-assed statistic. What do you think about that?" as he spoke, that familiarly irritating smile resurfaced.

"If you checked my scholastic record, you'll find that I never liked statistics." I spoke as I reached into my pocket. "OK, you got me! Look, this is all the evidence you need," and I handed him the folded, pink piece of paper.

I stood there, watching him deliberately unfold the paper crease by crease. After two bends, he read: *Encountering Police—Survive the Unexpected.*

"Wiseass! Just shut the fucking door!" Ricks spewed as he threw the paper onto the sidewalk, and dust and debris kicked up from the unmarked car's tires as it tore off down an adjacent alley.

And there I was, dazed and somewhat confused. I didn't know what Vicki had told them, but my little joyride and station visit confirmed my suspicions. Detective Ricks and his goons hadn't just randomly shown up at the pool hall. They were tipped, or they followed Vicki right to me. I felt a hint of guilt, when my conscience consciously blamed Vicki. Sadly, it appeared that all of my friends had expired faster than egg salad during a humid, steamy summer picnic. On top of that, the police were now scrutinizing my every move. It felt like a noose was tightening around my neck, and I hadn't committed any felonies. Yeah, sure, I sold a little grass, but it's not like I'd shot anyone. I rubbed my eyes and attempted to crack the stress out of my back. Where was Vicki? Did she tip off the cops and sneak out the back door? Or did she finish her drink like a lady and leave out the front door? Either way she was suspect. Once an ally, she had now become another problem, among a seemingly mounting mountain of problems. During my time with Detective Ricks, I had three voicemails that demanded product. Of the original thirty pounds, I was down to a little over ten. That meant once I sold the remaining weed, then I was finished with product and no supplier—unless I dealt with "the Chef." But he was a psycho that never saw, talked, or touched the product. He had so many layers of protection surrounding him that he was practically fed-proof. To contact him, I would have to throw the baby out with the bath water and hire a third party, because, as it stood, I couldn't make the same moves with the cops perched over my shoulder like an owl. Perhaps I could commission Crook to be my go-between. That's a proposition that I needed to deliberate because very few people had actually seen the Chef. He operated what authorities called a three-house ring, or "The Three Little Pigs." One house was the "kitchen"—that's where the product was cultivated. The second house was "storage"—this was where the product was clocked, packaged, and then distributed. The third house, just like in *The Three Little Pigs* was the brick house, or better described as "the vault"—this was where the money was accounted for, counted, and stashed. Each of the houses was rumored to be very nondescript, reflecting comfort not excess, necessity not lavishness, and therefore harder to discover. The Chef might be a reputed lunatic, but he was an insular lunatic with a very sensible way of conducting business.

CHAPTER 23

Crack, Bam, Bash, Burn

• • •

May 9, 2008, 7:33 p.m.

ACROSS TOWN, IT WAS WELL after seven thirty, and Officer Douglas neared the old woman's apartment building. He was following up on a 10-16. The closer he got to his destination, the more he could notice the heavy smoke that billowed off the rooftop. As he pulled up outside in front of the building, there stood a great many bystanders. They were adorned in colorful pajamas and slippers as most of them talked on their cell phones and smoked cigarettes. Officer Douglas parked his car and immediately jumped out.

"What seems to be the problem?" he asked.

"The building is on fire!" a nondescript voice from the assembly yelled.

"Some kids were playing with fireworks!" chimed another voice.

At that point, everyone started speaking at once, high-pitched, low-pitched, native, and foreign voices, all pounding for his ears' attention.

"Wait a minute; settle down! One at a time!" Officer Douglas calmly attempted to quell the crowd's antics as their voices grew louder and louder.

"Where's the old woman that lives in the upstairs apartment!" Officer Douglas shouted as he clicked his shoulder radio.

CLICK!

"I haven't heard her in days. She lives on the top floor!" bellowed a faceless mouth.

Suddenly, Officer Douglas's cell phone began to ring; he answered the phone. On the other end, it sounded like an elderly woman screaming in distress.

"Help! Can anyone help me? Five two nine, please! I've fallen and can't get up!" she continued to scream in desperation. In the wake of 9/11, the blueprint for heroic behavior had been designed. The mission was simple: enter, seek, locate, and rescue. Officer Douglas had lost someone that fateful September day. He was determined not to reproduce the helpless sting of not being able to save someone that couldn't save herself.

Officer Douglas shouted as he clicked the shoulder radio: "There's a ten-seventy-three and a possible ten-seventy at 18403 Progress Way. Officer going in! Requesting back-up!"

CLICK!

He ran into the smoldering building. As hungry flames randomly rose from the floorboards, he was instantly surrounded by smoke and fire. Officer Douglas flipped on his city-issued flashlight, which offered little assistance in clarifying images through the dense smoke. The odds of locating the screaming woman were already daunting enough, but the stakes were made more impossible as the fire chewed through the antiquated building. A collection of joists and ceiling beams came violently crashing down behind Officer Douglas. Right then and there, the fires of hell offered him a window of opportunity to turn, run out of the building, and wait for the fire truck to respond, with the rest of the bystanders. Was he scared? Of course, but he was a true, proud, badge-wearing boy in blue. Sometimes "your fear is your only courage." And he pressed forward. The area by the door closer to the floor was less smoky, so he crouched down, almost like an infant crawling for the first time, and struggled to hedge his way up the steps as he inched closer to where the screams echoed. Like a scene from *Ladder 49*, conditions had swelled well beyond three-alarm status as the building had begun to bend in defeat to the fire. Basic in layout, the apartment building featured one central stairwell that ran straight up to the top; each floor housed separate apartments that branched off to the left and the right. By his clouded estimation, Officer Douglas was halfway up the third floor.

As he ascended the stairwell, the smoke caught up to him. Suffocating, he ripped his shirt from his body and tied it around his face, in an effort to filter the unrelenting smoke that was crowding all around him like a lynch mob at high noon.

"Please help! Five two nine! Oh God, someone save me!" the woman's cries for salvation continued.

Officer Douglas narrowly avoided part of a collapsed ceiling as he breached the landing of the fourth floor. Smoke inhalation had become a major issue; his lungs were nearly asphyxiating, as he coughed and hacked out phlegm. No quit, no surrender was all he had on his mind. Fire is such an odd entity. Like snowflakes, no two fires are alike. But every fire has one common purpose and one purpose only, and that is to continue to burn until there isn't anything left to burn. Miraculously, he reached the top floor only to realize that he had gone one floor too high and had to double back down one floor. But as he returned to the mouth of the stairwell, it was then engulfed in flames, and therefore, exiting that way was nonnegotiable. Instinctively, he ran to the only window on the sixth floor and opened it. Fresh air swept into the building, creating an oxygen surge that acted like a growth hormone as the flames behind him increased in size and aggression. As the fire marched toward him, it forced him out of the window and onto the tiny ledge. Outside, on the west side of the building, he could see a large crowd of people looking up at him from the ground below. Where the fuck was the fire truck? He coughed and inhaled as much fresh air as possible while spitting out increasingly larger amounts of blood-stained phlegm. His resolve was intact, but physically he was nearly spent. The only thing left to do was to gingerly walk the thin line of the window ledge and come in through another window. Cautiously, he unsnapped his service revolver as he approached the next window. Using the butt of his gun, he shattered the square panes of glass, until he could use his foot to kick in what remained of the windowpane. But one part stubbornly refused to budge. Once again, he pounded the pane as hard as he could, yet it didn't move. To his surprise, the force caused his revolver to slip out of his hands, and it plummeted to the ground among the shrubs below. As a last resort, he repeatedly pushed his shoulder as a battering ram to force his body back into the burning building. On the third try, his body crashed through the window as he awkwardly launched into the apartment and fell onto his left shoulder. Now on the fifth floor, he ran along the apartment doors, blindly touching each door's number plate. But this took too long. Smoke had shoved itself into every conceivable corner until the smoke started to choke itself. Coughing uncontrollably, he knew it was now or never. Suddenly, he heard, "Help me! I'm at the end of the hall! Please hurry!" In an instant, he raced to the end unit apartment, and he felt through the darkness for the doorknob. Until his hand traced the door with the numbers 5-2-9. It was locked. Officer Douglas repeatedly kicked the door until he separated it from its hinges and started shouting over the raging fire.

"Hello, miss! My name is Officer Douglas; I am here to rescue you! Where are you?"

"Help me; I'm over here!" the voice of desperation cried one last time.

CA-SHHH!

Police Radio: "Officer Douglas, the fire truck has reported to the ten-seventy-three at 18403 Progress Way. Please correspond! I repeat; please correspond!"

CA-SHHH!

Ignoring the radio response, Officer Douglas crouched low and dragged himself through the apartment, searching for any signs of the old woman, but there was just too much smoke.

"I'm here, miss; where are you?" he screamed.

COUGH-COUGH!

"Can you see me? I'm on the floor right by the window! Please hurry!" The window was mostly covered by drapes except for the briefest of slits that allowed a glimmer of light from one of the streetlights to enter the room.

"Hold tight; I'm almost there!" were his last words.

Suddenly, a wooden baseball bat struck blow after blow on top of Officer Douglas.

CRACK-BAM-BASH-BURN!
CRACK-BAM-BASH-BURN!!
CRACK-BAM-BASH-BURN!!!

The cracks and bashes rang out until the bloodied, maple bat stopped striking Officer Douglas across the upper and lower rear cranial portion of his head. Unconscious, he lay silent as flames creeped around his body. Stepping through the smoke and shadows, his attacker wore an oxygen mask. Large in stature, the mysterious assailant quickly picked up a metallic box and fled out of the building and down the rear fire escape. Instantly, the fire had started to have its way with Officer Douglas's body. But he wasn't alone; there was another body lying next to him also waiting to be preyed upon by the raging fire. No two fires are alike, but their common goal is to burn until there isn't anything else to burn.

SNAP-CRACKLE-POP!

The smell of burning flesh and smoke filled the air just as the building's roof came crashing down.

CHAPTER 24

Slim Chances

• • •

May 11, 2008, 1:55 p.m.

I MAINTAINED A LOW PROFILE after I was picked up by the police. As a precaution, I tried to vary my modes of transportation. Today, I took two different cabs, the subway, and then a bus—just for the local grocery store. My money and what remained of my product were in a secure location, but motel food was beginning to affect my stomach. I was in need of actual nutrition. *SLIMS* was a popular local health market. It's amazing how expensive it is to eat healthy.

I spotted her as she reached down to grab a hand basket. A former polo player, she was dressed in a business suit, and the athleticism of her build was professionally on display. Initially, my neurons couldn't foster a connection between her name, her face, or her body, but once I heard her voice, everything fell into place. She turned, and our eyes locked momentarily; then she took a double take as her mind processed what her eyes had seen.

"Clint, how are you? It's me, Sasha!" she exclaimed with her arms wide open.

"Sasha Adair! I remember you! How, are you?" I smiled as we hugged.

"Wow! I'm impressed. It's been a long time. I haven't seen you since you transferred from USC. What are you doing with yourself?" she asked.

"I'm a pharmaceutical representative for a starter company," I lied. But what else could I say? Hey! I deal medicinal marijuana: by the way, if you're interested, an eighth goes for $65 and a quarter for $120. "What about you? You're a lawyer, right?"

"Yes, I am scheduled to start my new position on Monday. I'll be working to improve the social well-being for emotionally disturbed children," a proud smile followed her words.

"That sounds like the sort of thing that you would be doing. You always had an altruistic vision for society. Why did you leave the West Coast?" I inquired, attempting to divert away from questions that pertained to "all things me."

"Remember Jimmy Rubin? Well, he and I got engaged during the end of my senior year. Oh, but I think you had already left at that point," she said.

"Jimmy Rubin? That mop-haired fool! You married that Muppet?" I asked incredulously.

"That was the plan until I caught him in flagrante delicto. One day, I came home to surprise him, and I was the one that ended up being surprised. I discovered him in bed with his boyfriends. That shitty secret put an end to our engagement. His explanation was that he had to get in touch with the real person that was inside of him. After graduation, I packed my bags and headed as far away from that jerk and anyone connected to him," her words were calm, indicating that she had healed and was well beyond such foolishness.

"Ouch, that's not cool," I replied.

"What about you? Did anything ever manifest between you and that Asian woman?" she inquired.

"No, but we parted ways on favorable terms. I left school, once all that madness went down. I was just glad to get out," I added.

"Look, I'm supposed to be picking up a cake for this event, and I'm already running behind schedule. Too bad we didn't run into each other earlier—this would have been your type of event," she replied.

"No worries, what matters is we were able to reconnect right here and now—maybe next time," I concluded.

"OK, definitely! Here's my card; give me a call. I just purchased a condo near the Financial District. It's right on the water; we can meet for drinks and then walk to that new club *ROUGE*," she said.

"Sounds like a plan. I might need to ask you for some legal advice. What are your rates?" I joked.

"Oh, honey, you couldn't afford me." She laughed as she said those words. "But I could direct you to our pro bono department, and they would assist you," she looked at her watch. "It was good seeing you." We hugged and parted ways. "Take care of yourself, Clint," her words were genuine.

"I will—you too, Sasha. I'll definitely be in contact," I said, as I examined her card.

After we parted ways, I walked down the next aisle, turned right, and headed to the area marked *PRODUCE*. This section always sponsored unique levels of human activity. Today, it was this portly woman stroking a long, green cucumber, while her husband cuddled two mangos as if they were perky B cups. I was disturbed by this behavior. Distracted, I had to jerk my cart to the right to avoid running over a child that was crawling around on the floor. As I swerved, I slammed into a tomato display. The collision chased tomatoes all over the floor.

I looked up, just as she opened her mouth to speak. "You know, someone was planning on eating those. Seems like you can't get enough red in your life," she said in a pointed manner.

"Thanks for your help," I added. "Enough red you say?" I asked as she passed me the last of the wayward tomatoes.

"Yes, you bashed these tomatoes; then earlier you were talking to that redheaded woman by the door," she responded.

"What woman? Oh, Sasha—she's not a woman; she's a lawyer. I mean, she's an old friend. Wait, have you been watching me? Are you CIA or IRS? You didn't take my picture with your camera phone?" my words were playful in nature, but her reaction indicated that she didn't see any humor in what I said.

"First of all, check your ego! A proper lady doesn't have to stalk a man; she gets noticed through her presence," she spoke with an inexplicable style, combined with a heavy dose of defiance.

"You are beautiful, I must admit, but you and your girlfriend weren't too graceful, when you commented as you walked by me and my friend talking," I retorted.

"Oh, you heard that?" she almost blushed.

"You said it loud enough for everyone to hear. Look, I don't tell you how to stroke your girlfriend, so why should you worry about who or what I'm doing?" I replied.

"Wow, why don't you get some dip to go with that boulder-sized chip on your shoulder. Excuse me! I thought I would start a friendly conversation. Never again will I be so presumptuous. Here are your funky tomatoes; the rest are under that potato hopper!" she picked up her items and walked away, shaking her head in obvious disgust. Realizing that I was wrong, I rushed to offer her an apology.

"Excuse me, miss. I think you just met my evil twin brother; he has a very bad temperament and is severely socially maladjusted. Whenever he doesn't take his medicine, he makes a buffoon of both of us. Allow me to apologize for his ignorance. My name is Clint, and I would be honored to correct any frustration that he may have caused you," my words were confident and her demeanor slowly relaxed.

I smiled in my most charming manner, as I extended my hand as an olive branch. In vain, she attempted to just stare at it, until a smile spread across her face; then we formally shook.

"My name is Lourdes, and I accept your apology. In fact, I probably owe you an apology. My *girlfriend* and I (not the kissy-kissy kind) were rude and judgmental. Our comments were not fair," I could see inside of her deep brown eyes that her contrition was authentic.

"Hey, that's cool; we agree that we were both wrong. The past few days have been rough. I guess I must be on guard," I added.

"Times are crazy. People are dying overseas and right here in our own communities. Did you hear the story about the grandmother that killed her grandchildren with a homemade batch of Ambien-laced cookies?" she asked.

"No, I missed that one, but what about that nightclub shooting the other night?" I probed.

"At *EDIBLE GROOVES*?" her face sported an incredulous look as she responded.

"Yes, do you know that place?" I inquired. I wanted to tell her that I was also present when the shooting took place, but that information could have muddied our conversation.

"I was actually performing onstage during the shooting," her voice spiked with excitement, and her body trembled as she spoke. "Bullets were everywhere, and people ran in all directions. I was lucky to get out of there. My drummer took a bullet to the calf!" she exclaimed.

As she spoke, I realized that everything around me had gone silent. At that moment, time stopped, while everything and everyone around us became static. Just as our conversation gained momentum, her friend interrupted our flow.

"I've been looking all over for you, and now I see why I wasn't able to find you," Aki blurted.

"Aki, this is Clint. Clint, this is Aki," Lourdes's voice stumbled slightly as she introduced us.

"Pleased to meet you, Aki," I said as our hands shook like two kids jumping rope.

"Getting cozy in the produce section, I see. Has she asked you for your phone number? Clint, she hasn't had a date in Lord knows how many moons." Aki was a cute, candid, and unfiltered busybody.

Smiling as I looked into Lourdes's eyes, I said, "A proper lady doesn't ask a man for his number; it is expected that the gentleman asks her for her number," my words caused Lourdes to blush.

"You two are already too much for me! Please just exchange info so that we can go eat! Better yet, Dez, give me the list. I'll finish shopping. You two, do whatever it is that a proper lady and man do. I'll meet you in the checkout line. Nice meeting you, Clint," Aki said, and just like that, 1+1+1-1 became 2.

My eyes followed Aki as she disappeared around the corner. Finally, I had Lourdes all to myself.

"Lourdes, what do I have to do to ask you out?" my words were alive and direct.

"What about helping us walk our bags to the car? I'm a sucker for chivalry. Then, maybe, I'll give you my number," she stated in a playfully serious manner.

"History books show that chivalry died during the 1600s. Don Quixote, that poor misguided fellow," I retorted.

"Well, I guess I'm bringing chivalry back! If you want my number, you have to carry some lumber!" she quipped.

"Sounds fair. So, tell me, what are you ladies making for dinner?"

"Homemade, greasy, cheesy pizza! I love it!" she replied as her eyes enlarged.

"I dig pizza as well. There's this joint that serves the best pizza in town. I think that should be the site of our second date," I said.

"Second date? When was the first one? We just met! You're pretty confident, aren't you?" she snapped.

"I thought this was our first date. Similar to *E&H* speed dating. We met in a social setting and engaged in stimulating conversation. I thought women liked confidence blended with a fingerprint of aggression?" I asked as I smiled.

"We also like the smell of cologne, but too much can be offensive," she deadpanned.

"Duly noted," I responded. We caught up with Aki in checkout line number six. Lourdes and I gathered the bags as Aki retrieved her car. Ignoring the *FIRE LANE* sign, Aki whipped forward, stopped, lit her hazard lights, and popped the trunk.

"German engineering, nice!" I continued with my attempts at small talk with Aki. I learned some time ago that if you get in good with the best friend, then you're in good for good with the goods.

"That's what we forgot! We forgot the beer! I knew there was something missing," Aki announced to anyone that could hear her.

"No worries, we can get some on the way to the movie store," Lourdes replied.

"Well, ladies, your bags have been loaded. I guess I'll leave you two to your own devices. It was a pleasure to meet both of you," I said as I started to slowly walk away.

"Wait! Aren't we going to exchange numbers? What about the pizza?" Lourdes blurted.

"I was just playing with you. My number is easy to remember. It's 555-7234. What's yours?" I asked.

"Mine is 555-6489," her hair fell into her eyes as she leaned over the trunk of Aki's red coupe and jotted down my number. She had my attention; her face was cute, and her curves were supple. Lusting while looking, I stared so hard that I feared getting caught. So much for keeping a low profile, here I was in broad daylight, exchanging numbers, while any suit with a badge could be watching my every movement. But for some reason, with every word she spoke, I felt myself slipping.

I examined the decorative Post-it she handed me and directly asked, "What's your schedule like this week?"

"I have a few appointments; besides that, I'm pretty flexible," she responded.

"Cool, I will definitely give you a call," I replied.

As we reached to hug, she smiled and immediately thrust her backside back so that her pelvis was as far away from mine as humanly possible, while she patted my back with both of her hands. This was a purebred example of the classic "butterfly hug." It was good that she hugged me in such a manner; I was impressed by her modesty.

"Again, Aki, it was nice meeting you," I coolly added.

Additional smiles were exchanged, and eventually they jumped into the coupe and sped away.

I would later glean, that inside Aki's car they discussed what had just transpired. "He's cute. What does he do for a living?" Aki was in my favor.

"I don't know. I didn't get around to asking him. Do you want to date him? Maybe you should; here take his number!" Lourdes attempted to hand Aki the folded Post-it.

"I'm not the one he was checking out!" Aki refused Lourdes's attempted Post-it pass and continued to ask questions.

"Well, are you going to give him a chance, at least one date? Or was his charm and charisma all for naught? I think, after all the flirting, you owe him a date!"

"I knew you were watching! When we were checking out, I noticed that our cart didn't have any extra items. If you hadn't been such a busybody, maybe you would've remembered to get the beer. You probably just went around the corner and hid in the soda section," Lourdes smiled because she knew her friend quite well.

"Ha-ha, you know it!" Aki released a full-fledged chuckle.

"I might give him a chance. But I haven't decided. And I don't need you to push me into something I don't necessarily want to do," Lourdes cautioned.

"What's there to decide? You go to the restaurant and test his pockets and his manners. Just order the most expensive thing on the menu. Mmm, crab cakes! If he can't afford it or is just plain cheap, you'll know because you'll see him squirm. Then, when the food arrives, pretend that your stomach hurts. If he gets mad, you know he's not for you. After faking an illness, think of an excuse, any excuse; it doesn't have to be believable! Actually, the more unbelievable, the better, because a bad excuse further demonstrates that you don't like his company. If he's sane, he'll get the hint. If not, he might even call you an *EXPLETIVE*, and then you definitely know he's a no-no! Hey, if you don't give Clint a chance, then what about my brother? He was asking about you," Aki added this in an attempt at humor.

"David's married, so that leaves Jermaine? No thanks! You know that boy is crazy!" Lourdes exclaimed.

CHAPTER 25

The Fuzz

• • •

May 11, 2008, 2:43 p.m.

JUST LIKE A GREAT WHITE shark breaching the ocean's surface and devouring some hapless, unsuspecting seal, a gray late-model sedan came screaming toward me. Nearly hitting me, it came to a sudden stop, inches from where I stood. Two detectives wearing dark aviator sunglasses quickly apprehended me right in the middle of *SLIMS'* parking lot. I immediately knew that this trip to the station was going to be significantly different than the first trip. For starters, I was handcuffed and read my Mirandas. No one spoke as we rode in silence. The interior had an artificial new-car smell, not the actual new-car smell, but the one manufactured by a green-papered pine tree hanging from the rearview mirror. It had been years since I took a ride with handcuffs; it didn't take long for me to remember to engage my core. Without an engaged core, you were prone to slide off the vinyl seats and onto the floor.

Once we arrived, they drove around to the back of the station. The car stopped, and both detectives stepped out. The passenger-side detective opened my door and led me to the rear door of the stationhouse. *BUZZ!* We walked in as a heavy metal door slowly rolled open. At that moment, I started to feel like a prisoner, and the handcuffs seemed to get colder and colder with every step we took down a long, dark hallway. The next door we came to was flanked by two burly guards on either side. Keys clanked, and the door was pushed open. It was another ten paces until we stopped at the first door on the right. Equipped with a tiny window, this door was much smaller than the other two. One of the guards unlocked the dead bolt and opened the door, which revealed a barred jail cell. I was ushered in, and the cuffs were removed. The lighting was very dim, and I heard numerous voices, but could barely see any faces. So-called American democracy and its duped due process didn't reach dank, dirty corners like this one. The room smelled of piss, shit, and vomit. I entered as the door violently slammed shut behind me. Dirt was everywhere, and a rush of goose bumps made my arms feel like rough, dirty suede. I found a vacant corner and leaned back against the harsh, rigid concrete as time stood still beside me for what seemed like several slothful hours. Eventually, I heard someone call my name, the cell was opened, and two guards escorted me to an interrogation room. This room was already occupied by a man, seated, wearing a blue pinstripe suit with a reptilian briefcase. He talked on his cell phone as one of the guards instructed me to sit on the chair on the other side of the metal table. The man in the suit ended his phone call, opened his briefcase, and then motioned for the guards to leave.

"My name is Detective Dansbury. Is there anything you want to tell me?" the pinstriped suit questioned.

"Yes, why am I here?" I asked.

"We're here because your fingerprints are all over this nine-millimeter. It was found in the car where Vinny Vinzantinne's body was recovered. How do you explain that?" he held a clear, plastic bag with a red-and-white label that read *EVIDENCE*. Inside that bag was the nine-millimeter gun.

"I'm not talking to the police. I'm not saying jack-fiddly-diddly-spit until I talk to my lawyer!" I announced.

"C'mon, if you're so innocent, then what do you need your lawyer for? Only the guilty ask for a lawyer. Just admit you did it! I got three witnesses that can put you in the location around the time of Vinzantinne's death! Hell, after a few teary-eyed witnesses testify, I could get a conviction just like that!" as the friction between his left thumb and middle finger generated a snap, his confidence brimmed, until I asked the following question.

"I hear what you're saying, but I'm not biting. Answer me this, tough guy: which hand are the fingerprints from? The right or left?" I inquired.

Detective Dansbury began to yell as he answered. "All I hear is blah blah blah! Look at you; you don't even know the game!" he growled.

"You and I both know why you didn't answer my question regarding your smoking gun. Now who's the suspect?" I almost laughed at the elementary game of tick-tac-toe Detective Dansbury played.

"Let's change gears before we talk shop. Let me tell you about this woman I met up with last night," he took off his blazer as his words spun off course from our original discourse.

"Look, dude, I don't want to hear any fish tale about some strange you got last night!" I informed him.

"It's all interrelated; just hear me out. Look, I was on this date with this chick that had the most incredible ass. I mean, it was thick; it was round; it was astronomical! It almost had wings; it was perfect! The problem is the rest of her was soggy. My quandary? If the ass is right and the rest is wrong, do I have a reasonable reason to go anal?" he had a maniacal look that increased with every syllable.

"How should I know? Fuck her in her toes for all I care! Wait! Isn't sodomy illegal in this state?" I had become perturbed.

"Are you're suggesting I go missionary? That's it; that's my plan! I'll fuck her missionary style. It will be my homage to you, because where you're going, you're going to need God! Do you have any concept of what they're going to do to you? This cupcake stationhouse is just a dress rehearsal. Inside the big house, the officer-to-prisoner ratio is almost non-existent. That leaves a lot of eyes, hands, and dicks unaccounted for. You're about to become a bitch to ninety-nine different guys. I suggest that you walk around with Vaseline dripping out of your third eye. It should at least aid in reducing friction. But when those Mandingoes get a hold of you, they'll pump you so hard until your ass crack is as smooth as dirty suede. You'll be an ass hoe for the smokes in the pen!" he was practically yelling at a distance of less than twelve inches from my nose. Suddenly, my "good friend" Special Agent Detective Ricks entered the room. What a relief, because Dansbury had very bad halitosis.

"Dansbury, calm down! Get out of here; go cool off!" Dansbury sneered at me as he brushed by Detective Ricks. It was obvious this wasn't their first "Good Cop Bad Cop" routine.

"Forget about Dansbury; he's a good cop; he's just stressed, first baby on the way. Here, drink this," Detective Ricks spoke softly as he handed me a cup of coffee.

"Coffee? No thanks, I don't touch the stuff. Don't you remember during our first date? So, you're the good cop! Did you guys draw straws, or is your partner a natural asshole?" I verbally poked. Detective Ricks rose as if he was about to strike me, but he withdrew. He knew this precinct was under a watchful eye, and all of them had to be Boy Scouts. And I knew that no evidence against me existed. They were irked because I didn't crack under the pressure of their little demonstration. On the contrary, I took pleasure in talking smack.

"Well, that depends, Clint; tell me what you know about Vinny's death. And you and I could become good friends," I almost yawned as he asked the same questions.

"I'll tell you what I just told Officer Dicksbury: I don't know anything. I didn't kill anyone. I don't even know anyone that's killed anyone," I was amazed at their lack of professionalism.

"If that's your story, then stick to it. But when the lab results come back, if they conflict with your story, then I am going to charge you with first-degree murder! Do you understand the seriousness of that charge?" Ricks asked.

"Yes, I do. That's why I want to contact my lawyer, so that no one or no item gets confused during this process. I know how the fabrication of so-called evidence occurs. Right now, you know I'm innocent, and I know that I am innocent, but here we are dancing the same tired dance to the same old, tired music," I smirked.

"You'll get your one phone call; use my cell phone. I'll be waiting outside," he said as he passed me his phone.

I dialed Sasha.

"Hello," she answered sheepishly.

"Sasha, sorry if I woke you; it's Clint. I need you to come down to the precinct and represent me; they're trying to pin a murder charge on me," I implored.

"What? Clint, is this a game? I don't have the time or energy to fool around with your silly games!" she was irritated because my call threatened to snatch her out of the comfort of her high-priced California-king-sized bed.

"No, Sasha, I am dead serious. I need your help," I replied.

"OK, I'll be there as soon as I can!" she responded.

An hour later, Ricks, Dansbury, and the chief stood on the other side of the double-sided interrogation window as they watched and listened as Sasha counseled me.

"Have you talked to the niece? Did she supply you with the groceries that you need to cook this guy?" asked the chief.

"What she told me was run-of-the-mill stuff, generic like white house paint," responded Ricks.

"Do you think she's hiding anything?" the chief inquired.

"Not something, but someone...Clint Stoener! Dansbury and I have reason to believe that she has fraternized with him. Reports both confirm and deny that Clint was employed by Vinny Vinzantinne during the nightclub shooting," Special Agent Detective Ricks said.

"They make a cute couple," mocked the chief as he curiously continued to watch Sasha and me.

"I guess, if you're into that sort of thing!" snapped Ricks.

"What did he have to say?" the chief queried.

"A real cocky guy—he didn't say shit, but his past shows that he has played in the dirt before!" Dansbury added his heated two cents.

"What type of dirt are we talking about? Murder? Rape?" the chief inquired.

"Not exactly, just a few minor brushes with the law as a college student," chimed Special Agent Ricks.

"Chemicals? Powders?" the chief asked.

"Nah, just some pot," Ricks retorted.

"Then you don't have anything on him. Just make sure that you're following the LE Standards of Ethical Conduct. I don't want to repeat what we went through with the Munson case. The city is still paying that bill, and the mayor makes a point of constantly reminding me of that fact," the chief cautioned as he turned to both Dansbury and Ricks.

"Not true, his past demonstrates a proclivity for crime. Most felons committed misdemeanors before they jumped over to the felonious side of the fence!" Dansbury's voice began to rise as he spoke.

"Are you raising your voice at me, boy? Don't forget who's running the show! *Comprende?*" he paused. "Besides you're reaching. It was a nice try, but your blind shot in the dark failed. I want you to shift gears and focus all of your energy on Officer Douglas's murder and the corpse found beside him. I'm going to place someone else on the nightclub and Vinzantinne murder cases. Dansbury, I am going to transfer you to drugs and narcotics," the chief reported.

"This case is drugs and narcotics!" Dansbury implored.

"What! Because this Clint character sold a little weed at a hash bar? Sorry, pal, I know how this story ends. Look, we don't have any concrete evidence; cross him off our list after he and his lawyer vacate the building!" the chief demanded.

"With all due respect, sir, two weeks ago, informants at Rikers Island reported an inmate used another inmate/informant for a game of pin the tail on the donkey. Come to find out he was an alleged hired hand connected to the mobster Nicky Nicotine. And we've all heard the street tales of Nicky's hitmen killing rivals and sending mutilated heads and bodies to their families' doorsteps," Detective Ricks reported.

"Finally, some light has been shed on this mess," the chief's words were drenched in sarcasm. "How does this relate to Vinzantinne?" he asked.

"I did some research, and New Jersey police reported that a man was found dead on the doorstep of Connie Vinzantinne's home," Dansbury said.

"So," the chief replied.

"His name was Don Vinzantinne, Vinny's uncle!" Dansbury emphasized.

"Let me guess; the head was decapitated by shotgun, and the eyes were removed?" the chief asked.

"Yes, blind, dead men can't point out their murders even in the after-life!" Detective Ricks exclaimed.

"But, Chief, it goes deeper; these guys are all connected. I had the boys at public records run a few leads. Here's what they found. Two years ago, Vinny purchased fifteen vans for his downtown enterprises, and all receipts were paid to the order of Saul Motors, Inc., the same Saul that's also friends with Clint, the Saul that hosted a party the night of his murder. I bet dollars to doughnuts that Vinny, Saul, and Clint were all at that party!" Special Agent Ricks exclaimed.

"Hmm, so you really think Clint is a heavy hitter?" the chief asked.

"I'm not saying that he's in the Majors, but he's definitely in the AAA league. And what's the fastest way for anyone from the streets to make it to Fifth Avenue?" Detective Ricks riddled.

"The needle or the nose!" Dansbury chimed.

"Exactly!" Detective Ricks concurred.

"Have you put the screws to Stoener?" the chief questioned.

"I wanted to!" Dansbury growled as he glanced back at Detective Ricks.

"What other options are we working?" the chief asked.

"With that lying, double-talking asshole Carlos lying in the hospital, we need more pawns on the chessboard!" Dansbury exhorted.

"In due time, we'll get them. But for now, let Stoener go. He just might lead us to the answers to all our questions," the chief said, giving his verdict.

"Dansbury, where are we with Damon Nemo?" Ricks inquired.

"I'm still working on it. I should have something in a few days," replied Dansbury.

"Get me something, or you're off the case! Do you hear me?" the chief barked.

At this point, Sasha and I had finished our conversation. Detective Ricks informed her that no formal charges had been filed and that I was free to go. She evaluated my discharge papers, signed off, and issued a verbal threat against the chief and his department: "If you continue to harass my client without concrete evidence, there will be questions to answer before a judge!" then she drove me to my motel.

"Jeez, Clint! I guess some people will never change! They clearly have nothing, but they are determined to pin something on you. You have so much potential. How do you continue to get caught up in such foolishness? What gives?" she was visibly tired and frustrated, and I had given her every reason to be both.

"I have no words or excuses. I haven't been squeaky clean, but the charges they're implying are fabricated. You know that. I am not a killer," was the only explanation I could muster at this late hour. I thanked her, and we exchanged our good-byes.

CHAPTER 26

First Date

• • •

May 14, 2008, 8:25 p.m.

A FEW DAYS HAD TRANSPIRED since my latest interrogation, and things had become eerily quiet. With the authorities seemingly off my back, I took the opportunity to ask Lourdes out on a date. Our destination was a newly opened restaurant called *AFRODESIAC-PIZZA*. Cozy, this quaint cooperatively owned establishment served house specialties like collard greens alfredo and fried chicken pizzas topped with ground, watermelon pepper seeds. The menu was alternative, and the decor was a non-resolute style that wavered between Sicilian furnishings and volute woodwork. Lourdes was impressed by its ala mode ambience.

"I really like this place. How did you find it?" she asked, as her eyes shimmied in the light of the overhead purple, pear-shaped lamp suspended from a thin black cord.

"I don't recall but finding an Italian restaurant like this is like finding a skinhead with dreadlocks!" we both laughed at my simile.

"I wondered why you were so hush-hush. But this place is great; I would bring my mother to this place; she's a quarter Sicilian!"

"Interesting, so what's your family like?" I asked in an attempt to make meaningful conversation.

"Wow! You're just going to jump right into it like that! That's a long story; I don't know where to begin," startled by my questioning, it didn't make her uncomfortable, but she was definitely taken by surprise.

Just at that moment, our waiter arrived carrying two pies. One of the pizzas contained deep-fried catfish over a bed of smothered onions, and the other had feta cheese with Portobello mushrooms, whole garlic cloves, and kale.

"Could I offer you some fresh pepper for your meal?" queried the waiter.

"Yes, please. Just on this slice, right here," several seconds later, several sprinkles of black flecks fell onto my entrée.

"And for the lady?" he asked.

Lourdes's response was vehement. "No thank you. No, not even a speck!"

"I take it that you don't like pepper," I inquired.

"Yeah, my father worked at a spice company shortly after I was born. One day there was an accident at the plant, and he and another coworker were trapped up to their noses in fresh black pepper. Unable to move, my father inhaled, and the pepper caused him to sneeze uncontrollably. According to his coworker, who survived, my father sneezed so much that he started convulsing with violent seizures. Eventually, he had a massive heart attack and died before they could save him. Have you ever heard the theory that your heart stops beating for a split second when you sneeze? Well, imagine sneezing sneeze upon sneeze upon sneeze for nearly nine minutes straight. I stopped using pepper from the age of six after my mother explained how my father died," her mood had depressed.

"I am so sorry to hear that," I consoled.

"Look, I'm not into sympathy and a condolence speech; you can score more points with me if you make me laugh!" she said as she used her shiny knife and fork to cut through a pepper-less slice of pizza.

Suddenly, her phone rang.

"Oh, excuse me, I have to take this." Lourdes rose and walked from the table.

She spoke for three minutes, and about twenty-five minutes later, we were finished with our meal. She requested two take-home containers so that she could package our remains. The waiter brought the check, and Lourdes politely slid out of her chair and walked toward the bathroom.

When she emerged from the bathroom, I had placed three twenty-dollar bills under the check. Lourdes seemed to be sporting a glow about her.

"Would you like to have some fun?" she asked.

"Sure," I replied.

"Do you bowl? I know this great bowling alley I think you'd appreciate," she seemed eager to go bowling, so I followed her enthusiasm.

It took us some time to find the bowling alley, but once we got there, I was pleasantly surprised, as the DJ bumped the hottest music. This definitely wasn't your father's "Rock and Bowl." Outside, expensive autos filled nearly every parking space. Inside, everyone flossed. Upstairs, hip-hop music reigned supreme, and the clientele was mostly a cadre of hipsters sporting all sorts of styles. These Scot Wieland, Paris Hilton, Lenny Kravitz, and Kurt Cobain clones spent large dollars on a variety of bottles, cocktails, and shots. Woman after woman flashed highly defined waistlines through midriffs that displayed their jewel-encrusted navels. The lights were low, and people knocked down more booze than pins. We approached the hostess stand, and Lourdes did all the talking.

"We want one of your VIP booths downstairs," she insisted.

"OK, included in that seating area is your choice of two bottles of champagne, liquor, or wine, with ice, and your choice of juices. Your server will handle your orders. Follow me," the hostess said.

"I think you'll like downstairs." Lourdes spoke with a devilish smile.

"What's downstairs?" I wondered.

We stepped down a narrow, concrete stairwell. At the bottom were dimly lit, beehive-designed catacombs. I was instantly in the middle of one of the most unusual strip clubs that I had ever seen. *BUTZ MORE* featured crimson lighting and was as exotic as its name. The walls were velvet and suede, and the floors were covered in faux leopard skins. Shoes were not allowed, and each client was responsible for checking their shoes at the door. Traditional leather chairs were available, but apparently no chair was more comfortable than a cute, naked, obese woman with size 40 H breasts. For two hundred dollars an hour, you could enjoy your own ergonomic "human chair." These personified chairs provided you with a back rub and a whole lot of other affection. Not all the women were large. Ironically, it was the skinny women with the big breasts that made the smallest dollars. I forgot to mention that this place was BYOB, "buy your own breasts." Silicone was in abundance, but alcohol was only permitted in the VIP section. In the center of the club, I watched a group of international students as they inhaled euphoria from a bar that served fifty-dollar shots of flavored oxygen. Imagine, lines of people paying to get "gassed." VIP customers were able to order a gas tank to be delivered right to their table with the air either chilled or served at room temperature. The high provided by pure oxygen is very special. Your skin tingles, and if you're not careful, you could become induced into bold episodes of laughter. Lourdes implored me to sample a gulp of this and a taste of that. I admit this assortment of cute, cuddly, chubby chicks opened my eyes to an entirely different level of appreciation for fleshier women, especially after I sat within the warm enveloping flesh of a plus-sized blonde woman in her early twenties. This club's sole purpose was the promotion of titillating stimulation. Everything was sexually sideways, from the decor to the varied types of strippers, but the piece de resistance was the complimentary sex questionnaire that looked like this:

	BUTZ MORE		
	Getting to Know You Before We Fuck		
Part I Name:		Age:	Birthday:
Zodiac Sign:		Occupation:	
Address:	Apt#:	Phone number:	
City:	State:	Zip Code:	
Height:	**Weight:**	Measurements:	
Complexion:	Eye color:	Hair color:	
Favorite position:	Bi-Curious:		
Bi-Sexual:			
Favorite female nationality:			
Drug of Choice: Acid Coke Ecstacy Heroin Marijuana Other			
Twosome, Threesome, Foursome, Full-blown orgy (circle one)			

I chuckled when I read it. We both proceeded to fill out a questionnaire. When I looked up, Lourdes had completed hers.

"Are you having a good time?" she asked, almost shouting to be heard.

"Sure, who wouldn't enjoy this!" I answered.

"OK, time to pony up! Let's exchange papers. I am dying to read your answers!" she practically shouted over the background noise.

We passed our papers; my right hand slid my paper across the table to her left hand as she slid her paper across the table to my left hand via her right hand.

The responses on her questionnaire sort of stunned me. I wondered if mine had the same impression upon her.

"Hmmm," was all she said upon finishing her survey of my responses.

"Hmmm, what does that mean?" I inquired.

"That means what it means," she spoke as she slid her hair behind her right ear.

"How's that?" I asked.

"You are afraid of intimacy," she responded.

My questionnaire smudged a little as she pushed her left index finger to points of reference.

"Do you see, here on the back, where you said that handcuffs are a major tool for making love? For you, bondage affords you a level of control. You long for power, as opposed to affection. This is clearly evident in the response where you said that when your partner is about to climax, you enjoy teasing and making your victim...um...err...partner beg and plead for climactic mercy!" she reported.

"Interesting, you got all of that from one response? What else did you deduce?" I calmly asked as I slid my chair closer to her.

"I am inclined to say that your father cheated on your mother, and you blame your mother for loving a man that she had no business loving. I would further hypothesize that you have never loved, and if loved, you wouldn't know what to do because you don't know what love is," she poignantly stated.

"Hmmm," was my response.

"I know that was a lot; was I close?" she inquired.

"In my opinion, love is emotional suicide. The mere assumption that two people will feel the same way about each other at the same place and same time every day is incredulous. People love who or what they can trust. When in reality, love should be a timeless source of affection without a statute of limitations. Love is supported by understanding and forgiveness. I know people that won't open their hearts to a person, but they will tongue kiss their car, cat, or dog, simply for the fact that they know those items are incapable of emotionally harming them. We've all been at that place called hope, when we meet what we believe to be our 'soul mate' and instantly decide that we want to spend the rest of our lives together. But conditions can become unconditional, and love disappears. That's been my reality. I find it amusing that you judged me from a piece of paper that has my first name and a few superficial comments. And that's the picture you painted of me? Really? Well, try this suit on and see if it fits *you*," I emphatically stated.

"Lourdes, you my friend, are a bleeding heart and a casualty waiting to happen. You probably remember every breath of your first sexual experience. I wager to say that you still have the same underwear that you wore that night. Am I right, Little Miss Can't Do Wrong?" I asked in an almost scathing manner.

"Actually, I do remember everything about my first experience. It happened years ago, but it still feels like last week. I was sixteen with larger than normal features. I had a round butt and cantaloupe-shaped breasts. My first date was about to pick me up in fifty-five minutes. Ryan Jefferson had finally asked me out, and while I got ready, my freebasing stepfather barged into my room and had his way with me. What I remember most was crying and watching him use my bath towel to wipe my virginal blood off the tip of his shriveled, uncircumcised penis. He tried to soothe me by telling me how much he loved me and what we did was OK. Ever since then, I have searched for love. God! I can't even begin to count the number of beds or the various car seats that my bare ass has bounced on. But don't you ever make the mistake to tease me about my first time, because it's something that I have been dying to forget! So, do I believe in love? Yes! There has to be something beautiful, something that possess dreamlike qualities to counter the ugly-dirty daymares that I encounter and reencounter on a daily basis!" She buried her eyes and nose between her crossed arms and shook her head as if she was trying to shake all of the memories out of her head once and for all.

"Well, saying I'm sorry can't heal this situation, but it could help to heal the wrong that I have done. I apologize, Lourdes." I felt like an asshole.

Our conversation became silent; then I heard muffled breaths coming from her buried face.

"Lourdes, please forgive me! I'm so sorry," I pleaded.

"It doesn't matter; I'll be OK," she muttered with her face still hidden.

"Why? Of course, it matters!"

HA-HA!

"I was just pulling your leg!" she laughed as she watched my face flip from embarrassment to relief.

"What! You mean to tell me that you made that entire story up?" I asked.

"Of course!" she responded.

"Well, I guess that I deserved that!" I replied with egg on my face.

"Yes, you did!" she said, still laughing.

"That's cool. Hello, my name is Clinton Asshole. It's a pleasure to meet you!"

"Hey, would you like to get out of here?" she asked as she grabbed my hand.

"Sure," I replied.

We left *BUTZ-MORE*, got into my car, and drove out of the parking lot. Hundreds of feet ahead, a huge prism of red and blue police lights flickered as officers inspected an unoccupied car. I slowed our pace as Lourdes stretched her neck to gain a better perspective.

"Wait! What are they pulling out from under the car? Is that a body?" she shrieked.

"I'm not surprised; the murder rate in this city is constantly rising. People are killed for sport. Survival is serious. Five hundred bodies were dropped in the ground last year. Bail bonds and mortuaries have popped up like hamburger franchises. They're handing out coupons for coffins. Can you believe that?" I said.

"But I refuse to believe that times are more brutal now," she stated.

"You're kidding, right?"

"No, I most absolutely am not! Technology and mass media make news or crime larger than life," she challenged.

"Did you hear me when I said five hundred one people died last year? In earlier times, a death total of those proportions only occurred during wars between enemy rock-throwing villages. To say that times aren't worse now is just crazy. Lourdes, answer this: do you have mace or pepper spray in your purse?"

"Pepper spray, yes! It's hard to find mace," she replied.

"Did you carry pepper spray ten years ago? Did you even know anyone that carried any of those items ten years ago?" I asked.

"No," she responded flatly.

"Exactly, because you didn't feel threatened. I met this woman the other day that drives around with a butcher knife stashed in her glove box," I exclaimed.

"A butcher's knife!" she exclaimed.

"Exactly!" I emphatically replied.

Four hours later, we arrived at her place, had a beer, and went straight to bed. The time was so late that it was entirely too early in the morning to be going to bed. I couldn't sleep. I was restless, perhaps slightly horny, so I walked upstairs to Lourdes's rooftop deck. I sipped the warm remnants of my lager from a handless mug, as I stared up into the sky and identified a crowded clutch of clouds that resembled rabbits dashing across a dark blue field. Then I heard the creak of wooden steps moan like a Moog organ. When I turned around, Lourdes was walking toward me with a smile on her face.

"What were you thinking about?" Dressed in my oxford, she stared deeply into my eyes. I thought quietly to myself, "What's the deal with her wearing my shirt like a varsity sweater?"

"I was just wondering how long you've been at this apartment?" I asked.

"Just a few days. Our last apartment burned down," she replied.

"Our?" I asked.

"Yes, me and my mother. She lives in the downstairs apartment. What else were you thinking about?" she questioned.

"I find it amusing that you're wearing my shirt as if it's a varsity sweater, like we're dating. You barely let me kiss you," I verbally jabbed.

"Hey, I trusted you enough to stay over. And now that you mention it, that T-shirt looks familiar," she was quick; she could give as well as she could take.

I ignored her T-shirt comment. "And that's causing major problems for people all over the world. Some people feel that when a man can stay over, and the woman isn't menstruating, then they're supposed to have sexual contact!" I wasn't mad; nor was I serious; I was just testing her.

"There was; I kissed you," she replied. "I don't go putting my lips on random dudes, let alone on random places. If that's what you want, then I am the wrong girl!" she spoke with conviction.

"You should be careful; not all men are respectful! What if some dude wanted more than kisses and warm beer?" I was still testing her.

"He wouldn't have been able to get what he wanted," her countenance shifted to a more serious tone.

"Are you kidding me? Do you know judo? I'm just saying you should be more careful. I know that I am a respectfully hip dude, but I can't vouch for others," I said.

"Like the clouds you were just staring at, life is subject to your interpretation. You looked at the clouds and probably saw rabbits. But I see the bigger picture. I see an ocean," she said.

"An ocean? Interesting," I said.

"Yes, it is. What you aren't aware of is there are two reasons why you wouldn't have enjoyed my 'strange fruit' last night. One, I never fell asleep. I watched you the whole time. Two, I sleep with a twenty-two under my pillow," she deadpanned. I think what she said turned me on. I wasn't sure. But I think so.

"But you just said that you trusted me," I responded.

"When I said I trusted you, that meant I trusted that you wouldn't do anything to cause me to have to end your life," she was totally serious.

"What would you have done if I had made a move, a strong move?" I questioned, still testing her resolve.

"Honestly, I'd probably be wearing two silver bracelets as I explained to the police what happened while you bled to death," she fired back.

"Whew!" I couldn't stop laughing.

"What's so funny?" Lourdes was slightly annoyed.

"Confession: I got scared when I woke up. I thought that you were sleeping on your stomach because you were hiding something," I said.

"You mean this?" She brandished her gun. "Wait a minute! You mean to tell me that you thought I was a guy?" she asked incredulously.

"Pretty face or no pretty face, you do have big hands." I wanted to chuckle, but I didn't.

"Hey, the same could be said about you. If you hadn't come up to me in the market, I might have considered you a female!" she snapped back.

"I admit that I have a clean baby face, but I in no way look like a woman," I semi- vehemently responded.

"I didn't say a woman; I said a female. You know those pretty boys that spend so much time and money on their appearance that they become 'fee-males.' That's what you reminded me of when I first saw you. A pretty boy, almost too pretty!" Lourdes started laughing. "Well, I guess that's called a quid pro quo! What would you have done if I had been a man?" she inquired.

"I might have shot you!" I quipped.

"Ha-ha! That's cool! Well played!" she chuckled in the face of the harmonic moment we just shared.

"But women are the only true 'fee-males.' What about all of those Jerry McGuire 'show me the money' types? What's your take on those women?" I asked.

"Yes, some women do give guys a hard time when it comes to making money. But guys get off too easy. I mean, how hard is it for a competent man to make a decent wage in this country and carry his own weight?" she retorted.

"OK, so when you saw me, what type of impression did I make?" I couldn't resist inquiring.

"I had some idea that you enjoyed nice things," she replied.

"OK," I said.

"I don't know about the amount of money you make, and I don't care," she added.

"Well, what makes you different than any other female?" I inquired.

"For starters, I didn't sleep with you," she was quick to re-highlight that fact.

"Not yet," I spoke with words drenched in hopes and dreams.

"Slow down, cowboy! If I do decide to sleep with you, it will be my decision. It may or may not happen, but if it does, it will be my choice and not because of some green-and-white paper with funny old male faces on it," Lourdes was very serious in both her words and countenance.

"OK, I can dig it. What do you find to be worse: a woman that has sex for money or a woman that marries for money?" I asked.

"In my humble opinion, there is very little difference at all between the two. The woman that sleeps for money is a whore, and the woman that marries for money is essentially married to the money and is ergo a married whore," she deduced.

"What if that same rich, married woman slept with someone poorer than her husband?" I asked.

"She's a confused whore!" she announced. We both laughed. "You're crazy," she exclaimed.

"The feeling is mutual," I confirmed.

"Are you doing anything for breakfast?" she inquired.

"Nothing that I know of," I replied.

"I just started going to this family-owned, all-hours diner a few blocks down the street. Everything sucks except for their eggs and coffee. You're more than welcome to join me. We can play foosball there!" she added.

"Foosball? I haven't played foosball since college. Sure, why not? But pool is my game," I said.

"How about this..." Lourdes paused. "I'll treat you," she stated.

"Wait a minute; you and I didn't sleep together, and you want to buy me breakfast," I asked incredulously.

"Yes, just remember, if you order crab cakes, I might expect some sort of sexual satisfaction from you," she joked.

"Oh, then I am most certainly ordering the crab cakes!" I joked.

"Excellent, I'm just going to clean up, grab some jeans, and throw on some makeup. Finish the rest of your beer and meet me downstairs in about ten minutes," she smiled widely as she spoke. "You know what this means, don't you?" she asked.

"I don't know; what?" I replied.

"We're about to go on our third date!" she smiled again and finished with a demonstrative wink before she whisked herself down the stairs.

At that very moment, I started to feel something. I couldn't describe what I felt, but I started to feel something, something that was quite foreign.

CHAPTER 27

A Bloody Mess

• • •

May 15, 2008, 6:20 a.m.

THAT SAME MORNING, WHILE LOURDES and I ate breakfast, several discoveries were made within the local police precinct. Apparently two leads had surfaced.

A steely-faced detective, last name Perkins, was called in from the West Precinct. Two daughters and thirteen years on the force contributed to the gray patches that surfaced near the temporal areas of his head, evidence that age and stress had caught up with him. "Perks," as his friends called him, was only thirty-three years old, but he looked forty-six. The chief had called him in as a "consultant" to assist with managing his department's mounting load of unsolved crimes. Perks carried a large manila envelope, the type equipped with the industry-standard metal butterfly clasp, under his right arm and two plastic bags marked *EVIDENCE* in his left hand.

"Chief, we have confirmation about a suspect in that nightclub shooting. Look at this," he said as he spread several documents across the chief's desk.

"Give it to me without all the icing," the strain in the chief's voice was thick; pressure was mounting, and his weariness showed.

"This is what Forensics processed," Detective Perkins said as he handed him the bags.

"Besides the red wig and long, black rubber gloves in this bag, what the hell is that in the other bag? Is this some sick CSI-type joke? Is that what

I think it is? Who's responsible for this lunacy?" the chief's blood pressure rose exponentially.

"It's not a joke. It's exactly as it appears, and yes, it has been used. Disgusting, yes, it is. But that piece of evidence, though abominable, along with the wig and gloves were discovered on the floor of Vinny's office bathroom after the shooting. We're waiting for the DNA lab results. And there's more," Perkins added.

"What the fuck else is there?" the chief asked.

"This," Perkins passed a partially wrinkled envelope to the chief.

"Well, Goddamn soma' bitch cross carriers!" his countenance changed immediately. "Did you read this?" he asked Perkins.

"It was passed to me from Forensics. Yeah, it's bad; it's really-bad," Perkins added.

"Fuck!" the chief blared before the room became momentarily silent. "Two bombshells at once? Military personnel have a term for this: FUBAR! First things first, who does that disgusting piece of evidence belong to?" the chief inquired.

"My money is on Vicky Vinzantinne," Perkins replied.

"Has that been confirmed?" the chief responded skeptically.

"As of now, no, but from a murder standpoint, we don't have any evidence to charge, but that evidence was found in Vinny's private bathroom. Apparently, this tasty menstrual morsel of evidence didn't flush. As his niece, Vicki served him in many ways. It appears she's the only other person that had direct access to Vinny's bathroom, and right now, that's the simple blood and guts of the matter," Perkins reported.

"Are you telling me that a man like Vinzantinne has never had any other ladies in his office? That's shoddy! It's a long stretch until forensics and DNA testing are verified, I don't want anyone making any moves without my say so!" the chief insisted.

"Yes, Chief!" Perkins responded.

"Hey, when I do give the word, I want you to be the one to arrest Vicki Vinzantinne. I still haven't forgotten what her family did to you," the chief's words were sympathetic.

"I appreciate that, sir!" Perkins replied.

"Any other news?" the chief asked.

"I sent a vehicle past her residence last night and this morning with no success," Perkins said. "With your permission I'd like to send Officers Rodriguez and Mitchell over to her residence in a full-time surveillance capacity. Once the results are released, we can take her into custody and file a warrant for additional DNA samples, provided she refuses to cooperate," Perks was the consummate professional.

"That makes sense," the chief said as he despondently stared off into his own thoughts.

"Chief, are you OK? I have known you long enough to know when something is wrong," Perkins said.

"Yeah, I'm fine. On a more somber note, have you mentioned the contents of this letter to anyone?"

"No, you're the only one that has seen it; what do you make of it?" Perkins replied.

"Where did you get it from?"

"Officer Douglas—he gave it to me hours before he was killed," Perkins said in a monotone manner.

"Whoa! This was Douglas's? Do you think his death is related to this file?"

"Sir, with respect, I am not trying to tell you how to run your affairs, but the answer is there as plain as day and night," Perkins confirmed.

"I know what I have to do," the chief replied. "Look, you handle the Vicki angle. I'll handle this situation. Tell Dansbury that I need to speak with him ASAP. Let's keep this thing under wraps. With everything that's going on, we don't need any more negative attention."

The chief and Perkins went back several years. The chief respected Perkins as a detective, but he revered him even more as a person. The chief had even been at his first daughter's christening.

It took fifteen minutes for Dansbury to meet the chief in his office.

"Hey, Chief, sorry I'm late. I was questioning some lowlife stick-up suspect. What's up? Perkins said you needed to speak to me," Dansbury inquired.

"Yeah, take a seat. Why didn't you come to me with this?" the chief said in reserved manner as he passed the envelope to Dansbury.

It didn't take Dansbury long before he opened, read, and processed the personal accusations within the envelope.

"Chief, what the fuck is this? I shouldn't be the one on trial here! I'm looking at this, and none of it makes sense. Why would I sell out one of my brothers on the force!" Two prominent veins begun to bulge and crawl around his eyes like earthworms in wet soil. "Being a cop is all that I have. Chief, I've always viewed you like a father!" Dansbury implored.

"Were you aware that your former partner was found dead, beaten over the head with a baseball bat? A baseball bat that reports state was owned by you! The evidence doesn't look good," the chief shook his head as he spoke.

"My former partner is dead! Why would I kill him? And if I killed him, why would I use my own bat? That doesn't make any sense!" Dansbury was on the defensive, much like all the suspects that he had abusively interrogated over the years.

"Look, Dansbury, I know that this doesn't make any sense, but I just got off the phone with Internal Investigations; they know about the kickbacks that you received. Tell the truth. What? Douglas caught you in the act, and when you offered to cut him in, he refused, and you took a totally different option! That's why he dissolved your partnership? How could you do that? He just started his family!" suddenly, two uniformed officers walked into the chief's office.

"You're arresting me? C'mon, Chief, you can't arrest me; I'm innocent! I would never harm Douglas! This is a set-up!" Dansbury insisted.

"Settle down, Dansbury; I'm just trying to get the facts; everything will be fine. Let me take you into custody. Hand me your badge and your revolver," the chief commanded.

"Can you help me out, Chief?" Dansbury was beyond desperation.

"It's bad. Not only was a positive print match pulled off your baseball bat, but a potential eye witness saw you climb down the fire escape seconds before that apartment building burned to the ground. Look, yes, it's bad;

it's very bad. Just place your holster on the table and put your hands up against the wall. C'mon, son, let's be smart about this," the chief calmly advised.

"Nah, Chief, fuck that!" Dansbury drew his revolver and swallowed half of it.

"No!" yelled the chief.

But Dansbury squeezed and—

BAM!

The violent blast splattered Dansbury's blood and brain matter all over the furniture and into the chief's coffee. His body fell back and then slowly streaked blood on the wall all the way to the floor. As he slumped over lifeless, with his eyes and mouth wide open, Dansbury died.

CHAPTER 28

Forever Young, I Want to Be Forever Young

● ● ●

May 14, 2008, 10:47 p.m.

Sasha called to notify me that the authorities wanted to speak with Vicki on suspicion of several counts of first-degree murder. I knew that it was just a matter of time before they started breathing down my neck. I needed to disappear. I needed cash, and a lot of it, and I needed it quickly. An associate on the south side owed me. If I could collect, then my situation would become incredibly flexible. Fearing being tailed, I switched motels last night after Sasha dropped me off. Today, I sat in Yellow Cab number 26. The driver was a simple, hip elderly man that kept a clean cab, and his route recognition was superior, devoid of modern technology. He was entertaining; it was a pleasure being in his presence. As we spoke, he told funny stories that distracted my mind from jumping around in all sorts of directions. Slender in build and well groomed, he donned a blue-gray foam trucker hat, a recent birthday gift from his youngest grandson. Slink was what his friends called him; I addressed him as Mr. Anderson. At this point, he was well into what turned out to be the craziest of the three anecdotes that he shared during my ride. Every story would always start off with him saying: "Hey, young blood, let me slide this through your ears, and tell me your vibe."

"Hit me," was all I could muster.

"One night, I visited my then wife, Isabel, while she was in the hospital recovering from emergency back surgery. On this particular night, I left the hospital in order to shower and grab a change of clothing. Once I got home, I noticed that there was something different about our bedroom. It took me a while, but I finally realized that the bed had been slightly shifted. For some reason, our bed had been pushed an extra six inches to the left. The divots in the carpet provided conclusive evidence, and the picture over our headboard was off center. This prompted me to kneel and look under the bed. My eyes quickly found a solid oak box. Quite miffed and against my better judgment, I pulled it from under the bed and opened it. What I found was fifteen thousand dollars, six condoms, and twelve eggs. Immediately, I returned to the hospital to confront my wife. Heart racing, I asked Isabel about what I found," he continued.

Isabel replied, "Oh, that box! It took you long enough to find it! Over the two years of our marriage, whenever we had bad sex, I would put an egg in the box," she replied.

"Instantly, I thought this was a compliment," Mr. Anderson said as we made a right turn through a faded crosswalk. "So, I can make your body really rumble when we tumble in the sheets, eh?' I boastfully asked my wife," he stated.

"Not exactly, those eggs represent the times we had terribly, bad sex, she replied.

"Really?" I asked.

"Remember when you thought we had a sewage leak and our bedroom smelled like shit? Well, that was actually the other thirty eggs that somehow cracked!" she mercilessly corrected me.

"Embarrassed, I asked, Well what about the fifteen grand and the six condoms?"

"The six condoms are all that remain from a pack of one hundred, and the money is what I made using the other ninety-four," she belligerently replied.

"Isn't that some fucked-up, funny shit!" Mr. Anderson asked me while he adjusted the rearview mirror.

"Wow! I agree; that's whore shit," I replied.

He turned back to look me directly in the eyes. "Listen, friend! That's a true story!" he avowed.

172

"I said whore shit, not horseshit!" I chortled.

"Oh, OK, I got it!" he chuckled.

"I guess that explains why she's your ex-wife!" I quipped.

We both laughed as he slowly pulled up to a stop sign.

"You can let me out right here. Keep the meter running; I shouldn't be too long," I informed him as I left the cab.

I walked one and a half blocks until I came to a cell-phone vendor. I needed a burner. I entered the store and bought two prepaid cell phones and exited the store. I had just gotten back into the cab when my old cell phone rang. Was it the feds? Should I answer it? Despite all my inclinations otherwise, I answered the phone.

"Hello, Clint," it was Vicki.

She sounded shaken and spoke in scrambled codes. It was hard to understand anything she said.

"There are ten million reasons for people to act like maniacs. Not easy to believe one mistake could cause so much pain. You need to meet me ASAP. I need you to see me; I need you to see me! I have to go; I've already been on the phone too long!"

CLICK!

The address she gave me was in a seedier part of the city, not too far from where I currently stood. This wasn't the type of area Vicki would frequent—crackheads and pimps, yes, but not Victoria Vinzantinne. Something wasn't right.

I hopped back into the taxi and asked Mr. Anderson to drop me off a few blocks from the address that Vicki gave me. Minutes later, I paid him and thanked him for his service. Before he drove off, he gave me his cell-phone number and told me to call if I needed him to pick me up.

Before entering her motel room, I called the number that Vicki called me from, but I got a busy tone. Then I proceeded to room 112, knocked on the door, and there was no answer. I turned the knob; to my surprise it was unlocked. I opened the door, and I was mortified at what I saw. Every inch of her body was in the far doorway swinging. I initially saw her feet and then the rest of her beauty suspended in death. A television announcement announced an APB for a Caucasian female in her mid-twenties wanted for questioning.

VIA TV: "Her name is Victoria Vinzantinne and she could be armed and dangerous! Don't take matters into your own hands. If you see her, contact the authorities immediately!"

Still in shock, I walked closer to the television, and I noticed a piece of paper. It was a note addressed to me. It read:

My Dear Sweet Clint,

If you are reading this then my worst fears have become my reality! God, How I have loved you over the years. Remember when we stopped having movie night? Well I never told you but that was because of my Uncle Vinny. He never liked you. But my feelings for you never died! in fact when you left for the West Coast for the longest time, I felt like a part of me left with you. My life didn't feel the same. And when you returned and I saw you again in my Uncle Vinny's office my heart nearly jumped out of my chest. But I knew no matter what I felt or what we felt we would never be able to be truly together. Don't get me wrong I thoroughly enjoyed our random secret hook-ups but I needed more. So in order for us to be together I did what I felt I had to do but I couldn't control the gun. It just jumped out of my hands and I missed Uncle Vinny. But the bullets flew and bodies dropped I couldn't do anything to stop it. Even after dropping the gun it kept shooting and people kept dying. But that scumbag of an uncle finally got what he deserved. I was just trying to do the world a favor and do us a favor so we could be together. But I failed. And now the police are after me. I can't live in prison away from you. So here I hang. Clint I left you a surprise in this room something close to my heart. Find the key to your success and go to my uncle's office look behind his bookcase and you'll find what you need to make it Xmas in July. I wil always bejefjdkufgooggjdkgjgnkfjgfkdghj

Your Undying lover,

Vicki—

Oh yeah, I almost forgot 4 to the left, and stop on 5, then 2 times to the right, 3 times to the right and stop on 9, then 3 times to the left and stop on 72, then 1 time to the right and stop on 24.

I followed Vicki's directions and searched every nook of the room to no avail. My whirlwind of emotions almost blocked my reasoning, until it dawned upon me that Vicki's favorite area of a bedroom was the bed itself. I checked through the pillows, sheets, and linens. I still didn't find anything. I reread the letter twice until it clicked, the lines: "I left you a surprise close to my heart" and "key to your success" became clear. If my interpretation was correct, what I sought was a key, and I knew exactly where it was. I wasn't too thrilled at what I had to do. Grabbing a chair, I climbed up and faced Vicki's dark, dead eyes. I stabilized her body by wrapping my left arm around her waist, as I used my free hand to rip the necklace off her neck. The momentum of my jerk shifted my balance, and I fell off the chair. As her lifeless body violently swayed from side to side, I grabbed her feet to stop her from swinging. Next, I wiped everything down and reorganized the room. I left after I made an anonymous call to the authorities disclosing Viki's location. With her note and key in my possession, I walked as calmly as possible to the nearest bus stop. Anxious and confused, I stopped and called Mr. Anderson. Eleven minutes later, he picked me up outside of a convenience store. I gave him my motel address as I barely swallowed the emotional vomit lodged in my throat. She was such a beautiful person. In her death, I realized how much I loved her. Damn, Vicki! Too young and too soon! I couldn't help feeling somewhat responsible. I just sat there: dumb, numb, and void. My head hurt, and my eyes filled with grief and sadness as streetlamps flickered and woke up as we drove. The picture of Vicki, my sweet, beautiful angel, chased my every thought. I wish that she could have stayed that way, but forever young is how she died. In death, she finished a life filled with unfulfilled promise, which ended in sadness and pain.

CHAPTER 29

Swiss Cheese?

• • •

May 14, 2008, 10:52 p.m.

CHEESE WAS RESTLESS; HIS PROMISE to stop sleeping with sex workers only lasted a few hours. On the phone, he had already talked to the woman on the other end for forty-five minutes, but their conversation had reached an impasse.

"Trust you? Woman, I barely trust God!" he barked.

"Hey, one time I started going to Bible study because I was trying to sleep with this religious girl. In fact, it was the first time I had ever been to church. I was raised by my grandfather; he was old, so we would never go anywhere. On Saturday evenings, he would iron our shirts and suits. We would go to bed early; then he would wake me up even earlier on Sunday mornings. While I showered, he fixed oatmeal and toast. After breakfast, we would get dressed; then we walked into the living room, and he turned on the television as we watched his favorite evangelists. That was my grandfather's idea of attending church. His crazy ass even gave me a dollar to put in an old pie tin that he said was the collection plate. I don't know what surprised me the most: the fact that God was something more than a televised preacher man in a suit, whose show preceded episodes of *Happy Days* and *Leave It to Beaver*, or the revelation that the one dollar I religiously placed in the pie tin was my entire allowance. I lived with my grandfather until complications with his liver overran his life," Cheese said, finishing his first soliloquy.

"I'll tell you how that relates to the church girl if you stop interrupting! After a while, we went on date after date, and it took me six months before she let me feel her up. Six whole months! That's six months of worship, six months of Bible school, six months of prayer meetings, and the list goes on and on. Between blue balls and 'Glory Hallelujah,' I started to go crazy! So, to answer your question, no, I don't trust you. And, no, I can't continue to stall him. He's bound to get suspicious," Cheese said to the woman on the other end.

"God? Not God! We're talking about you-know-who! And, no, I don't need to hear your fucking vaginal confessions! The biggest sin with women is that they have a sex organ between their legs and they have been made to believe that this organ is the best object in the world, that it's so powerful, that it can make a man want to leave his wife and kids for it, or that it can magically force compulsive liars into men who whisper truthful tales between the sheets," Cheese replied.

"I know what he knows. He doesn't know anything. But I need to know more," Cheese demanded.

"No, bitch! This isn't reality television! You can't make an omelet out of empty eggshells! Everybody knows why you fuck. I learned a long time ago that it's very hard to erase a dark pencil line drawn six times in the same place without tearing the paper. You are not as fine as you think you are. Your breasts have started to sag like two UUs," he said, "and I have too much pride to believe in your stretched-out crotch," Cheese's honesty was brutal.

"Yes, the head was flu-like. That shit was sick; I can't lie. Your jaws are tighter than two AA batteries in a child's toy. But trust you! No! Just get me the info that I need, and I'll take care of you," he said. She agreed to his terms and hung up the phone.

CLICK!

Cheese turned on his stereo, and music automatically started playing, as he spread his freshly ironed outfit across his bed. As he stepped into the shower, a sudden, authoritative knock pounded his front door. Wrapped in a towel, dripping wet, Cheese approached the door and peered into its peephole, but it was empty. As he retraced his steps back to the shower, the amount of water droplets increased in numbers as they dotted his parquet floor. Moments later, the same knock banged through his door, only this time it was harder and for a longer length of time. Again, Cheese looked through the peephole, and again, he drew a blank. Seconds later, his phone rang. Cheese walked over and answered the call.

"Hello…Hello…Who is it?" he asked.

"Cheese, you dumb-ass motherfucker, what were you thinking?" Damon was on the other end, and he was miles away from being remotely happy.

"Look, Damon! I know you're mad, but it was a judgment call; everything happened so fast! The noose was about to tighten around Vinny's neck! He was going to flip! Word around the station was he faced a minimum of fifteen to thirty years for some priors unless he cooperated. I didn't think he had the stones to pull it off; thirty years is a mighty long stretch. That's when I made an executive decision," Cheese protested.

"Executive? You don't even have junior partner status! I never gave you permission to touch him. I was aware he was working for the cops. That was negotiable. Did you get him to tell you where the shipment is? No, of course not! Because you don't know about the package. Do you have any idea how much fucking money your so-called executive decision just cost me? The Saul situation was different. But Vinny was reasonable!" As Damon screamed into the phone, his ears turned beet red.

"Sorry, boss, I didn't know! I thoug—"

"That's the problem; you're a chimp, and I don't pay you to think!" Damon admonished.

"Sorry, boss, give me a chance to make this right!" Cheese implored.

"Sorry, boss?" Damon mocked, with a whimper. "You want me to make it right? Where are you right now?" Damon asked.

"I am at my place," Cheese replied.

"Sit tight; I am on my way over. I'll be there in twenty minutes. I think we can sort this out," Damon hung up the phone.

CLICK!

As soon as Damon hung up, there was another knock on the door. Instead of checking the peephole, Cheese tiptoed to the nearest coffee table, pulled the bottom drawer open, and grabbed his revolver before he cautiously approached the door. There was a moment of silence as the music in his apartment stopped playing, while Cheese continued slowly toward the door, but before he could get there, he heard a loud familiar *CHK-CHK*. It took him a millisecond before he realized what was about to happen. Instinctually, he dove, narrowly escaping a harrowing barrage of bullets that sliced through his apartment. Frantic, he crawled across the floor as a hail of bullets continued to penetrate the walls in search of his body. Grabbing his car keys, Cheese miraculously slithered through an undersized bedroom window. The shooting continued as he raced naked and afraid to his car. Panic stricken, fumbled movements forced the keys to slip through his fingers. Leaning over, he abruptly swiped the keys from the car mat and shoved them into the ignition, turned, started, and pressed the gas pedal as hard as he could; all four tires screeched in pain as he sped out of the parking lot. A total of 120 bullets were shot into his apartment, yet only one had struck him, as bullet sixty-nine was the one that went in and out of the fleshy part of his rear right deltoid. Cheese was about a mile away from his apartment as he sat at a red light, while his heart raced as he looked back over his left shoulder for evidence of any pursuing headlights. Seeing nobody behind him and a green light in front of him, Cheese began to crack a smile when...

BOOM!

His car exploded before he could make it through the intersection. Mangled car parts mixed with assorted body parts, as intense heat and fire created a foul odor of gasoline and burning flesh. Moments later, an all-black van with tinted windows pulled up beside what was left of Cheese's wreckage. The van's right-side window slid down as the passenger drew a .50-caliber Desert Eagle and pumped several bullets into the smoldering car. The shooter was none other than the infamous Rico.

"Now, let's go find that package," Rico said as Damon nodded and then applied pressure to the gas pedal, and their black van with a license plate that read *Saul Autos Inc.* spun around the corner and disappeared into traffic.

CHAPTER 30

Invading Shadows

• • •

May 15, 2008, 4:58 a.m.

SINCE VICKI'S DEATH, WHENEVER TIME faded deeper into darkness, I couldn't rest. Trash trucks, honking horns, people's voices, and dogs barking were just a few of the culprits that stole my sleep. Like a bug crashing into a windshield, my mood was wrinkled. Vicki's lifeless body haunted my dreams. She was in two separate dreams last night. In both dreams the cord was still tied around her neck. During the first dream, I remembered speaking to her, but she just stood there without responding, slowly rocking from left to right with a sadistic smile on her face. What kind of conversation do you have with a dead woman while you're dreaming? I woke up in a cold sweat, disturbed, shaken, and confused. In the second dream, she came to me, with her eyes wide open like a zombie, screaming in a high-pitched voice sharp enough to cut glass: "Clint, did you get the key? Clint, did you get the key?" I woke up ASAP, found her note and reread it several times as I searched for answers.

After several deliberations, I knew I had to go back to *EDIBLE GROOVES*. Full-blown paranoia had set in. My head was heavy, too heavy to deal with this situation sober, and the *NO SMOKING* sign didn't abort my intentions. I walked into the bathroom and turned the shower dial all the way to hot. In minutes, the bathroom steamed up. Next, I started a pot of complimentary coffee. As it brewed, I rolled a healthy-sized joint of Purple Haze. As I opened the bathroom door, the steam rushed past me like an angry bully intent upon assaulting the first cold air it met. I walked in and disappeared amid the remaining steam. The toilet seat was already down, and I sat and proceeded to light up. A series of deep inhales and slow exhales filled and exited my lungs as if I was in a cannabis Lamaze class. Face lost in the steam, thoughts lost in the Haze, my mind started to slow down, and relaxation finally made an appearance. Lost in a daze, I sat on the toilet so long that my legs became as stiff as porcelain. Anything to escape "the shadows," I didn't like "the shadows." The shadows in my mind were dark, dank, dirty, and filled with uncertainty.

CHAPTER 31

Rico and Damon

● ● ●

May 15, 2008, 12:12 a.m.

RICO, STILL PROUD FROM RIDDLING Cheese's car, reloaded his gun as Damon drove toward Amsterdam City via Route 30.

"Well, what brought you back?" Damon asked.

"The cocaine," there wasn't a moment's hesitation in Rico's response.

"Yeah, white powder always makes any story better. Now that I have your undivided attention, let me bring you up to speed," Damon said.

"How much are you talking about? If I recall, you said that our share would be roughly nine million dollars on the streets," Rico added.

"More like twelve million pure, and with the right dance moves, maybe thirty million or more," Damon confirmed.

"That's a lot of coke! Killing Saul was the right thing to do; he was a long, frayed thread in a ball of loose ends. But Vinny had value," the usually stoic Rico started to crack a smile.

"You're damn right. That's a lot of coke! That's our coke. Not anyone else's, that's our coke! It's time we claim what's ours!" Damon emphasized his point by violently poking his left index finger into the black van's freshly detailed dashboard.

Rico was still trying to imagine how the only source to a thirty-million-dollar shipment was now dead. "Vinny would still be alive had I stuck around. I knew this was too much for you to handle," Rico said, calling Damon out.

"Fuck you! I told you Cheese should've never been brought on. But no, you had to have another dirty cop on the payroll, as if Dansbury wasn't enough," Damon said.

"Fuck you! You can never have enough blue-shaded assholes on your payroll!" Rico began to point the business end of one of his .50 Desert Eagles in Damon's direction.

"Get that shit out of my way! Like that's the first time I've had a gun in my face. I never gave Cheese the OK to touch Vinny. That's why Cheese is dead now; if you hadn't killed Cheese, then I would've! What the fuck kind of name is Cheese anyway? I should've shot him on that principal alone. Fuck Cheese!" Damon started to raise his voice as Rico nodded in agreement.

"Where are we headed anyway?" Rico asked.

"I'm dropping you off, and I am going have to pay an old friend a visit," Damon stated.

"For what?" Rico inquired.

"I want to ask God for forgiveness for my past, present, and future transgressions," Damon joked.

"What if God doesn't hear your prayers?" Rico pressed.

"Then I am going to shoot the messenger!" deadpanned Damon. "While I'm doing that, can you slide through the hospital and 'tuck' our friend in for good?"

"It's about fucking time we put that mook to sleep!" whenever Rico discussed murder, his member would harden. This guy got a hard-on about violence.

"Here, take this and reach into the bag on the floor behind you. Grab two more niggers, and *finish* the job," Damon said as he passed Rico a new cell phone.

Then Damon increased the pressure on the gas pedal until the speedometer read ninety miles per hour. They drove without fear; they lived without fear and made money without fear.

CHAPTER 32

Clint's Disheveled Monologue

• • •

May 15, 2008, 6:36 a.m.

I DECIDED THAT I WOULD implement project: *EDIBLE GROOVES* on the seventeenth; that gave me the better part of two days to prepare. The steam was long gone as I stared into the bathroom mirror searching for the truth. Something was missing. Premonitions screamed that Saul's murder was linked to whatever Vicki's note had attempted to tell me. When I thought about it, there were entirely too many criminals at Saul's party for there not to be some sort of connection. I struggled as I tried to figure out how to ensure my safety in the face of danger from the authorities and other criminals. What if Vicki's note led me to a cash grab, and I was able to run away to sun and fun? The inherent flipside of that was—ah, well, I didn't even want to commit any energy thinking about the blood and violence of what might be. But I didn't want to be blinded by the dollar and establish faith in a random key that I'd retrieved off a dead woman, friend or no friend. And what was I searching for?

The catch: there was probably someone watching the building, waiting for me to make a move. Mind spinning, I could not stop talking to myself.

I knew the situation was flimsy. I had no ability to examine all the angles. This wasn't poker with a kitty of cash. I was face-to-face with a zero-sum game. Theoretically, I had everything to gain and l-i-f-e to lose. Life or no life, fuck it! I'm all in! Let's do it! I had just sold myself the dream, and I was ready to stick my neck out so far that my ears and shoulders started to hurt. A change of identity was what I needed, and I knew exactly where to get one. The more I spoke, the more I believed that this plan could work.

Now that my plan had an outline; I still needed to fill in plenty of blanks. First, I needed to go to my safe-deposit box; that's where I kept my *big* gun. Second, I needed to get into contact with the identification specialist. I figured it made sense to request a building inspector's disguise equipped with authentic blueprints and building zone codes. In about forty-eight hours, I would know how this story ended. Only time would tell if my plan was the beginning of a renaissance biography or a short graphic novel detailing my demise. I decided at 3:59 p.m. to go into my local bank to collect contents from my safety-deposit box. Then I would shoot across town to meet the ID specialist by seven thirty. If all went smoothly, I'd be back to check out of my motel by ten p.m. Then I'd be that much closer to disappearing.

The sun had risen by the time I exited my motel room. Blinded, my eyes burned in confusion as they adjusted from the transition of relative darkness to the bombardment of unmitigated sunlight. I summoned the first available cab and went directly to the bank. The presiding representative escorted me into the safety box room and then made himself scarce. It had been some time since I'd opened this box. My number was 420. I keyed it open and was instantly reminded as to why I'd purchased this box. In addition to the ten thousand dollars, the box also contained two discreetly packaged firearms. One was my handgun of choice. The second represented the crazy spoils of drug dealing. Some people will barter anything—for example, the "Say hello to my…" gun from the movie *Scarface*. A B-list movie director won it in a card game and later traded that gun with me for a thousand triple-stacked ecstasy pills. How was I supposed to register a firearm of that magnitude without grabbing the ATF's unwanted attention? So, I had a gunsmith dismantle the iconic firearm; then I buried it within four separate cream-colored envelopes deep inside my security box. The other envelope was white, and it contained my nine-millimeter. I collected the cash and the white envelope and locked the box before I notified the bank representative that my business was complete.

Just as I left the bank, I got a call from the ID specialist and was informed that we would need to reschedule our meet and greet. He told me that I would be provided with the time and place within twelve hours. Feeling exposed, I needed a safer place to crash for the next few hours, so I decided to call Lourdes.

RING!

"Hello," her voice was almost hoarse; it sounded raspy like an upset raspberry.

"*Hola, chica, como esta?*" were the first words that came out of my mouth.

"Peace! I was just thinking about you. How have you been?" she asked.

"I am well." It was a lie. But we'd had such a great time the last time we were together. I knew I had to see her again. "What are you doing right now?" I inquired.

"I'm actually free tonight; after that I don't know. I just got accepted to the Peace Corps! If I accept, then I will be somewhere in the Caribbean for two years," I could hear the happiness in her disclosure. I'd always wanted to join the PC, but then life happened.

We agreed to meet at her house for early evening cocktails. To kill some time, I disappeared into a movie theater. I was employing the stick-and-move strategy that worked so well for Ali. I only hoped to attain similar success minus the Parkinson's.

CHAPTER 33

A Taste of Sugar

• • •

May 15, 2008, 9:27 p.m.

THE DECISION TO MEET LOURDES before I stepped into the proverbial lion's den proved to be a great idea. Tequila was our cocktail of choice. Several drinks later, as she stood in front of me, I realized that she was one of the most beautiful women that I had ever encountered. Her big brown eyes sparkled and beckoned me to make a move. I was mesmerized in her presence. I was giddy. She possessed an uncanny ability to blend devout feminism with unbridled sexuality. This synthesis broke my insular resolve. Words were exchanged, kisses kissed, and clothing was removed as I traced the soft lines of her bare back with the tip of my left index finger.

"Ouch! I don't mean to sound like a whiner, but maybe you should think about cutting your fingernails," as she spoke, she employed a slick, almost silk-on-glass manner of sarcasm.

"Missy, my nails are clipped," I responded.

"Well, maybe you should try some lotion. I have some balm on my dressing table," she pointed to the vanity over her right shoulder.

I found the balm and rubbed her shoulders, neck, and lower back. I'd once dated a massage therapist while I lived on the West Coast. She could do the most wondrous things with her fingertips. I smiled as I employed some of the techniques I had learned from Valentina. Gingerly, additional balm was rubbed into Lourdes's lower back, thighs, and all over her tightly clenched butt cheeks. I liked the fact that she kept the doors to her buttocks shut tight. Even if a lady enjoys an occasional session of backdoor lovin', a true lady always kept her cheeks clenched together until proper dues had been paid. I wondered what type of tales her tail could tell. Maybe I should start spanking her? No! It was too early for that. I asked her to turn over so that I could address her feet, legs, thighs, and other erogenous zones. She obliged. The further I rubbed, the more aroused she became. As my hands continued to explore her body, her facial expressions became distorted, and her speech stuttered in incoherent syllables. I felt my desire manifesting, and I couldn't hold back any longer. Before I broke, she pounced on top of me, and we rolled over each other. She mounted me, and I would eventually mount her. We practiced this exchange several times during the dawning of night. Lourdes was comfortable being on top. I put my hands on her hips, closed my eyes, and listened to her moaning escalate until her shouts of sexual gibberish were heard in every corner of her room. My pulse quickened, and my brain donated its very last drops of blood into my anaconda. Head spinning, the world around me became all warm and fuzzy. She was well versed in the art of orchestrated hip thrusts. Forty-five minutes and a variety of orgasms later, beads of sweat cascaded from her nipples. After a quick sip, we found ourselves in the barrage of another explosive session. Rolling around between the sheets, we were like two teenagers without a care in the world. But in the crevices of my mind, I knew that police surveillance made me hotter than some four-hundred-pound stripper's thighs. The equation of my success was simple: grab whatever treats were available and flee the scene without being seen. And then I could be off to destinations unknown. But now I had a new challenge: what to do with the Lourdes? She was a taste of honey to which I was fast becoming addicted. I should've known better. With our amorous session finished, I wanted more: more words, more laughs, more intimacy, as we fell asleep wrapped inside of each other's arms.

When I woke up, I discovered that she'd left. The red Post-it on her headboard read that she had an early-morning meeting and didn't want to wake me because I was sleeping so peacefully. I laughed out loud as I finished reading the note. I now knew how it felt to be left in bed after a night of coitus. "Well played, Lourdes, well played," I thought. Her departure brought out the feelings that I recognized earlier. Only this time, they were multiplying exponentially. Was I fearing the unknown? Indigestion? Butterflies? Or was it the dreaded *l* word? Love, the intersection of a simple verb coupled with the nexus of two potentially complex nouns. Why was I so consumed? Who knows? Did what I feel even matter? In the next forty-eight to seventy-two hours and some odd minutes, I would probably be dead.

CHAPTER 34

Southern Discomfort

● ● ●

May 16, 2008, 10:01 a.m.

Minutes after I left Lourdes's home, I called Sasha. I needed her to check for any affidavits filed in my name, and I also wanted information about Vicki's situation. But Sasha sent my call to her voicemail, so I left a voicemail. Today represented many challenges. I had an open confirmation that the ID specialist and I would meet this evening, but I still hadn't been given the when and where. Feeling paranoid, I called Sasha again. This time she answered, confirmed that she had received my message, and said that she would acquire the information that I sought. I also supplied her with a list of names of people that were at Saul's the night of his murder and said I needed more background information. Her timeline was at the end of the day. So much insanity had transpired in such a brief span of time; I really had no ability to trust anyone. I took three cabs to get back to my motel. Stopping on the way, I picked up a sandwich and some beverages. Hungrily, I wolfed down the food and beverage and then closed the shades on my eyes while I attempted to gather my thoughts. But the pull of extreme exhaustion forced me to fall asleep. When I woke, I discovered that I had missed two phone calls. One number was Sasha's, and the other number was foreign to me. I dialed Sasha.

RING!

"Hello, Clint," her voice was filled with energy; I knew she had information to share.

"Sasha, thanks for calling me back. What do you have for me?" I asked.

"Two things: you'll be happy to hear that there are no current affidavits connected to you," she said.

"Well, that's good news. What else did you find?" I was anxious.

"It didn't look good for your friend Victoria. The authorities are purported to possess fingerprints, GSR, and DNA evidence. The DA was prepared to prosecute her to the fullest extent of the law," Sasha reported.

"Really? That's terrible. Is there anything else that I should know about?" I asked.

"Oh, this might be miniscule, but the coroner's report determined Vicki's death a suicide by way of strangulation. I noticed the police report mentioned that forensics found two spots of blood clotting or hematoma around her neck. The cord she used to hang herself created the first bruise, but there was a second bruise much smaller than the first. The report seemed to yield suspicion that Victoria might have been the victim of a post mortem crime, as if a necklace or chain had been snatched from her neck after she died," Sasha reported.

"Wow, that's thorough! Thanks, Sasha; how much do I owe you?" I asked.

"How about dinner at Bouley's? I have a feeling, if I take you on as a client, you definitely will bring me a totally different array of experiences," she chuckled as she spoke, yet we both knew she was dead serious.

"The French restaurant? Sure, I can do that; you tell me when you're free, and we'll make it happen," I said.

"I'll have my secretary check my schedule, and we'll coordinate. You be safe, Clint!" she replied.

CLICK!

Time had revealed many secrets. Poor Vicki! No sooner had I gotten off the phone with Sasha than my phone rang. This time the unknown number came up *ANONYMOUS*.

"Hello." I had an allergic reaction to answering mysterious phone calls.

"This is a recording. The Phantom is confirming tonight's appointment at the Patterson Barn off the Batten Kill River at eleven p.m. Be sure to be on time, or he'll disappear. Make sure you have the buy money," the recording beeped and ended.

CLICK!

And just like that, the voice was gone. I guess his moniker, the Phantom, was aptly assigned. When he took a client, he made their original identification "vanish" without complications. It was closing in on quarter past four. After rolling around with Lourdes all night, I really hadn't had a chance to rest. Twenty minutes later, I had logged onto www.zzzzdreams. bed. My alarm was set for 8:00 p.m. Surprisingly, I slept rather soundly.

By the time my alarm went off, I had already been awake for about thirty-five minutes. It was time to make moves. The Phantom's message was emphatic about punctuality. I wanted to be there ahead of schedule to scope the place out. Freshly showered, with five thousand dollars in tow, my motel clock read 9:00 p.m. I headed to the Batten Kill area. Attempting to switch things up, I shelled out some cash to borrow one of Crook's mother's touring sedan.

By the time I pulled into the vast field surrounding Patterson Barn, I was amazed to see all the other cars. *HAZE PRODUCTIONS* was sponsoring this outdoor rave concert. The atmosphere reminded me of the grainy, black-and-white footage of a nineties concert. Bonfires were all around; some blazed over fifty feet high, as twenty-something coeds, entranced, ritualistically danced in their glow. The time was 10:25 p.m. By quarter to eleven, I was approached by a pair of twin brunettes that had a fat joint of some Ickey Woods, asking me for a light. I chuckled, as I looked around at all the surrounding bonfires and these two claimed they couldn't find a light. We had just started our cipher when my phone rang. Again, it read: *ANONYMOUS.*

"Hello," was my industry-standard response.

"Yeah, meet me by the barn on the side nearest the river," the voice instructed.

CLICK!

I took one final toke and then apologized to the twins for my rapid departure. They asked if I wanted them to flash me their breasts before

I parted ways. I told them I'd take a rain check, and I walked toward Patterson Barn.

The walk was longer than I expected, but as I got closer to this side of the party, the vibe had demonstratively changed. It was like a masquerade party. Everyone was adorned in masks and gothic garb. Feeling overexposed, I unbuttoned my shirt and tied it over my nose and around my face as I continued walking. My image probably resembled Billy the Kid stalking his next bank victims. As I rounded the far-left corner of the barn, I almost interrupted this couple fornicating. Several paces removed from their moaning and groaning, I approached a group of masked characters standing around a burning trash can. Something told me that the Phantom was intermingled within this group, specifically the person that wore a Casper the Friendly Ghost mask. They laughed as they drank from plastic cups.

"Yo, Casper, come here; I need to speak to you," I said in the direction of the trash-can crew. Sure enough, the person behind the mask came over and introduced himself.

"The Phantom, at your service. Grab a cup. I do all of my business over drinks," as he spoke, he poured me an all too large portion of Southern Comfort.

I took a small sip and instantly felt that piercing sensation of heat in the pit of my stomach. It tasted like cough syrup. I'd never liked SC. Even back in school, everyone that knew me knew that I hated Southern Comfort. One night of drinking, I survived the worst hangover I've ever had. Today, I still refer to it as Southern Discomfort. Not wanting to risk offending the Phantom's hospitality, I slowly sipped in a manner that gave the impression that I drank, as we discussed business.

"Everything clear? Are all parts lubed and in motion?" I asked, as my stomach winced as I watched him guzzle an extended pull from the bottle of SC.

"If you have half the green, then I have half of your product," the Phantom curtly replied. I gave him the envelope containing five thousand dollars. It was agreed the driver's license, passport, and shot records would be obtained during our next and final meeting. I stood calmly as he passed the envelope to one of his associates, and I judiciously "sipped" the formidable remnants in my cup. Once the count was confirmed, the Phantom motioned for his colleague wearing a Kermit the Frog mask to give me a bag that contained zoning building blueprints, an official city zoning uniform, and a zoning identification card. Everything looked legit in the dark of darkness.

Before the Phantom and I parted ways, we planned to meet in twelve hours, or approximately noon tomorrow, to complete our business. We shook, and I left with over half my cup intact. Once I was out of sight, I dumped the remaining contents into the grass. I walked directly to Crook's mother's vehicle, opened the door, started the engine, and drove toward the city. As I drove, I stopped at a red light, and the people beside me in a yellow muscle car looked at me strange. It wasn't until I looked in the rearview mirror that I realized I still had my shirt tied around my face. Ridiculous—I needed more sleep. Unfortunately, by the time I got to the motel, I wouldn't have long to sleep. Since money never sleeps, neither do the schemes that go toward earning it.

CHAPTER 35

No Skinny-Legged Jeans, Please

● ● ●

May 17, 2008, 8:12 a.m.

SOMEONE ACROSS THE HALL SLAMMED a door, and it jarred me out of my sleep. Jeez! I checked my phone. The Phantom had left a voicemail informing me to meet him at 9605 Red Run Street. Our meeting had been pushed up almost three hours, for 9:15 a.m. I showered and adorned myself in a fresh set of clothes. A portion of the Phantom's message instructed me to bring the uniform. Apparently, he had contracted a tailor to alter the building inspector's uniform. Though completely legit, I didn't possess the girth to fit into the uniform's thirty-eight-inch waist and fifteen-inch neck. About the only thing that fit me was the hat labeled "one size fits all." Following a few rejections, I was finally able to convince a taxi driver that my trip would be well worth his efforts. We drove seemingly halfway across the city to a section where people had parks and more grass than they could occupy. All the streets were lined with trees. Maple seemed to be the most popular selection. Thirty-two minutes later, we pulled up in front of 9605 Red Run Street; a brownstone was tucked away at the end of the block. I paid the cabbie and approached the front door.

Posh in nature, this mammoth exterior door was adorned in stained glass and gold ornate features. I rang the bell. As I waited, I shuddered while I reflected on my childhood visits to the tailor. I didn't know everything, but I thought that if another person touched any part of your penis or scrotum more than once, that was not tailoring—that was sexual assault. Seconds later, I was buzzed in. Boy, I hoped the tailoring industry had changed over the last twenty years, or we were about to have a problem, the Phantom or no Phantom. When the door opened, to my surprise, my eyes were introduced to a sensational woman. Her eyelashes, eyebrows, lips, and hair were meticulous cared for, and she spoke with some sort of French-English accent.

"*Bon-jour*, Cl-int, my name is Mar-ie-cella," she spoke with a syllabic emphasis that was mildly distracting.

"Greetings, Mariecella, the Phantom sent me," I replied, still somewhat skeptical.

"Ze Phantom as jou say will not be joi-ning us. It's j-uz you zend me," she replied.

"OK," I muttered.

"C'est bon; zest' get start-ed, shall we?" she said.

"Sure, let's do it," I followed her down a long hallway that was littered with pictures of her in the company of numerous famous faces.

Mariecella instructed me to take a seat; then she explained the services she was going to provide. I passed her the bag containing the uniform, and her bust hung effortlessly in my face as she bent over to remove the bag's contents. But I wasn't interested in all of that. After collecting the pants and shirt, she told me to stand on a small, square platform surrounded by five mirrors. I obeyed, and she acquired my dimensions with a faded, yellow tape measure, and to my pleasure, my nether regions were not encroached upon. Then she directed me to occupy one of the nearby dressing rooms so that I could change into the uniform.

When I walked out, she bent over in laughter, humored by the way my body swam in the oversized uniform.

"Oh, *mon dieu, mon dieu!*" was all she spoke between laughs.

Once her laughter subsided, she quickly made a series of bold chalk markings around my torso, waist, and legs. When she got to my legs, all that I could think was, "No skinny-legged pants, please!"

After the markings, I was instructed to return to the dressing room and change into my clothes. I passed Mariecella the uniform over the dressing-room door. Once I was fully dressed, I followed her to the sewing room. This room was completely barren except for a high-end sewing machine, the table on which the machine rested, and three old chairs. Mariecella sat behind the machine, and I sat in the middle chair, watching her seamlessly operate. A mere forty-five minutes later, she announced: "Ar zous readee to zee thee rezultz?"

"Yes," I felt a tingle of excitement, like I was a preteen about to go trick-or-treating alone for the first time.

We returned to the dressing room, and I opened and closed the door to the original room as I slipped into the uniform. Then I exited the dressing room.

"Voilà!" was all she said. Sure enough, she was correct, as I stood in front of the mirror; the costume had transformed into a convincing disguise. Once I put on the hat and badge, I resembled an official city employee. As a bonus, for authenticity purposes, she applied a discreet amount of gray costume make-up to my eyebrows and hair to further augment my appearance. I thanked her, gave her the final payment owed to the Phantom, and then she provided me with my new driver's license, passport, and shot records. I preemptively called a cab as I changed. Upon exiting the dressing room, I thanked her again and said good-bye before I disappeared into the taxi.

I was about ten minutes away from Mariecella's home before I concluded that Mariecella was the Phantom. This delayed revelation shoved a loud chuckle out of my mouth. The cabbie smirked at my outburst as we continued back to my motel.

It was after one o'clock when I keyed back into my motel room. I only had a few hours before I was going to put my new identity to use. I was so close to discovering what awaited me at the end of the rainbow.

CHAPTER 36

Now or Never

● ● ●

May 17, 2008, 2:23 p.m.

MY PLAN WAS ALL LAID out, but the monotonous rigors of repetitively reviewing each move and countermove filled my head with omnipresent toxins of paranoia. As I stood in front of the mirror, I could hear and feel my racing heartbeat.

"Fuck!" I needed stillness of heart. I drank some warm tea, I tried meditation, but both offered no results. Frustrated, I rolled up the fattest spliff I could manage, plugged in my MP3 player, and inserted a small, soft earbud into each ear as I headed to the bathroom for a hot box. I figured if I was going to go out, I might as well go out on a roll. I ignored my usual steam-shower routine.

Flick-flick went my lighter until it produced enough fire to ignite the honey-brown end of my blunt. Several drags later, all my fears and tears vanished into the sky. I didn't know how much my heartbeat dropped, but I could confirm that I was numb, and my paranoia was held hostage by the smooth, mellow nature of my high. It was now or never! No reason to prolong what needed to be done, I had done my due diligence; I had planned my plan, and now it was time to execute. I scooped up my bag, which included my gun and the key. I made sure I had my necessary documents before I walked out of the motel. This time I decided to take the back stairwell, as the music in my ears banged the latest *DIRTY SUEDE REMIX ALBUM*:

"The press is literally masturbating...feds investigating...while I'm dinner dating...a money-hungry lady named Satan...or "Louise Cypher"...She saw my "ices," and her eyes spread like ISIS...So before coffee and after ice cream...I scream why do we strive for... the dichotomy between rich and poor...not totally sure...some too broke to spare time...too rich to spare a dime...why do we strive for...morality or impracticality...I look around, and all I see are all of thee including me...doing all sorts of things for all the wrong things...Why do we strive for...a bigger house that has a much bigger door...bigger bills and a mortgage insecure...like a child with zits or a woman with itty bitties...I know it sounds silly...but I'm asking...huh, really?...Why do we strive for...the stone the builder refused...should've been the one that he used...When buildings crumble, then everyone's confused...Why do we strive for...the man with the style...or the woman with hair bought by the mile... Apparently appearance appears to be coherently realistic...when it's just an image...or an exorbitant gimmick...Why do we strive for...artificial celebrity...egocentric longevity...so we can elevate or simply levitate...like David Blaine...our egos insane...Why do we strive for...to separate the faces...run the same races...hiding behind masks in esoteric spaces...Why do we strive for...unsurprisingly...with dinner inside of her and the bill in my hand... Louise asked me the number of zeroes in my account...I said, actually my accountant is still counting it...whether a hundred or a thousand...a mountain of zeroes still amounts to nothing... Disgusted by my discussion...she jumped up out of her chair... knocked over a glass...didn't even care...grabbed her bag and got the hell out of there...Now isn't that something...It's 2008...What will you strive for?"

The song spoke volumes. In hindsight, perhaps I should've examined how it related to my decision, but I was too committed to pull out. I took a detour, walked out of the motel, and turned left into the back-parking lot.

I paused, reached into my pocket, and produced an American Eagle cigarette, lit it, and pulled several tokes. After a final drag, I tossed the cigarette on the ground and crushed the life out of it. Being environmentally conscious, I picked up the butt and tossed it into a nearby green-and-white Dumpster. One right turn combined with another right turn led me to the main street, where I hailed a taxi. I gave the cabbie the address to a location two blocks from *EDIBLE GROOVES*. Fifteen minutes later, with the meter paid, I hopped out of the taxi and walked to my destination, but my steps were interrupted by a rambunctious bug. Buzzing spastically, this pesky bee sparked a transcendental voyage as my thoughts rippled back to a time during my youth when I watched a yellow jacket and a cricket wage war. The urgency of my situation interrupted my reflection; now wasn't the time to reminisce. The stakes were too high.

Before I knew it, my steps had brought me close to the front door of *EDIBLE GROOVES*. I still had my garage key, so I backtracked to the lower garage entrance and slid the black strip on the back of the entry card through the scanner; surprisingly it still worked. The parking lot was completely empty except for two black vans that had black-and-white *Saul Autos, Inc.* borders around their license plates. Seeing this caused my heart to skip a beat, and I pulled my gun from my bag, tucked it into my pants under my shirt, and cautiously proceeded to the elevator. I pressed the button for the thirteenth floor; the doors opened and then closed, and I was on my way up. Several seconds later, I exited the elevator and walked through the lobby of Vinny's office until I came to his office door. I reached out and was relieved to find that when I turned the knob, the door opened. So far, so good, I thought. Vinny's office was exactly as I remembered; eerily, nothing had been touched or rearranged; it was almost like business as usual. Vicki's note mentioned "look behind the bookcase and you will find what you need to make it Xmas in July." You couldn't miss the bookcase; it was about the size of a large door. I searched all over for a secret keyhole, but my search proved fruitless, until I looked on the sides of the bookcase, and there it was, a keyhole, hidden behind a small crevice between the bookcase and the nearly adjoining wall. So far, Vicki was true to her word. I inserted the key, and the bookcase slowly swung open until it came to a stop. There in front of me was a large safe door approximately five feet by five feet. I immediately pulled out Vicki's letter and followed her direction regarding the safe code.

> *4 to the left, and stop on 5, then 2 times to the right, 3 times to the right and stop on 9, then 3 times to the left and stop on 72, then 1 time to the right and stop on 24.*

When the safe dial stopped on 24, I paused and took a deep breath as my heart raced with uncontrollable anticipation. I was so close, but I couldn't discount the fact that this could be booby-trapped or connected to an alarm or anything for that matter. Oh well, I turned the safe handle and pulled the door. What I discovered was that the safe was in fact an entrance to a completely different room, almost like a condensed warehouse within a warehouse. This other room was filled with five large barrels. I struggled as I unscrewed one of the access caps and wafted my hand from the access hole up to my nose. What I smelled was very strong and strangely familiar. I had only smelled that smell one other time in my life, and that situation would never allow me to forget the smell of what I smelled now. The five barrels had the following labels: *AMMONIA, BLEACH, EMULSIFIER AGENTS, CORROSION INHIBITOR*, and *PROPELLANTS*. The more I sniffed, the closer my memory came to recall what the familiar smell represented. Then it hit me: I smelled LC! Also known as liquid cocaine. Whoa! If each of the five barrels contained forty-two gallons per barrel and each gallon weighed about 8 pounds, that would equate to a total of 336 pounds per barrel. Therefore, five barrels multiplied by 336 pounds per barrel was about 1,680 pounds, or roughly 764 kilograms, of liquid cocaine cleverly concealed in barrels labelled "cleaning supplies," I quickly did the math in my head. Cocaine per gram was currently $2 in Colombia and about $2,000 per kilogram, while a Dominican Republic kilogram fetched about $9 per gram or $9,000 per kilogram, and New York prices registered about $110 per gram or $110,000 per kilogram, and those prices escalated the farther north you went. If I used the New York market as the industry standard at $110,000 per kilo, then I was looking at an absurd $84,000,000 of liquid cocaine. That price could substantially appreciate once the street distributors "tap-danced" on it. I couldn't begin to fathom how many problems this type of cocaine weight could create. To turn a proper profit, I'd need a chemist to convert it to powder form and then a connect for a wholesale exchange, not to mention all the protection I'd have to hire. Thanks, but no thanks. I was instantly annoyed with Vicki; she knew I didn't deal with coke. Just before I began to curse her government name, I discovered a five-inch Zero Halliburton stainless-steel executive case on the floor behind the fifth barrel. I opened it and began singing Vicki's praises. The suitcase was filled with stacks and stacks of Benjamin Franklin faces. There were four rows by four rows equaling a total of sixteen stacks of nothing but crisp hundred-dollar bills. "Jackpot! Thank you, Vicki!" I thought time and time again, as I wiped down everything. I was extra mindful to wipe down the safe dial. I closed and locked the safe before closing the bookcase. Cautiously, I wiped the bookcase itself, as well as the doorknob to Vinny's office. With the Zero Halliburton in hand, I even wiped down the buttons in the elevator. After I exited the elevator, I heard police sirens closing in on my location. Was this the end? Had Vicki set me up? Swiftly, I walked past the black vans and left through the back door of the garage. Now street side, I pulled my cap down over my face and continued walking across the street. I walked an additional three blocks before I grabbed a taxi and called Lourdes. She was home, and I told her that I wanted to see her tomorrow night. She obliged. After exiting the taxi, I immediately entered my motel room and packed up my belongings and inspected the Zero Halliburton to make sure there wasn't a tracking device hidden somewhere within the money. Once inspected, I stuffed my duffel bag with the money and ditched the Zero Halliburton inside of the custodial trash cart before I caught another taxi.

CHAPTER 37

Everyone Has a Plan until They Get That Phone Call

• • •

May 18, 2008, 3:52 a.m.

IT TOOK SOME TIME BEFORE I was able to find a suitable motel, but once I did, I spent all night and well into the dawn of the next morning counting cash. The more I counted, the more I started to plan for a brighter future. I had about two additional stacks left, and I estimated my total was approximately $1.2 million dollars, or twelve thousand hundred-dollar bills to be exact. I figured I probably had about another two thousand bills to count. But I could barely keep my eyes open. I had grown quite weary, and eventually I blacked out with cash in my left hand.

While asleep, I dreamed that I had won the state lottery, but such was life, and all dreams had to come to an end, as I had to discover shortly. I woke up staring at the reality of over a million dollars. It was hard not to wake up with a smile when you saw that much cash. Then I got *the* phone call, the one that I most definitely should have ignored.

RING!

"Hello, motherfucker; this is your destiny calling!" The voice was deep, direct, and uncompromising. I didn't recognize it, but I was more than disturbed by what it was saying. It fostered a quick recognition that my life was in danger.

"You've been a very naughty boy; you stuck your hands in a cookie jar that didn't belong to you!" the voice continued as I listened with laser-focus.

"Here's what you're going to do. You're going to return that package back to where you found it, and maybe, just maybe, I'll let you live. You have four hours; then I'm coming looking for you!"

CLICK!

Talk about a downer. How did the voice on the other end even know who I was and how to get in contact with me? I was careful to make sure to hide my face from any cameras in *EDIBLE GROOVES*. Maybe someone had spotted my image on one of the cameras outside of the building. Maybe I wasn't the first person to get to Vicki; maybe there had been someone there before I got there. Or maybe, just maybe, her death wasn't a suicide. What was the truth? The truth about life? I thought of something I'd read while in college. Many of us so-called existentialist hipsters believed that we were part of a grand scheme or plan, and our personal evolution was beyond the power of a supernatural enigma like Nietchze's Superman, and therefore, we were the sole controllers of our destiny. Forgotten within all this was the singular fact that none of us could predict the future, and that fallibility made each of us equally vulnerable. All humans, no matter how pious, we're all driven by something. As for me, I was totally guilty of greed to the tune of an unearned $1.4 million windfall that I thoroughly intended to keep. But now, I was presented with an unknown challenger. And the threat that I had just received was jarring. I was personally fed up with all of these surprises, so I decided to add a few of my own.

CHAPTER 38

A Panicked Man Almost Drowns
Himself and His Saviors

● ● ●

May 18, 2008, 9:42 a.m.

I TOOK MY TIME BEFORE I checked into a different motel. To secure my found treasure, I shoved a large sum of the $1,350,000 into my security-deposit box and then contacted the only person that I could trust. We agreed that we would meet around 8:00 p.m., so we could prepare for whatever or whomever was headed our way. My new motel had a few more amenities than the previous one. Time evaporated as I lay across my bed, eyes closed, while I tried to clear my mind before my seven-o'clock departure. By the time I arrived at C & J's, it was five minutes past eight. At their age, Crook and Juice were too old for their two-level apartment; it always resembled a frat house in both appearance as well as smell. Beer cans, beer bottles, ashtrays filled with cigarettes, sports magazines, and porn covered most of their living space. After I climbed the stairs, I knocked on their door. Juice greeted me and informed me that Crook was "pinching one off." Juice was surprisingly cordial, but Crook was the one I wanted to see. Moments later, I heard a sigh of relief and the toilet flush before he exited the bathroom.

"Apologies for these conditions," Crook said as he picked up an opened beer and indiscriminately drank its contents and then released an insane belch.

"No worries," I replied. But I was plenty worried.

"Dude, why the long face, bro? I told you we got you!" Crook said as he picked up the large shotgun perched by the sofa. *CLICK-CLACK* went the chamber as he stuffed it with shells. For some reason, as he spoke, Crook looked shorter and his shoulders appeared more-narrow than the last time we met. Truthfully, this dude looked frail, but his munitions were strong.

"Once we finish this shit, make sure you have the other half of the bread you owe," Juice chimed in; his gaunt face had dark circles around the eyes. We agreed $25,000 up front and the other $25,000 once I was safely out of the city—chump change in comparison to the remaining $1,350,000.

"Crook, Juice, I need to talk to both of you for a minute." The sofa moaned as I rose.

As we walked into the kitchen, Juice threw on a long-sleeved T-shirt.

"OK, what's up?" they asked in synchronicity.

"Are you two sure no one has the layout of this apartment? Can you remember all of the males and females that you've had over here in the last few weeks?" I asked.

"Of course, the only males that have been here are you, me, Crook, and...Cheese," Crook said.

Cheese! I couldn't believe what I'd just heard. That information was so very wrong on many different levels. Cheese was at Saul's house the night he was killed. On top of that, Sasha's background investigation later confirmed that Cheese was identified as the undercover police officer that was found in his car burned to a crisp a couple of nights ago. My mind raced in all directions. If Cheese was a cop, or even worse, a narco, then were these guys also cops? Also, if Cheese wasn't strictly undercover, then the cops probably knew about this place, and if that was the case, then our position and safety had been placed in jeopardy. The fact that Cheese was dead, and these guys didn't know or acknowledge that he was dead made me even more nervous. In my eyes, the only reassuring factor was the wacky booby trap that they'd constructed on the top floor of the apartment. While all of this was going on, I was unable to hear that tiny little voice in the back of my head that was screaming, trying to grab my attention.

Run away, Clint! Run away!

For the briefest of moments, the room went completely silent, and there it was, that tiny little voice, nearly hoarse from screaming at the top of its tiny little lungs.

Run away, Clint! Run away!

That was all I needed to hear. Like a claustrophobic trapped inside of an elevator, exiting their apartment was all I wanted.

"Yo, fellas, I need to step outside for a smoke and some fresh air; give me five," I said.

"That's cool. If you're going to the store, grab some Pringles!" Crook was a certified junk-food junkie.

"Sorry, bro, it's probably just a smoke break, but I'll see what I can do. Maybe I'll swing by Late-Mart." I pulled my cap over my head and looked at those two poor saps for probably the last time. I knew when things went down, it would be swift and heavy. The elevator was still broken, so I opted for the south-side stairwell; that route would allow me to leave through the back end of the building. They lived on the ninth floor, and I hadn't gotten to the fourth floor before the commotion began.

Their front door got bashed in, and then the shooting started. They didn't know what hit them. Sadly, that's what joining ROTC will get you, two shots to the head with one left in the chamber. My plan was to get to the touring sedan as soon as possible. I'd scooped Crook's keys on my way out and ran down the back stairwell and then out the back door and around the corner. My eyes scanned the darkness until I spotted the sedan, entered it, and started the engine. Suddenly, without warning, something that felt like a brick struck me in the face. A second blow sent me crumbling into the steering wheel.

CRACK!

"Kill the fucking engine!" commanded an oddly familiar, yet not totally familiar, voice. I was stunned and disoriented, yet still coherent enough to reach for my gun.

CRACK!

Another blow struck me in the back of my head. With my consciousness lost, I drifted off to a memory of me being in our backyard with my father as we watched two insects battling: a yellow jacket and a cricket. The yellow jacket's stinger acted as a gun before the cricket was able to throw its hands up in surrender. Compromise was never an option. The yellow jacket proceeded to fire off his stinger like a Russian Luger and repeatedly penetrated the cricket's exoskeleton. These shots rendered the cricket helplessly paralyzed, and the yellow jacket started to rapaciously feast on the fruits of its fallen foe. I could still hear the crunching sound of the yellow jacket's mandibles chewing through all edible parts. That day, I'd learned a valuable lesson and a reminder that we were all susceptible to being predators or prey in all phases of life. To this day, I still remembered the remains of the cricket. I saw it, and I still couldn't believe what I saw. The stickiness of criminal riches urged the yellow jacket's maniacal behavior.

"Daddy!" I yelled as I struggled to reconnect with reality.

SMACK!

His stinging slap returned me to my senses.

"Your daddy isn't here! Shut the fuck up! Get out of the car and start walking!" His gun poked my back, and I obliged.

"Not so fast, my friend! Move slowly!" barked the unidentified voice. The aggressive nature of his voice was further complimented by the clicking sound of a bullet being loaded into the chamber of the gun that he now pointed directly in the back of my head. One false move and I was dead.

My mind quickly regained traction. It was at that point that I pinpointed the owner of the voice. I only knew one person that used the phrase "not so fast, my friend." The voice spoke again.

"Look, everyone upstairs is dead, and before the cops come, you're going to lead me to the money, or you will be dead too!" As we walked back into the building, I had two guns: one shoved into my back and the other shoved against the back of my head; ironically one of the guns was mine. We took the north stairs, as our steps squeaked against the freshly waxed floors, and the voice commanded, "Walk faster!" I had heard all that I needed to hear. I was fully certain I knew the person behind the mask.

"Take me to the money!" pressured the voice while the guns were shoved deeper into my head and back.

We hadn't even entered Crook and Juice's apartment, and I could smell the pungent aroma of nitroglycerin, sawdust, graphite, and all the other components of gunpowder and death. The door had been left ajar, as we walked into the split-level apartment. Blood was everywhere. The scene resembled a *Cocaine Cowboys* dustup. Two people lay dead in the kitchen, one portly Hispanic man was slumped over the dining-room table, and three bodies lay dead on the stairwell landing. Two additional nameless, dead faces riddled with holes lay outside the upstairs bathroom. My knees buckled; my mind raced into every possible corner as I plotted my escape.

"Keep moving! Take me to what I'm here for!" Despite the boisterous display of violence and the slow way I moved, the police still hadn't arrived—so much for the motto "to protect and serve." My mind raced faster. I knew that I had one ace left, and if I played it just right, then maybe, just maybe, I could get out of this fiasco alive.

We found Juice facedown across his bed with two shots to the head, execution-style. As I scanned the rooms, I realized that we hadn't stumbled upon Crook's body, but a trail of blood stretched across the floor in the direction of the rear bedroom window. Blood even stained the opened window's frame; this gave me hope that Crook had made it out alive.

"Stop stalling, motherfucker! Where's my money?" Growing more and more impatient, he emphasized his words by giving me another smack across my head with the gun nozzle.

"What you're looking for is on the top floor," I said.

At the top of the steps was a landing that fed into three bone-white doors. Each door had a unique European sign nailed above the upper framing. From the left to the right, the doors were labeled as follows: *PRIVATE, NO SMOKING,* and *NO ENTRY.* A shattered, reprinted black-and-white Picasso lay in ruins in front of door three. All three doors were equal in size and dimension, and each door was adorned the identical brown doorknobs.

"What the hell! Is this some type of game?" Police sirens finally raced closer. "Open the fucking doors!" the voice with two guns demanded.

With time shifting to my side, I shucked and jived toward door 1, *PRIVATE*. Grasping the doorknob, I flung it open. The room was empty. Next, I walked to *NO SMOKING*. I grasped the doorknob, and I flung it open. The room was empty. Seeing nothing, the voice became furiously impatient.

"Stop wasting time! Open the last fucking door!" the voice demanded.

Slowly, I approached door 3, *NO ENTRY*, and fumbled the knob between my fingers as if I was having trouble opening it.

"For Pete's sakes, get out of the way!" the voice impatiently shouted, and I stepped aside as quickly as possible.

I turned my back as I heard the doorknob being turned, and the door was pulled opened.

"You see that's how you open a—"

CHOOM!

I didn't even turn around. I was well aware of the dangerous capability the twelve-gauge shotgun we rigged to door number 3 possessed. His head was almost blown completely off. It wasn't necessary for me to sort through his remains; Carlos, a.k.a. Felix the Cat, was dead. I remembered his brash voice from our poker game at Saul's house. He was an impulsive gambler; he bet high and played fast. These tendencies made him the perfect candidate to get his head blown off. Knowing all of this, I took extra care to pick up my gun, and I wiped it down. Then, I quickly dismantled it, before I dropped its parts down the trash chute. Dodging all blood, I ran down the stairs and out of the building. Things were crazy, but I was clean: no GSR, no gun, no nothing. As far as I was concerned, I was an innocent citizen who just happened to be at the wrong place at the wrong time. I felt bad, because I'd panicked and hired Crook and Juice to help save me, but in the end, they wound up drowning in their own blood.

Suddenly, I heard footsteps running behind me. As I turned, I recognized the long-haired woman as she ran past me. It was the woman I met at Saul's party.

"Morgan!" I screamed. Ignoring my voice, she continued to run. And before I could run after her, I heard the loudest…

BOOM-BOOM-BOOM!!!

Cheese and Juice's apartment building exploded. The thrust sent me sprawling and the back of my head slammed against the stone-cold street. Concussed, I woke up in a local hospital.

CHAPTER 39

Tying It All Together

• • •

May 23, 2008, 4:22 a.m.

After I was released from the hospital, Sasha drove me to the police precinct. My head was bandaged, and I suffered from head-splitting migraines. I never liked police stations; they reminded me of doctors' offices with handcuffs. Whenever I walked into either one, there was a high probability that somehow, some way, I was going to get screwed.

As the police interviewed me, my head started writhing in pain. No matter what I said, these morons seemingly refused to comprehend what I was saying. Part of the problem stemmed from the fact that I was being interrogated by two individuals that I had never seen nor spoken to before; one of them was called "the chief." As we spoke, I wondered about Officer Dansbury's whereabouts.

"Listen, for the fifth time, those people were already dead when I got there! I was the one that called the shooting in!" I sold it hard, but I was still responsible to make sure they bought it. Suddenly, the interrogation-room door opened, and an all-too-familiar face walked in, Detective Ricks.

"Hello, Clint; you're the hipster with the hip answers. By the looks of you, it looks like karma caught up with you. Well, here's a question: If you had nothing to do with what happened, then why were you there in the first place?" he interrogated.

"I was looking for this girl I once knew, but I couldn't find her. I guess she moved." This was a lie, but it couldn't be confirmed and that's the kind of lie.

"Oh, now that Vicki is dead, you need another booty call?" Ricks snorted.

"That was totally unprofessional. Hey, Chief, is this how you run your shop?" Sasha barked at the tired, puffy-faced old man as I looked into his wrinkled eyes.

The chief paused and tossed his hands in disgust before he violently shook his head. Then the chief turned to Detective Ricks and the other interrogator. "C'mon, fellas, there's no use interrogating this guy. Lawyers and the Internet have produced a smarter brand of criminal. He's right; we got no gun, no GSR, nothing. Let him walk!" the chief said in exasperation.

"I have no problem with that," I softly quipped as Sasha helped me to my feet.

"Now wait a minute, Chief! Let me at least ask him just a few more questions while we have him here. I mean, am I the only one looking to do real police work?" As per usual, Detective Ricks was always trying to be a super-cop.

"I'm not sticking around for this! You have ten minutes!" The chief slammed the door extra hard as he exited. The noise from the door made the pain in my brain practically unbearable. I almost winced but I didn't want to look weak.

"OK, understand me here, Clint. What are the names of your associates that were murdered in that apartment building? There's no identification on any of the bodies, even that brunette, the one with her pretty, little throat slit whom we found in an upstairs closet. What gives?" Ricks queried.

"Like I said, their business is not my business," I quietly replied.

"Well, what is your business? Is being hip, or too cool for school, your business?" Special Agent Ricks asked.

"Sure, hip is good," I slowly responded.

"And how would you define hip?" Ricks asked.

"The state of hipness is twofold." I used my right index finger to motion for Detective Ricks to come closer. "Hip is knowing that the thirst for all things hip is insatiable," I whispered.

"That's all you have to say?" Detective Ricks exclaimed.

"That and the idea that I'm in the business of minding my own business, and right now my business is booming," I softly quipped.

"Explain to me why everyone you know has a ton of dirt under their fingernails. Doesn't all of this dirt make you feel dirty," his logic was weak.

"I'd only feel dirty if there was dirt under my fingernails. But if you look closely, my nails are clean." I extended my right middle finger for further evaluation.

"Ha-ha, very funny, asshole! I know you have something: a name, a reference, maybe something that you heard," he was beyond desperate. I could see that this case was like sand sliding through a child's fingers at the beach. It was sad, even pathetic. I really felt sorry for these lames. I had the advantage, and they knew it, but I figured maybe I could toss him a bone and do myself a favor in turn.

"Look, now, I don't know if this is hard information, but I heard somewhere about this guy named Damon. He's supposed to be a connected thug. His last name is Elmo…Enema…I don't know," I said.

"Nemo—Damon Nemo!" Ricks was ecstatic, as if he'd won at bingo night. He pointed to a picture of Damon tacked onto the wall. I noticed that my photo was also tacked to that same wall. I wanted to ask why, but I had bigger birds to catch. "Is this the guy?" he asked.

With a quick glance, I said, "Maybe. I've never seen him."

"Sources confirm that this man, J. D., known to some as the Razor and to others as Damon Nemo, is in town, possibly visiting relatives. He has a stepmother that allegedly lives in the city. Her last known address was 18403 Progress Way. But that burned down," Ricks stated.

"Well, what are you sure of?" I sheepishly rubbed my eyes and looked at the clock on the far wall.

"For starters, we're sure of her name and where she's from. Besides that, the investigation is still pending," Ricks reported.

"Are we done here?" I yawned as I spoke. This yawn was fabricated with the purpose of adding fuel to the fire.

"Confident, hip, and cocky—how do you pull it off? Always in the middle of guilt, but never guilty. Let me show you the door! There it is, connected to that knob. Use them both and get the hell out of my sight. I'm through with you!" he pointed me and Sasha out.

Standing, Sasha said, "To answer your question, when you're innocent and true to yourself, then everything else falls into place. You should try it sometime," she turned the knob and walked out behind me.

After I left, the chief rushed back into the interrogation room.

"Clever move mentioning the old woman's address," the chief said before he lit a cigar.

"Did you see him rub his eyes when I mentioned it? I'm telling you, Chief; I think all three of them are in it together!" Ricks folded his arms as he spoke.

"You might be onto something; do whatever you need to; just bring me the results!" the chief replied. Later that evening, the authorities released a public service announcement requesting assistance in locating the whereabouts of Damon Nemo; a reward was offered for any information that led to his apprehension.

CHAPTER 40

The Sting of Christianity

• • •

May 19, 2008, 1:08 p.m.

ON THE WAY TO SEE the Pastor, Damon received bad news. Not only was he wanted by the authorities, but Rico had called to share more bad news.

"Did you hear about that thing?" Rico asked.

"Yeah, I'm on top of that. I am meeting with the Pastor. Then I'm going to head to the stash house until things settle down. What do you have to report about our friend's bedtime story?" Damon asked.

"Yeah, that's a problem. I had the hot cocoa and the bedtime story ready, but when I arrived, he wasn't there!" Rico exclaimed.

"What do you mean—he wasn't there?" Damon's voice spiked.

"Just as I said, he slipped out. It doesn't take a genius to know who helped spring him from the hospital," Rico said.

"Cheese!" Damon deduced.

"That fucking worm—I'm glad I put him to sleep. Did you hear about the dustup last night? The streets say that Carlos was a part of it, and now he's worm food," Rico reported.

"Good riddance! When I finish my business, then I'll meet you at the spot," Damon said.

Damon's destination was across town, in a wealthy suburb, built around an opulent church made possible by the lavish tithes supplied by its congregation. Lawyers, doctors, politicians, and professional athletes called this church their place of worship. Every Sunday, the congregation paraded around the premises in their colorful clothes and gaudy jewelry.

The Pastor, once a cold-blooded hustler, was blessed with a smile and a gift of gab that could steal a cub from a lioness. But for the last twenty years, he had gone "on the straight and narrow." He even eschewed alcohol. The congregation viewed him as if he was their father and they were his children. He called all of them "my son" and "my daughter," or "my child," and his financially bloated constituents absolutely adored him. They would take up special collections to buy him excessive gifts. During the blizzard of 2007, the Pastor was given a Range Rover HSE 4.6 with all the trimmings. His congregation felt that he should be safe and comfortable as he visited the elderly (which he never did) or delivered soup to the needy (which he also never did). Or how about the 5,200-square-foot colonial they bought him for Christmas three years ago? Selfless was his image, but he was a dirty fraud like so many others of his ilk.

Damon rang the bell outside of the church. Recognizing Damon through the peep slide, the Pastor smiled and opened the left side of the main door. The door opened, and lightning pierced through the sky, as rambunctious thunder forced heavy rains to fall.

"Damon, my son, come in out of this nasty weather! Here, give me your coat," the pastor said.

"I don't think that will be necessary; I just need to talk," Damon said as he shook rain off his face.

"Of course, follow me. Are you thirsty? We have apple juice, orange, and possibly some leftover communion wine?" offered the Pastor.

"Some sacrament sounds good," Damon replied.

The Pastor was small in stature, every bit of five foot five; his tiny feet dragged along the floor as he escorted Damon to the kitchen. Damon had known the Pastor for over thirty-five years. But today's business dealt with the religion of money and drugs, not the enlightenment of the soul. The Pastor ambled his way to the refrigerator as Damon took a seat. Seconds later, the Pastor produced two glasses that contained red liquid, while his knees and other joints cracked as he lowered his body into one of the plush leather chairs. His arthritis was rumored to be the result of the Pastor's favorite vice; he loved to court beautiful women. This might be offensive to some radically devout Christians, but at least he wasn't preying on little boys.

"Yes, my son, how may I help?" the Pastor asked.

"Pastor, I've fallen onto bad times. I need your help to get me out of the country," Damon said.

"I'm flattered, my son, but I don't have the powers to call off the hounds. You knew the policy," the Pastor's voice was always smooth and even.

"There has to be something you can do?" Damon implored.

"My son, I remember your father very well; we shook hands many times. He was a great man that didn't get the chance to see the rest of his days, an honorable man in a dishonorable business. What would he say about you?" the Pastor asked as he turned and looked Damon squarely in his eyes.

"Pastor, with all due respect, my father was half the man you are; isn't there anything that you can do for me?" Damon was vulnerable. He knew the Pastor was the only person that could help him.

"Son, what's done is done. The authorities are closing in as we speak. You've strayed from God, as evidenced by the television reports and the phone call I just got from my informant at the police precinct. It would take a miracle of epic proportions. Excuse the cliché, but it's the truth," the Pastor calmly replied.

"What about a contribution of epic proportions?" Damon was desperate.

"I'm listening," responded the Pastor.

"What if I ceded my downtown properties over to you, as well as one of my offshore restaurants? Then could I buy my way out?" Damon inquired.

"You could, if you sweetened the deal by including your strip club." When it came to business, the Pastor was the shrewdest of the shrewd.

"Would that guarantee my safe passage?" Damon asked.

"I can't promise anything with the deacons. To be honest, if they had it their way, the contract would've been signed, the hit men hired, and the guns bought. Tell me what happened in Jersey City?" the Pastor inquired.

"Pastor, I wasn't thinking; you know Rico. When he gets going, there's no telling what could happen," Damon replied.

"Wait—you still associate with Rico? Never mind, we'll discuss that later," the Pastor said.

"Do we have a deal?" Damon asked.

"Yes, my secretary will draw up the papers," the Pastor replied as they sealed the agreement with a handshake.

Checking his watch, the Pastor said, "Excuse me, my son, I need to make a few calls."

"Thank you, Pastor; thank you, Father!" Damon said as he took his final sip. Minutes later, he walked down the hall and joined the Pastor's strikingly attractive secretary. Three hours later, the contracts were drawn, signed, and notarized. Damon met the Pastor in his study, where he was reading a large Bible with enlarged print.

"Here are the contracts, Pastor. They are signed and sealed for your approval. Look them over; I'm going to hit the head," Damon reported.

Pressure can and will cause problems for even the most stubborn personalities. Damon had just surrendered a large fortune, but his feeling of newfound optimism was a weight off his shoulders. Confident, he patted the Pastor on his left shoulder and walked down the hall, turned right, and went down another hallway into a stark white bathroom. Through the only open window, a puddle of rainwater gathered on the floor. Unknowingly, a large wasp had followed Damon into the bathroom. Noticing the puddle on the floor, Damon grabbed a hand towel and started to rotate his left and right hands to twirl the towel until it was as taut as a cord. As the wasp buzzed by his ear, he released the towel from his right hand and used his left to whip the towel in the wasp's direction.

SNAP!

The towel appeared to smash the wasp against the mirror. But when Damon looked in the sink, he was surprised to find it empty. After scanning the floor, the wasp was nowhere to be found.

"Where are you, you little bastard?" he thought out loud.

Before he could search any further, he felt a deep, cold, sharp, stinging sensation in his neck. The horrified mirror image of the Pastor repeatedly stabbing him in the neck added to the pain as his own blood blotched the pearly white room.

"Ouch—shit! You fucking-fatherfucker!" Damon pulled the protruding knife out of his neck and threw the Pastor to the floor. Automatically, he tried to use the hand towel to stop his blood from spewing from his carotid artery, as a stream of urine concurrently flowed down his left leg.

"Why did you do that!" he blurted as he continuously tried to dam his neck with his left hand. Eyes the size of saucers showed his disbelief, as his skin rapidly became pale.

"You messed up. You lost my cocaine; then you killed the only woman I have ever loved. I just confirmed that it was you that killed your mother. That apartment fire was a pathetic ruse. She and I were once lovers!" screamed the Pastor.

Too weak to put up a proper fight, Damon fruitlessly lunged at the Pastor. He struggled to remain standing, until his legs buckled, and he eventually slipped and fell. Defeated, he labored to breathe; his head made a thud as it crashed against the floor while his death crept up through the once all white flooring.

COUGH!

"Don't you want to know who has your...*COUGH!*...coke...*COUGH!*... money?"

Bereft of remorse, the Pastor had the contracts and the revenge he sought. He kneeled and stroked Damon's hair as he said, "Don't you worry, my son; I have everything under control. Now, may your wretched soul travel safely to hell," the Pastor said, as he mimicked making a cross over Damon's body.

After releasing an extended fart, Damon died.

CHAPTER 41

What's the 411?

• • •

May 20, 2008, 11:37 a.m.

DETECTIVE RICKS STOOD AMID THE charred ruins of Damon's apartment building as darkness began to reign and the day passed its torch to nightfall. Ricks was trying to establish a trail on the man named Damon Nemo. He flipped open his cell phone and made a call. Getting no response, Detective Ricks was visibly disgusted; he hung up and proceeded to walk across the street. After crossing, he approached the first building, walked up its stairs, and knocked on the front door. After several attempts, he turned to walk back to his sedan. Before he could get to his car, a series of locks could be heard unlocking as someone began to open the apartment's front door. Turning quickly, Detective Ricks focused his attention on the opening door. Once open, a stunningly attractive, international-looking woman stood under the doorframe.

"Greetings, ma'am; my name is Detective Ricks, and I'm looking for this woman," he held up a black-and-white photo and allowed the woman to examine it.

"Her name...I can't recall, but she lived in the building across the street that burned down. So many people suffered that day," she said as tears ran down her face.

"Can you tell me any information about this man?" he handed her a black-and-white photo of Damon Nemo.

"Look, I can't help you. I don't know this man! Who are you to come around here asking those types of questions? You can't protect me; your whole precinct couldn't even stop a building from burning down!" she abruptly took one step back and disappeared behind the now closed door.

Baffled and infuriated, Ricks walked back to his unmarked car. Suddenly, a hidden voice from the shadows of a nearby alley grabbed his attention.

"I might have seen who you are looking for." The voice came from a man that donned a tattered, oversized, dirty jacket. His shoes were run over, and if you were just a few feet away, you'd quickly realize that he hadn't bathed in quite some time.

"You did? Tell me more!" Ricks implored.

"A few days ago, right before the building started burning, I was lying right over there, and when I opened my eyes, I saw a man in a dark jacket carrying a baseball bat and a can of gasoline climb up the fire escape," the homeless man spoke with a hitch as he repeatedly scratched his sore-infested neck.

"Wait a minute: you saw a man climb up the fire escape? How does this help me?" Ricks grew impatient.

"It was minutes before the fire started. I also saw the cop that ran into the building before he died," reported the homeless man.

"You mean to tell me, you saw the person that set that fire?" inquired an intrigued Ricks.

"I can do you one better; I saw the man in your photograph and another man from out of town climb up the fire escape," added the homeless man.

"How did you know the other man was from out of town?" Ricks asked.

"Because he looked like Jed Clampett, or maybe a Walton. After a few minutes, they came running down the fire escape. Jed threw the bat in the Dumpster; then both men sped off in a black van!" the more he spoke, the more he scratched his neck.

"Do you know anything else?" asked Ricks.

"Yes! But any more information is going to cost you; I need to eat! *THE PAPER BAG* is at the end of the street; meet me there in about five minutes," the homeless man said.

"No, I'll drive you," Ricks demanded.

Dark clouds had completely chased the sun away. Inside *THE PAPER BAG*, hunched over in a window booth, the homeless man ate, while Detective Ricks watched him from his unmarked car. Clearly needing a course in etiquette, the homeless man's face barely separated itself from his plate; he only raised his head when Detective Ricks flashed his headlights. Licking the plate clean, he hurriedly ran outside and approached Detective Ricks's car. At that moment, a black, late-model van pulled up; the rear right window was wide open as a masked man brandished a large double-barreled shotgun and squeezed the trigger several times until both the homeless man and Detective Ricks were mortally wounded. As the van sped off, the license plate border read *Saul Autos, Inc.* Rico was at the wheel; he had a few loose ends to clip before he disappeared. With Damon dead, he was now in charge. Rico was a deadly, slippery character well deserving of his moniker, El Serpiente.

CHAPTER 42

In Case You Were Wondering

● ● ●

SEVERAL MONTHS HAD PASSED SINCE my departure from the East Coast. I now lived on the outskirts of Denver, Colorado. Due to migraines from my explosion-induced head trauma, my plan was to lie low. Once the fall season had passed, I would make my permanent residence somewhere where the temperatures rarely dipped below eighty degrees. Lourdes came with me to Colorado, and we were both in agreement regarding climatological preference. After we enjoyed an extended period of fun in the sun, she still planned to enter the Peace Corps in Haiti. I figured I'd stay in Haiti, or maybe I would find us a nice villa in the Dominican Republic.

I was currently out shopping for Lourdes. I wanted to surprise her with something unique and avant-garde. As I walked through the park, a crunchy, Denver-bred yoga couple directed me to a vintage clothing store off Main Street. It was called *OLD SEWS* and was owned by a middle-aged couple. The husband was laid back, but the wife was one tough customer.

Before I entered the store, my eyes caught a blind man in very plain clothes with a seeing-eye dog. The dog sniffed the ground. Eventually, the dog became bored and led the blind man to the corner of the street. I grabbed the shop's door handle and walked inside. *OLD SEWS* was filled with a myriad of clothes from days gone by; it was a retrograde paradise. So many items yet not enough time: Lourdes and I were scheduled to meet for sushi in forty-five minutes. I riffled through a stack of jeans until a jacket hanging in the window caught my eye. It reminded me of one that

I regretfully hadn't purchased on my first trip to Europe. It looked like it would fit Lourdes perfectly.

"Excuse me, miss, may I see this jacket?" I asked.

Suddenly, the doorbell jingled. The visitor was the blind man. He appeared to be in the later years of life. His facial features were drowned out by thick, dark, black protective glasses. He just stood there. He didn't say anything. He just stood there motionless and breathing heavy. I could identify with what Luke Skywalker felt in dealing with Darth. I had a hard time focusing while staring into those Vaderesque glasses. This guy's vibe was spooky.

"May I help you, sir?" the wife's words cut through the waves of mounting tension. Even though I had clearly been there first, she addressed the blind man. I guess it was "Old Man's Day."

"Yes, I was told by a lady friend that you sold women's toiletries and unmentionables; is that true?" the blind man mumbled.

"No, you have been misinformed, sir. We resell women's clothing, not women's unmentionables," she replied dryly.

"Not even hosiery?" he continued.

"Not even hosiery," this time her response had more bite to it. She was a no-nonsense type of business owner.

The blind man didn't say anything else and led his dog out of the store.

Without losing a beat, the owner turned her energies in my direction. She briefly stepped over to the window and took the jacket off the mannequin.

"Here's the jacket," she said as she passed it to me.

"You can try it on and see how it fits," she pressed.

"It's not for me; it's for my girlfriend. Can I bring it back if she doesn't like the way it fits?" I queried.

"Provided you keep your receipt, we allow fourteen days from the point of purchase, for full refunds," she replied.

"What type of fabric is this made of?" I asked.

"It's brushed suede," she responded.

I held the jacket up to the light and examined it. "What's this dirt mark on the right arm?" I demonstratively pointed it out with my left index finger.

"Oh, that? You can hardly see it. It'll come out if you dry-clean it," was her response.

"Then why didn't you dry-clean this jacket before it was placed on the rack?" I retorted. "Whether it's just dirt or a dirt stain, it's still a dirty stain," I said.

"Look, smarty-pants, I'll take twenty-five percent off the sticker price; will that satisfy you?" she said.

"Sure. What's the total after discount?" I asked as I pulled out my wallet.

"With the discount, your total comes to forty-two dollars and zero cents," she announced.

I gave her a fifty-dollar bill, and she gave me my change.

As she wrapped the jacket up in brown recycled paper, she sardonically said, "Looks like you're the proud new owner of a vintage *dirty suede* jacket," she almost laughed at her words.

"*Dirty suede*, cool," I replied.

Lourdes loved the jacket. As for me, I was happy with her and the logistics of our newfound life. But I still had the key that opened the safe to all that liquid cocaine. I checked on www.publicrecords.net and discovered that within the next four months, Vinny's building was scheduled to go to public auction. I was debating on going back and buying the building and then figuring out what to do with all that cocaine. As I said once, and I would say it again, greed was a crazy affliction. Here I had $1.4 million tax-free, and I was seriously contemplating buying a building just, so I could sell cocaine. Insanity, right? I had plenty of time to think about it. But I had already made up my mind, as the $1.4 million apparently was not satisfying enough. I wondered how this was going to play itself out. We should see. I sighed and thought, "Once a hipster, always a hipster."

THE END

E P I L O G U E

The day before Lourdes and I were scheduled to leave for the Caribbean, I had just arrived home from a therapy session with Dr. Wiesenthal and I logged onto my computer and discovered the following mysterious e-mail:

From: Mulli, Rebecca [rebecca@prettygirl.com]

HIDE

Sent: Wednesday, October 31, 2008 at 4:20 PM

To: Stoener, Clint [clint@dirtysuede.com]

RE: A PROMISE

Clint…it is very disheartening that I haven't heard from you. It is more unfortunate

that I heard you've already found a new girlfriend…All it took was for you to force me

out of your life before you found a new lover…I have been thoroughly miserable since

our separation at JFK…Clint…Life is full of decisions…But remember we reap

whatever we sow…And it is ultimately up to you to decide for yourself how you would

like people to remember you…It is not what happens to us…But how we deal with

it…That's what molds our character…I advise you to take a step back and think about

what we shared… Does your new girl suck your ---- and ------- as well I do?!...I doubt

it!...Might I suggest that you look at yourself in the mirror and ask yourself what you

are willing to lose in the face of your new reality?...Please don't worry about

contacting me…But be advised that this isn't the last time that we'll speak…I

PROMISE YOU.

Sent from my EYEphone

swag. "Stuff we all get," a discolored, inferior, low-quality form of marijuana.

antifreeze or freezers. Covert term for cocaine, as its application tends to numb or freeze body parts like gums, noses, and the brain upon contact. Cocaine is also referred to as "snow."

on the arm. When a drug dealer is able to procure a quantity of drugs without paying for the product until the product has been sold. This is essentially the antithesis of COD (cash on delivery).

crystals. Refers to the sparkles reflected on certain strains of well-cultivated marijuana buds.

two niggers. A racially stereotypical reference made by Damon. While on the phone, Damon asks, "Will two niggers be enough?" Damon is actually referencing two handguns. It is Damon's belief that some minorities are like guns; they are both black and highly prone to kill. The colloquialism referred to procuring two black nine-millimeter handguns.

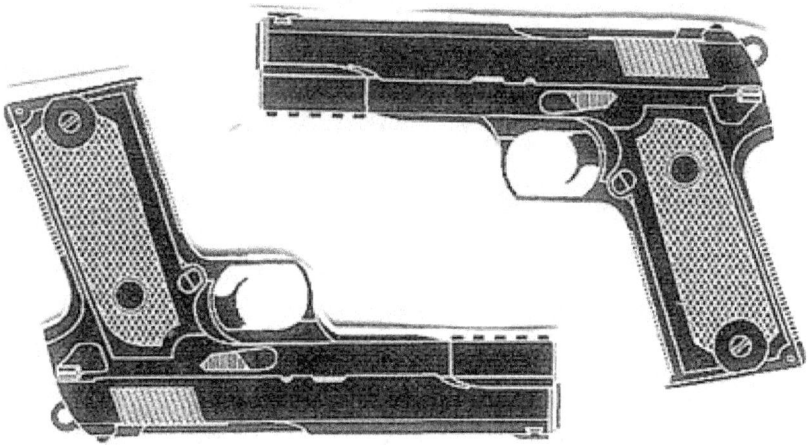

alternative subject matters. Conversational material usually dealing with drugs and/or sexual activities.

stash box. Any device that is used to hide illegal contraband. Some stash boxes are rudimentary in nature, whereas others are very sophisticated. The sole purpose of a stash box is to assist in alluding detection by the authorities.

schedule 1 restricted list. Controlled substances that are purported to be highly likely to be abused and are considered to have no current medical use within the contiguous United States.

the product. Drugs: marijuana, cocaine, hash, amphetamines, ecstasy, heroin, and so on.

game of T & D. Truth or dare.

Larry Wong. A fictitious character from the movie *King of New York*.

piker. A petty gambler; small-time player in "the game of life."

John. The desperate, sexually deprived males of society that solicit prostitutes or call girls in order to fulfill their sexual wants, needs, and desires.

rubbing one out. Masturbatory behavior.

Hank Moody. A fictitious character that embodies a carefree sense of cool.

man dance. A euphemism for a fight.

bat and dugout. A covert smoking device indigenous to the West Coast and the northern section of the East Coast. It consists of a ceramic cigarette (the bat) that can be packed with marijuana and then smoked. Upon completion of the smoking session, the bat is then housed in a wooden box called the dugout. (See illustration.)

Ponce de Leon. A Spanish explorer who reputedly discovered the fountain of youth when he journeyed to Florida in 1513.

the fourth stage of death: Putrefaction; onset time after death, thirty-six to forty-eight hours.

remaining piece. The last part of a joint or blunt; a roach.

examples of marijuana

Sativa-produces a mental, cerebral high, which provides energy that can transform into creativity, conversation, and other forms of stimulation.	Indica-users experience a "couch-lock". An Indica high numbs the body and induces supreme relaxation.
Blue Dream	Blue Berry Crush
White Widow	Girl Scout Cookies (poly-hybrid)

Christopher Wallace's "Ten Crack Commandments." Written by the rapper Notorious B. I. G., this song educates its listeners on how to maneuver through the drug game.

GSR, gunshot residue. The shooter squeezes the trigger; upon collision between the bullet and the firing pin, a multifaceted substance is produced as the bullet exits the gun barrel; burning gunpowder, smoke, and other particles also exit the barrel of a firearm and attach themselves to the shooter. The GSR can travel anywhere between twelve and twenty-eight inches or upward to three to six feet. If apprehended in a timely manner, authorities can test suspects for GSR. If results are positive, this may become a key point of evidence regarding determining the identity of the shooter.

10-16. Police code for domestic disturbance.

mark. 1. A person involved in a game in which one or more participants have been "marked," or identified as the target that all other participants have predetermined that they would prey upon. Essentially, the mark is marked for defeat even before the contest has begun. 2. Analogous to sexual behavior as prescribed for the aforementioned *John*. A mark represents the desperate, sexually deprived males of society that solicit prostitutes or call girls in order to fulfill their sexual wants, needs, and desires.

10-70. Police code for fire.

10-73. Police code for smoke report.

burner. A disposable cell phone or an unmarked gun that may or may not have a serial number.

E pills. Ecstasy.

tool. 1. Some type of firearm, whether professionally manufactured or unprofessionally manufactured. 2. A person that is perpetually uncool.

backdoor lovin'. Jim Morrison of the Doors sang a song with a similar title. Backdoor lovin' is a not-so-esoteric term that conjures images of anal intercourse.

hardening member. Male erectile behavior.

Ickey Woods. A high-quality strain of marijuana.

hot box. 1. A tight, condensed smoking area devoid of ventilation that eventually becomes inundated with marijuana smoke. 2. A very attractive female.

roach. The unsmoked remnants of a blunt or joint.

tap-danced. Refers to a drug dealer's unscrupulous practices in an effort to maximize profit; they will take a drug like cocaine and cut it up and add other inferior ingredients (e.g., baby powder, sugar, flour, laxatives) in order to increase the amount of product and thereby the street value.

spliff. A Bob Marley–sized joint or blunt.

five-inch Zero Halliburton stainless-steel executive case. A silver metallic security briefcase equipped with a combination lock. Typically, this type of briefcase is used in transporting an array of valuables.